THE
SILENCE

SUSAN ALLOTT is a British author who lived and worked in Sydney in the late nineties. She now lives in London with her children and her very Australian husband.

THE
SILENCE

SUSAN ALLOTT

THE BOROUGH PRESS

The Borough Press
An imprint of HarperCollins*Publishers* Ltd
1 London Bridge Street
London SE1 9GF

www.harpercollins.co.uk

First published by HarperCollins*Publishers* 2020
1

Susan Allott asserts the moral right to
be identified as the author of this work

A catalogue record for this book is available from the British Library

HB ISBN: 978-0-00-836130-3
TPB ISBN: 978-0-00-836131-0
ANZ TPB ISBN: 978-0-00-838977-2

This novel is entirely a work of fiction.
The names, characters and incidents portrayed in it are
the work of the author's imagination. Any resemblance to
actual persons, living or dead, events or localities is
entirely coincidental.

Typeset in Adobe Garamond Pro by
Palimpsest Book Production Ltd, Falkirk, Stirlingshire

Printed and bound in the UK by CPI Group (UK) Ltd, Croydon CR0 4YY

FSC
www.fsc.org

MIX
Paper from
responsible sources
FSC C007454

This book is produced from independently certified FSC™ paper
to ensure responsible forest management.

For more information visit: www.harpercollins.co.uk/green

For David

1

London, 1997

In a basement flat in Hackney, the telephone rings. It's two in the morning. Isla Green stands in the hallway, pyjamaed, barely awake. She is entirely sober. A good thing, if a little fragile; a little surprising. No tide of shame waits for her, no bloom of pain. She feels clean in her skin, like a schoolgirl. She can taste toothpaste in her throat.

On the third ring she reaches for the receiver. It's Dom's voice she will hear if the answerphone picks up, and his voice will set her back. It's three months since he left and every day she means to wipe the message. She lifts it to her ear just in time.

'Hello?'

It takes her a second to place him. 'Dad?'

'I didn't wake you, did I?'

She doesn't know why she's gripping the receiver. Why a trill of fear has sounded in her head. It's good to hear her dad's voice, which is more Australian than her own these days. He's

1

got the time difference wrong, that's all. At the end of the street a police siren starts its upward loop and cuts out. Its blue light flashes silently.

'What time is it there?'

'I don't know.' She stretches her free arm above her head, arching her back. In the eight weeks and three days since her last drink, she has been sleeping like the dead.

'Shall I call back later?'

'It's fine. Is everything ok?'

'I wanted to talk to you,' he says. 'Your mother doesn't know I'm calling. She went into town.'

She sits down on the carpet. This is the thing she couldn't put her finger on, that she should have known was wrong from the start. Her dad hasn't called her in the decade she's lived in London. It's her mum who makes the phone calls, leaves messages on the answerphone. Her dad writes letters. He hates the phone.

'What is it?'

'I didn't want you to hear it from your mother. She hasn't taken it well. I wanted to tell you myself.'

She drops her head between her knees. She thinks, if he's going to die, I'll need a drink. Cold, practical thoughts: she will finish this call and she will put her clothes on. There's an all-night takeaway at Clapton Pond where they sell six-packs of beer under the counter.

'The police came to see me,' he says.

'The police?'

'They're looking for a woman I used to know.'

Isla lifts her head. She's sweating. She runs her hand through her damp hair. 'What woman?'

'She was a neighbour of ours, back when we first moved to Sydney. You wouldn't remember.' He coughs. 'It looks like she's been missing a long time. Nobody's seen her in thirty years.'

The police car crawls past outside, swinging its blue light across the walls.

'What's this got to do with you?'

'The police think her disappearance is suspicious,' he says. 'They think I was the last person to see her, before she went missing.'

'And were you?' She tries to sound calm. 'Were you the last person to see her?'

'I can't have been. She moved away with her husband. I told them there must be some mistake.'

He lights a cigarette, exhales. She thinks of Dom, smiling behind a flame.

'Is she dead?'

'They think she must be.' His voice is quiet. A bad news voice. 'There's no record of her at all, in all that time. Her father died last month, left her most of his estate, but she hasn't come forward. Her brother's been asking around, trying to trace her. He turned up a few things that the police are looking into.' He laughs unconvincingly. 'One of those things is me.'

Isla finds a line of stubble along her shin. She runs her thumbnail over it, back and forth, until it hurts.

'The cops are searching through their records,' he says. 'They keep records of people who died without being identified.'

3

'What if it turns out she was killed?'

'That would be the worst-case scenario, love,' he says. 'That would mean a murder enquiry.'

'Jesus.'

'Look, I don't want you to worry.'

'But if you were the last person to see her –'

'I wasn't.' He shouts it. 'I told you, I wasn't.'

Isla rests her head back on her knees. In the part-light she sees unopened post on the doormat, soiled with the tread of her lace-up boots. Her bike, leaning against the wall, its basket stuffed with junk mail. On a hook by the door, the smart coat with the belt that she wears to the office. All of it familiar, unchanged.

'Are you there?'

'I'm here,' she says.

'Sorry to snap at you.'

'Dad.' She feels hot, but her skin is cold. Her pyjamas cling to her. 'What was her name?'

He hesitates. 'Mandy.'

Mandy. Isla smells a hot iron against cotton sheets. Eucalyptus.

'She looked after you a few days a week, before you started school. Back when your mum was working at Hordern & Sons.'

'She had a washing line strung out across her yard,' Isla says, remembering as she speaks. 'I used to hand her the pegs when she hung out her laundry.'

'Did you?'

Isla can't recall Mandy's face but she remembers being in her presence. Being liked by someone she liked. An easiness about her company that made other people seem less than her.

'Your mother wants to cancel the party for my birthday,' he continues. 'She's been upset since the police called round. She can't put it out of her mind.'

A door slams in one of the flats upstairs. Raised voices. Isla sits up. She understands now why he called.

'Does she believe you, Dad?'

'I don't think so. No.'

She cradles the phone. New connectors are opening in her brain these past few weeks, fuelled by mineral water and sleep. Unbidden memories startle her on the bus; on the escalator at Bethnal Green; as she sits in traffic on the Essex Road. Her life has an awful clarity now the protective, hungover fug is gone. She sits cross-legged on the carpet, in the middle of her life, in its crisp, central crease. She is thirty-five years old, tall and lean; striking, people say. A body that has been neglected but is still strong, surprisingly resilient. A thick head of hair, cropped short at the back; blonde strands on top that grow up and out, like a dandelion. A woman whose life took a nosedive, who is getting herself together, who needs to be careful. Whose father is silent at the end of the line, asking her wordlessly to come home.

'I could come back for a couple of weeks,' she says. It's the only thing to say. 'I could help with the party. Get Mum to see sense.'

'Could you?'

'I think so. I'm owed some leave.'

'That would be wonderful, Isla.' His voice has lifted. 'What about the apartment? Aren't you buying a place?'

The apartment. A two-bed on Sinclair Road with high ceilings and a Juliet balcony. It's beautiful, well-located and well over budget. They close in three weeks. She rubs her forehead with the heel of her hand. 'I can deal with it over the phone,' she says.

'Can they spare you at work?'

'They'll have to.'

'Are you sure this is a good time for you?'

No, she is not sure. She doesn't want to be in Sydney, where there are empty hours to fill and people she hasn't seen in a decade. She wants to sleep and work and hide.

'I'm sure,' she says. 'It's about time.'

Rain falls hard over London as the sun comes up. Isla lies on the surface of sleep, refusing the dreams that want her to be four years old again, walking through rooms that are familiar but not home. She starts the day, dresses herself. Her dad's voice is loud and scared in her head, playing on a loop, acquiring a strain of panic. She makes coffee, tells herself she does not need anything stronger. She is over-thinking this whole thing. He is not lying.

2

Sydney, 1966

Mandy supposed Steve must always have opened his gifts this way. A ham-fisted rip-and-crunch of the paper; a quick kiss and a 'thanks darl', and that was it. No ceremony. No comment on the way she'd lined up the stripes on the gift wrap. He did appreciate the gift itself, mind, so long as it was something practical that he could use or wear, that wasn't too different from anything he already owned.

Nothing new there, except Mandy found it aggravating this year, and wanted to thump him. She knew she was being unreasonable. Why would he notice the paper? He was the same man she'd been married to for seven years. And it was daft that she'd done that with the stripes. She'd become a woman who was uptight about gift wrap. How had that happened?

She sat beside him on the bed and turned her gift from him around in her hands. A bigger box than she'd expected. She picked at a piece of tape with her thumbnail and peeled it, slowly, free of the gift wrap. She did the same with the tape at the other side of the box.

'Why don't you just rip it, Mand? We'll still be here for New Year's at this rate.'

She gave him a look. 'I feel like taking my time.'

Turning the box onto its side, she reached her hand under the wrapping and managed to slide it free, without any tearing of the paper or damage to its hollow structure. Steve picked up the paper, as if to crush it, but thought better of it and put it back where it was.

'A watch!' She hadn't expected that. 'You got me a watch?'

He sat up straight, arranging the pillows behind him, and smiled. 'Let's see it on you.'

She fixed the tiny buckle and turned the watch so its face was centred. It was designed for a woman with bony wrists. A frail, skeletal woman who couldn't lift the weight of anything bigger. It made her arm look huge and muscular. She hated it.

'There. Fits nicely. Just snug,' she said. First lie of the day: 'I love it.' Second lie: 'What a nice surprise.'

Steve shifted onto his side and pulled her down to lie next to him. 'Merry Christmas,' he said. He reached around and stretched his hand over the flesh of her backside. 'I knew you'd like it.'

She moved closer against him so he couldn't see her face. Her nightdress crackled with static against his pyjamas. 'You dark horse,' she said into the warm meat of his neck. 'I thought you were getting me the necklace I showed you.'

'What necklace?' He rolled her away from him and pushed her hair from her face. 'You didn't mention a necklace.'

'It's all right.' She brightened her voice. 'Sorry. It's a beautiful watch. I didn't mean –'

His eyes moved side to side, trying to remember. 'You didn't say anything about a necklace.'

'I showed you, is all. In my catalogue. A gold chain with a pendant.' She held a finger to the base of her neck, where the pendant might have hung. 'I showed you a while back. It had a small letter A for Amanda. A pendant.'

He shook his head. 'You have to spell it out, Mand. If you want a necklace, tell me you want a necklace. You can't expect me to pick up on a hint like that.'

She smiled, and pinched his face until he smiled back. 'D'you like the jacket?'

'I love it, darl. Good for the truck when I'm driving at night.'

'That's what I thought.'

She turned her back to him and picked up the gift wrap the watch had come in, red with gold bells, still holding its box shape. From this position on the bed she could see one of Steve's socks beside the wash basket, where he must have thrown it and missed. He'd left his new jacket on the carpet at the foot of the bed, and the striped paper was torn, strewn across the floor. The Christmas cards she'd arranged on the chest of drawers had fallen sideways, and the water needed changing in the glass vase where she'd arranged a few orchids earlier in the week. The rest of the house could do with a once-over. She ought to get moving.

'I could take it back,' he said, sitting up. 'The watch. I kept the receipt. I think.'

'Don't be daft.' She balled up the gift wrap in her hand and wondered how long she could pretend to like the watch. Not much past Boxing Day, she figured. 'I'm hungry.' She swung her legs over the side of the bed. 'You take a shower and I'll get breakfast going.'

'No rush, is there?' Steve patted the sheets where she'd lain and looked up at her hopefully.

It was only nine-thirty, according to the Timex, and already she felt like a bitch. She ought to get back into bed with him, she knew that. Start the day again. Morning sex was a tradition she could get behind, as a rule. More her bag than Christmas. But the fun had gone out of it lately, and she couldn't bring herself to fake it.

'You know it's been weeks, since we—'

'It has not.' She tightened her grip on the ball of paper. 'It has not been that long,' she said, smiling through the third lie of the day. 'You're exaggerating.'

'Come back to bed, Mandy.'

'The Walkers are coming over before lunch. I need to get the house clean.'

'It's nine-thirty, Mand—'

'I know the bloody time.'

'So are we still trying then or not?'

Her heart thumped at the question, the starkness of it in the morning light of their bedroom. It was typical of Steve to come out and say the thing that needed saying; the thing she was trying to pretend was not a thing.

''Course we are. Not right now, is all.'

'My timing off again?'

'Don't go on about it, Steve. Just – leave it. Please.'

He thumped a pillow with the palm of his hand and his face flushed a dark red. He didn't look at her. 'Righto,' he said, to the pillow. 'I'll take a shower.'

In the kitchen she leaned against the counter, rubbed her hands over her face and let out a sigh. So warm in here. She turned to look out at the yard, opened the window and got a burst of noise from the cicadas. The heat was taking a grip; you could feel the strength of it, even at this hour. The cloud had burned off already. It was going to be a belter of a day.

She nudged the back door open and sat on the step to light a cigarette. Holding her arm out, she tried to like the watch, to reconsider it. It was a nice enough watch, if you could forgive it for not being the necklace she'd wanted, and for being too tiny for an ample woman like herself. It had a gold-plated strap and a small oval face, with notches where the numbers should be and a dial on the side which moved the hands around. She'd have preferred a watch with numbers on it, since the whole point was to tell her the time. Why would you leave the numbers off a watch?

But that wasn't it. She disliked the way it sliced time into prim, breathy little ticks. She'd never noticed seconds before, and now they were twitching around the dial, interfering with her natural rhythm. That was why she'd never owned a watch, come to think of it. She liked to do things as and when she was ready, in her own time. The watch was trying to push her around.

She heard him singing in the shower. He was good-natured, her Steve. Didn't take the hump for too long. She sat back against the door frame and smoked her cigarette, watching the horizon, a fine blue line just darker than the sky, visible through the tea trees at the back of the yard. She could hear the waves from here, whenever the cicadas took a breather: a low boom; quiet; another boom. That was a rhythm she could appreciate.

'You'll need to give those up, Amanda.' Steve was standing in the kitchen with a towel around his middle, dripping on the lino. His skin was paler from the neck down, and the hair on his chest was blacker than the hair on his head. 'Meant to be bad for you. For your lungs. I read an article in the *Herald*.'

'I know. I read the same article.' She turned back to the yard. 'You have the odd ciggie yourself.'

'Let's pack 'em in together, then.'

'Since when did you get to be a health fanatic?'

He sat down next to her, holding onto the towel, knees together. It was a squeeze, the two of them side by side on the back step. His skin was damp, soaking through the sleeve of her nightdress. She could see the tracks of the comb through his hair.

'It can be bad for the baby too, they reckon.' He watched her crush her cigarette into the ashtray. 'Bad for the unborn baby.'

'I didn't read that part.'

'It said it can cause the baby to be born too small.'

She looked out at the yard and managed not to say that she thought a small baby sounded better than a big one, from a logistical point of view. 'I'll give up if I get pregnant,' she said. 'How's that?'

'Mandy.' He reached out and held her hand. 'You'll make a great mum, you know.'

She moved her thumb back and forth across the palm of his hand and kept her mouth shut. He didn't know. He could hope, was all. If she turned out to be anything like her own mother, she'd be a disaster. Mandy had a growing fear, which she would not speak out loud in case it became irreversibly true, that she was very much like her own mother. Her own mother, for example, would have snubbed a kind, well-intentioned gift from Mandy's father, would have returned it the minute the shops opened. Mandy looked down at the Timex on her wrist and dropped Steve's hand, hoping he'd go off and get dressed now, leave her alone for a bit.

He didn't budge.

Steve also didn't know that Mandy had not yet stopped taking her daily contraceptive pill. Every morning, as she popped the small, white tablet from its foil bubble, she told herself this was a temporary situation. When she was ready for motherhood, she would stop taking the Pill and get herself pregnant and that would be that. The time would come, surely, when she would long for children; she would need to be pregnant and be unable to think of anything else. Louisa next door had told her she'd felt that way before she fell pregnant with Isla. She'd felt ready, and that readiness had been all-consuming. Mandy would have that feeling one of these days, Louisa had told her. But Louisa didn't know either.

Mandy leaned in against Steve and felt his chin on her head; his good, strong arms around her. She let her head rest against his shoulder. Shoulders like an anvil, her Steve.

'I'm sure you're right,' she said.

Fourth lie of the day. Mandy knew that this lie, the Baby Lie, was the one that made everything else a lie, and made it pointless counting the small, polite ones. She also knew, in a quiet, buttoned-down place, that she was falling out of love with her husband. And she wasn't fighting it, this fading out, this dimming of the light. Because it made the lie easier to tell.

'I was thinking,' he said. 'I might set off on this job first thing tomorrow. Get it over with.'

'Oh?' She managed, she hoped, not to sound delighted. 'First thing?'

'Might as well crack on. Won't be any easier if I leave it.'

'You're probably right, love.' She could smell the sea spray in the air. 'You'll be gone a few days, then?'

''Fraid so, darl. You know I'd sooner be home with you.'

'I know.' She stood and put her cigarettes in the drawer under some serviettes. 'I do know that.'

3

Ivanhoe, New South Wales, 1966

Steve saw her first, kneeling in the dirt at the edge of the creek. She looked happy enough. Five or six older kids with her, poking at something in the water with a stick. He turned away, kept his foot on the gas and hoped to God she'd run off before Harry spotted her. His shirt was wet against the car seat. He hummed a tune, to break the silence, and let himself believe he wouldn't have to do this one; he'd tell Ray they couldn't find her. With any luck they'd have a busy few months and it would go on the back burner. He'd be able to sleep tonight.

No such luck. The kid jumped to her feet and started shouting at the others to come and see, come and look at this. Waving the stick in the air. Steve kept driving, kept humming, and she kept waving the stick and yelling. What did she have to go and do that for?

'There she is!' Harry jumped clean out of his seat. 'Over there, by the creek.'

Steve braked. Turned off the ignition. 'Well spotted, mate.'

Harry wandered over to her, nice and easy, for all the world like he was her favourite uncle come to visit. He started talking to her, squatting down by the water. Steve knew what he'd say: 'I'm going to take you for a ride in a police truck.' He always said that. 'And then you're going to have a little holiday.'

Steve climbed out of the truck and waited. Harry held his hand out and the girl took it. She was taken with him, you could see it. Looking up at him and smiling. With any luck they could do this nice and quick without a scene.

'There's a baby too,' Harry said, just loud enough to reach him. 'A boy.'

'Do we need to do that today?'

'I should say we do.' Harry looked at him like he was out of his mind. 'Get the job done, mate. No sense dragging it out.'

Steve looked away, over at the creek where the kids had been playing. They'd all cleared off. It had gone quiet; just a dog barking, a door slamming shut. Someone must've raised the alarm. They'd be hiding their kids under the beds, in cupboards. The older ones would have made it into the bush by now.

'I'd just as soon leave it.' He kept his voice low. 'Why don't we leave it, Harry? It's never easy when it's a baby.'

'It's not meant to be easy.' Harry held the car door open for the kid, still with the nice guy smile on his face. 'You wouldn't be here if it was easy,' he said, shutting the door behind her.

'Not easy for them, I mean.' He glanced up at the house behind them, where the family lived. 'It doesn't seem right, does it?'

16

'Jesus, Steve. What are you saying?'

Steve stared back at Harry. Another dog started barking, closer than the first. 'Nothing,' he said.

The kid leaned out the window. 'Where am I going on holiday?' She was looking wary. 'Can I say goodbye to Grandpa?'

'I'll speak to him,' Steve said. His voice sounded fake, like an actor with a bit part. 'I'll let him know.'

'Get a bloody move on,' said Harry. 'And don't let 'em get to you. It's been signed off.'

The house was quiet. Tin-roof verandah and a dog sleeping in the shade. He knocked, not too loud, but footsteps came right away. He braced himself.

'What's wrong?' An old fella answered the door. He was darker than the girl: black skin and white hair, like a photo negative. What Ray would call a 'full blood' Aboriginal. He was none too happy to see a copper on the doorstep, and he'd clocked the truck down by the creek too. 'What's the problem?'

A baby cried quietly in the front room, out of sight.

'I'm here about the kids,' Steve said. 'You the grandpa?'

'What d'you mean?' He took a better look at the truck and saw the girl through the window. He reared back in shock. Tried to push past, hollering her name. *Dora.*

'Listen. Don't make this hard on yourself.' Steve gripped him by the shoulder and shoved him back into the house, just enough force so he knew this was serious. 'Let me in.'

It was dark inside, and a tight knot of flies was frantic over a piece of meat on a plate near the stove. Three empty beer bottles lined up next to the sink. The baby was propped up on the couch in a singlet and a nappy. He'd gone quiet, big wet eyes following Steve as he moved.

'Where's the mother?'

'Out,' the old fella said, and looked at his feet. 'Her sisters help with the kids. There's three sisters and five cousins. Plenty of us to care for the younguns.'

'Look, mate. We've been told to take the baby. Orders from above.'

The old fella shook his head. 'You can't.' He picked the boy up and held him tight, both arms across his body. 'We're a loving family. We look after the kids.'

A fly thumped against the small window and dropped to the floor. The room was stifling. Steve started feeling separate from his body, like he might not be in charge of himself. He didn't know what he'd do next. He locked eyes with the baby: a steady gaze, wise and sad. Something in Steve shifted then, standing in that small room in Ivanhoe, although he barely felt it. The slight loosening of a knot.

'I'm not going to take him,' he said. 'You get to keep the boy.' The old bloke didn't react. Steve didn't know if he'd said what he thought he'd said. 'I'm going to leave him here with you. I won't take him. But his sister's coming with me, mate. Foster family's lined up already.' He went into automatic. 'She'll be looked after. She'll get a good education. Good start in life.'

The old man started to cry then, his face stretched long and trembling. 'Can I see her?'

'Best you don't. Stay here and keep the baby quiet. Or else I'll have to take him.'

Steve heard the old man wailing as he shut the door behind him. White, hard sunlight after the dark of the house. The dog lifted its head and got up on its haunches, barked at him until he was off the property.

He shook his head at Harry as he got into the truck.

'No baby in there,' he told him. His hand trembled on the ignition. He wanted to cry himself, now he was out of there, away from the old man and his despair, his grief. He had no reason to cry next to that, but still his throat ached and his eyes threatened to well up. He was a lily-livered, poisonous bastard. He couldn't even look at the girl in the back.

'I changed my mind,' she said, swinging round in her seat. 'I want Grandpa.'

'Your grandpa says to be a good girl.' He said it without turning. 'He says to sit down nice and quiet and don't muck about.'

He reversed back a few yards and a great cloud of dust rose up around them. The old bloke was out on the verandah as he pulled away, then he was chasing the truck. Steve crunched through the gears, put his foot down and drove blind through the dust till he'd gone.

19

4

Sydney, 1967

Mandy had taken her eye off of Isla for one minute. Two, maximum. She'd been right there in the wet sand, a few feet away, digging with her hands. Mandy stood beside the little hole Isla had dug; the damp heaps of sand beside it. The hole was full of water. A huge great wave had come and covered the beach, wetting the tip of Mandy's towel. Which was when she'd looked up and found Isla gone.

She searched up and down the beach; strode off in one direction shouting Isla's name, then went back the way she came and did the same thing. She must have missed her. She kept calling. There were too many little girls in blue swimmers on this beach. All of them looked familiar from a distance and became strangers as she drew closer. Panic seized her. Her legs became heavy and slow. She stood on the shingle and faced out to the water, calling again, her voice lost to the boom and crash of the waves. The heat of the day, the laughter and movement, became nauseating; the gulls sounded shrill and full of dread. She waded into the sea and shouted, 'Isla! Isla!'

The waves were coming in tall and strong. She tried to head back to shore but a wave rose up and she was caught in the swell, lifted off her feet and carried powerfully to the beach, where she landed on her forearms. Pulling herself to her knees, she imagined Isla drowned, her neck broken, her lungs full of water.

She hooked the straps of her costume back over her shoulders, coughing. Further down the beach, Isla waved, and ran towards her through the shallows.

'Mandy!' Isla was wearing red swimmers. Red. 'I saw you in the water! You got your hair wet!'

This was why Mandy didn't have children. It was scary, and exhausting. She crawled onto the beach where their towels were laid out and sat herself down. Christ Almighty.

'You went swimming!' Isla threw herself onto her knees in the sand. 'Did you like it?'

'Not much.' Mandy laughed. She pushed Isla's flattened, gritty hair out of her face. 'I didn't see that wave coming.'

'You said you don't like the water.'

'I don't!' Mandy pulled her costume away from her skin and saw she had sand all over the place, thickly gathered in the folds of her belly. 'Let's go and get showered. Your mum will be back soon. We should head home.'

Isla shook her head. 'She won't be back yet. She went shopping. I reckon she'll be ages.'

'It's getting choppy out there. That's enough for today.' Mandy stood and reached for her towel, flicking the worst of the sand out of it. 'Tell you what. Next time we'll catch a shark and take it home for lunch. How's that sound?'

Isla nodded, and picked up her own towel. 'Tomorrow, can we?'

'Don't see why not.' She nodded up at the showers at the top of the beach. 'You have first shower. I'll be right behind you.'

Mandy's legs were heavy as she followed Isla up the coastal path towards the house. She stood a moment under the shade of the tea trees, listening to the waves, getting her breath back. Steve would be home soon. He'd been away over a week, so he must have finished the job. She had a bad feeling about this one, she didn't know why. It was getting harder for him as time went on. And it was getting harder to deal with him afterwards.

Her skin turned cold, thinking of it. She found her sundress, sandy and damp at the bottom of her bag, and pulled it over her head, brushed the dried sand from her skin and climbed the last few yards to the bottom of her backyard. The best she could hope for was that he wouldn't get back before she'd had a chance to open the gin.

'Mummy's back already!' Isla ran across the yard towards her. 'She's back! She didn't even get any shopping!' Isla stopped and attempted a handstand, leaving one foot on the grass, one bent leg pointing skywards. She stood up and lifted her hands above her head, triumphant. 'That's why she's cranky, and much too hot.'

Mandy followed Isla across the grass to where Louisa was

waiting for them at the rear of the house. She looked gorgeous, as usual. Tall and elegant in a pale blue dress, perfectly upright, and that dark slab of hair down her back. Mandy felt plump and crumpled in her presence. 'You should have let yourself in, Lou. Door's open.'

'I've only been waiting a few minutes.' Louisa held her arm across her forehead to block the sun. 'I was quicker than I expected. Thanks for having her.'

'Don't mention it. We had a great time.' Mandy pushed the back door open, dropped her bag on the lino and switched the electric fan on, more for Louisa's benefit than her own. 'Come in and I'll fix you a drink. You look like you need a pick-me-up. I know I do.'

Louisa took a coaster from the kitchen table and fanned herself. 'Sounds wonderful.'

She seemed nervy, smiling too brightly, Mandy thought. She tried to catch her eye, but Louisa sat down at the table and stared out at the yard, kicking her long legs out in front of her. The sun was pulling back behind the house, and Isla was skipping up and down, her shadow folding over the plant pots and the coil of garden hose.

'Is anything wrong?' Mandy asked.

'Still can't get used to Christmas out here,' Louisa said, without turning round. 'It hits me hard at this time of year, you know.'

Mandy did know. Louisa was so homesick you could feel it coming through the walls. She reminded Mandy of her mother in that way. The British accent and the pining for home, always fed up with this country. Her mum had never let up about the stinking heat, as she'd called it. Forever fanning herself and looking for the shade. Nothing had cheered that woman up like a dark bank of cloud.

Louisa turned to face her. 'I made a down payment,' she said, waving a fly away. 'I went into town to make a down payment.'

'On what?'

She glanced out at Isla in the yard. 'Fix me that drink and I'll tell you.'

Mandy flexed the ice tray and dropped a few cubes into each tumbler. 'Happy New Year, Lou. Here's to 1967.' She knocked her glass against Louisa's. This was her first toast to the New Year. With Steve being away she'd thought she might ignore it, but in the end she'd had a few drinks and stayed up past midnight on her own. She took a long sip of gin and wondered, was it unlucky to bring in the New Year on your own? An omen of some kind?

'You got a new watch?' Louisa reached for the Timex, which sat on the kitchen table, curled around the salt and pepper.

'Got it for Christmas.'

'It's beautiful.'

'D'you think?' She felt the alcohol reach her, its welcome lift. 'I can't get used to it. Never had a watch before.'

Louisa wrapped it around her own wrist and fastened the buckle. She stretched her arm out to look at it, turning it back and forth. Her arm was damp with a fine sheen of sweat, Mandy noticed. Even her sweat was lovely.

'You should wear it,' Louisa said. 'It's elegant.'

Mandy smiled and took the watch from Louisa. 'That's the problem,' she said. 'I'm not the elegant sort.' She buckled the watch, keeping it loose so it didn't pinch.

Louisa sat back and lifted her hair, pulling it into a comb. The soft hair at the nape of her neck was wet, stuck to her skin.

'What did you say about a down payment, Lou?'

Isla bolted past them, straight through the kitchen into the lounge room. 'Isla, don't run!' Louisa called. 'Slow down!'

Isla jumped onto the couch to look out the window. Mandy took a swallow of gin and waited.

'Steve's back!' Isla held onto the back of the couch and sprang up and down, her backside in the air. 'He's back, Mandy!'

Mandy stood at the window and looked out. Steve had parked up already, and the truck was filthy, as always. Mud-caked wheels; brick-red dust at the fenders. The windscreen was covered in muck but for the small double-arc of the wipers.

Steve turned the engine off and slumped over the steering wheel, resting his head on the bridge of his hands.

Mandy's stomach turned. 'Here we go,' she said, as he lifted his head. She stepped away from the window, afraid to catch his eye.

'Here we go!' Isla leapt off the couch and turned a pirouette. 'Here we go!'

'Isla, stop jumping around.' Louisa stood in the doorway with Isla's sandals in one hand. 'We should get going.'

'No rush. Don't feel you have to leave.'

'No, we'll be off. Steve will want a bit of quiet, if he's been away.'

Mandy nodded and stubbed her cigarette out in the ashtray on the coffee table. She could see from here, he wasn't going to keep it together on account of company. 'I hope he's not too cut up, this time.'

Louisa made a sympathetic face but didn't reply. She was miles away. Troubles of her own.

'It's not an easy job,' Mandy said. 'He takes it hard.'

Louisa walked through to the kitchen with Isla, making for the back door. She didn't want to meet Steve out the front, most likely. It was best avoided, this whole business. Mandy would have avoided it herself, given the chance.

5

Sydney, 1967

Isla jumped from Mandy's back door into the yard, clearing the gap between the paving stones. She was glad she was going home. Steve's truck was dirty again because he was a policeman and he had a dirty job. He had told Isla this. A dirty rotten job but some bugger's gotta do it. It got him cranky like Isla had never seen.

Mummy was standing at the rear of the house, talking to Mandy about grown-up stuff. Isla knew they would forget she was there if she stayed quiet. She prodded at the space between the paving stones with the tip of the hose and squatted down to see if any creatures appeared. They hid in the cracks and you had to budge them out. She had disturbed a spider once which made Mandy scream and say two bad words.

'Very drastic,' Mandy said.

Isla liked the sound of drastic. She said the word quietly to herself as she pushed the hose around the edge of the paving stone nearest to Mummy's feet.

'Please don't say anything,' Mummy said.

Isla kept small and silent, her knees by her ears, until Mandy spoke again. 'You don't do things by halves, Lou.'

A line of ants emerged from the base of a large plant pot. Isla put the tip of the hose in their path and watched them scatter. A few ants crawled onto the hose and she held it against her bare leg to see if one of them might run over her skin.

'I thought it was getting easier,' Mandy said.

Isla looked up to see Mummy shake her head.

'I thought the job was helping. You were making friends. Out of the house.'

'But now there's the baby,' Mummy said. 'I can't go through that again.'

Isla dropped the hose and stood up. 'I'm not a baby,' she said.

Mummy put her hand on her belly. 'I know you're not,' she said.

'I'm four.'

'That's right,' Mummy nodded. 'Silly me. Sorry, darling.'

Mandy gave Isla a wink. 'Four and a half,' she said. 'Isn't that right?'

Isla winked back. Mandy had taught her to wink. Mandy could do good faces with her eyes crossed and her tongue out. If you did a face Mandy would give you a score out of ten. Isla's highest score was a seven. She squatted back down and saw the ants disappear into a gap in the concrete.

'Listen to me,' Mummy said. 'Keeping you talking when you need to see to your husband.'

'Takes my mind off it,' Mandy said. 'Where is he, anyway?'

Mummy knelt down beside Isla and pushed the straps of her swimmers up onto her shoulders. She wiped Isla's face with her thumb. 'Come on,' she said. 'Let's get inside before we burn.'

Isla ran to the side of the house and waited for her mum beside the hedge that grew between their house and Mandy's. It was hot in the passage between the houses and the bins smelled bad. They didn't collect the rubbish over New Year's and the stink got worse every day. Isla leaned into the hedge. The seawater had made her skin tight and she liked the scratch against her back.

From the other side of the hedge, Isla heard Mandy's voice. 'Come inside. Don't you want to come in?'

Isla crouched down to look through the low branches. Steve was sitting on the top step of his verandah and Mandy stood behind him with the front door open. Steve had his hand over his face.

'Come in,' Mandy said. She stood beside him and touched his arm. 'Please, love. Come in.'

Steve didn't move. Mandy waited a little while and then she shut the door and went back into the house. Isla listened. Her legs ached from crouching down and she wanted to go inside but she was frozen there in the hedge, waiting for it to start. Steve's shoulders began to shake and he made a high, thin noise before he broke down and cried.

29

'There you are.' Mummy held her hand out and twitched her fingers. 'What are you doing?'

'Look.' Isla pointed through the hedge at Steve. 'Look. He's crying again.'

Mummy reached for Isla's hand. She lifted Isla away from the hedge and picked twigs from her hair. Behind them, Steve sobbed and moaned. Mummy seemed not to notice. 'You're getting straight in the bath,' she said.

'He's crying,' Isla repeated.

'Who?'

'Steve.'

Mummy stood still. She held Isla tightly by the hand and listened. 'So he is.'

The air was thick with a bad, rotting smell. A cloud of flies hummed around the bins.

'We shouldn't snoop,' Mummy said.

Isla followed Mummy up the steps of their own verandah, stepping over the tiles with the cracks in them so bad things wouldn't happen. Andrea Walker had told Isla about the cracks. Andrea was nearly ten and she lived across the street in a house with stairs. She was going to be in Fifth Class at school after the holidays and she knew about all the Kings and Queens of England. There was practically nothing Andrea did not know.

Mummy found her keys and put them into the lock. 'Poor man,' she said. 'He must have had a hard day.'

'The children don't want to go in his truck,' Isla said.

Mummy looked down at Isla. She brushed a fly away from her face. 'What did you say?'

Isla felt less sure this time as she spoke. 'The children don't want to go in his truck.'

'Where did you get that from?'

'Steve told me.'

'Did he?' Mummy pushed the door open. 'What a strange thing to say to a child.'

'It's true,' Isla said. When there was no reply she said it again, louder. 'It's true!'

Her mum's voice reached her from inside the house. 'I didn't say it wasn't.'

Isla sat down on the step. Mrs Walker opened her front door and threw a bucket of dirty water over her roses. The Walkers had a car and Mr Walker drove it to work and back every day. The only other car on their street was Steve's truck. Isla could see it from here, parked up with one wheel on the kerb. The windscreen was dirty with red mud.

'Isla?' Mummy was calling her. 'Come in and shut the door.'

Isla tried not to look at Steve as she turned around. Her greatest fear was that he would try to take her away in his truck. Mandy had explained that Steve only took children from problem families. You don't need to worry, she'd said. But Isla had not been reassured by this. Not at all. At the edge of her vision, Steve was a dark shape, hunched over, watching her.

6

Sydney, 1997

Isla and her mum sit in traffic at the lights crossing Anzac Parade. The sky is bright blue and the streets are over-lit, artificial-looking under a strong sun. Telegraph poles cast sharp shadows. The buildings are low, the streets are wide and the schoolkids laugh easily, keeping to the shade in their wide-brimmed hats and cotton dresses. Isla regrets her black jeans and heavy boots. Nobody wears black in Sydney. She feels like a tourist. A sullen, tired, uncomfortable tourist in a city with the brightness turned too high. She'd forgotten it was this hot in May. And she'd forgotten – maybe she'd never faced it before – that she doesn't fit in here.

'Tell me honestly. Is it a bit short?' Louisa looks at herself in the rear-view mirror and touches the softly layered hair at the back of her head. 'I think it suits me. What do you think?'

Isla smiles because she doesn't know what to say. She has envied her mother's long, dark hair her whole life. Without it she is no longer remarkable. She could be any woman in her

32

fifties. You might think, if you caught her eye in the street, that she must have been beautiful once.

Louisa is waiting for a reply. She fluffs her hair up at the sides.

'It must be easier to manage,' Isla says. 'With you swimming every day.'

'Exactly. It's dry by the time I'm back inside.' Louisa nods at her reflection and inches the car forward. 'I like it. I was sick of all the combing and blow-drying.'

The lights change. Isla watches a man in a suit and tie push himself along the footpath on a shiny, adult-sized two-wheeled scooter. It looks like a monstrous version of the one Isla had when she was six. He weaves through a group of pedestrians, smiling broadly. Isla wonders if she is hallucinating.

'You look thin,' Louisa says.

'Do I?'

'And pale.' Louisa's eyes move over Isla's hair and face before she turns back to the road. 'Are you taking care of yourself?'

'I just spent twenty-four hours on a plane.'

'Don't be clever. You know what I mean.'

Isla stares at the road ahead. Her teenage self wants to jump from the car.

'I've been going to the gym,' Isla says. She is thirty-five years old. She has a career and a life and will soon own an overpriced apartment with a Juliet balcony. 'I've been swimming every morning before work. Getting fit.'

Louisa nods and frowns, glancing again at Isla as she changes gear. 'The sun will do you good,' she says.

An empty bottle of orange juice rolls back and forth by

Louisa's feet as she drives. Isla's feet are pushed to one side by the shopping bags, old newspapers and unpaired shoes in the footwell. She wonders how her dad tolerates the state of the car. He is a man who hates mess, and her mum – contrary to her stylish appearance – is a woman who would happily live in total disorder. They have argued about it their whole marriage.

'I'm looking forward to Dad's party,' Isla says.

Louisa brakes and they both fly forward, slamming against the seat belts. An empty sandwich carton joins the orange juice bottle at Louisa's feet.

'Sorry.' Louisa swears quietly at the van driver in front of them, who is sounding his horn at a kid on a skateboard. 'Sorry,' she says again. She looks at Isla and blows a strand of hair out of her eyes. 'I wish I hadn't invited half the street to the party.'

'I'll help you,' Isla says. 'Let me take care of it.'

'I don't know what I was thinking.'

'It'll be fine, Mum.'

'And now—' She kicks the sandwich carton away from the clutch. 'And now there's all this business with the police.'

'Couldn't we forget about that for the day?'

'Everyone knows, Isla.'

She swallows. 'Knows what?'

'The whole street knows the police have been to see us.' The car stalls as the traffic moves on. Louisa turns the key in the ignition, cursing. 'They know your father's a suspect.'

'Suspect?' Isla laughs, and it makes her throat hurt. 'I think that's taking it a bit far.'

'Let's hope so.'

Isla stares at her mum as she checks the mirror, pushes her sunglasses onto her head. 'Do the police really think Dad's behind her disappearance? This Mandy woman?'

'Yes,' Louisa says. 'They really do.'

'That's insane.'

Louisa tries to start the car and pointedly does not reply. The sun beats hard against the windscreen. A car behind them sounds its horn. Isla thinks she might put her fist through the window in response to her mother's disloyalty, her coldness, which is at once staggering and entirely familiar. She shuts her eyes and sees her blood pulsing.

'Mum.' Isla digs her fingernails into her palm. 'Surely you don't think—?'

Cars pull out behind them and overtake as Louisa turns the ignition, stalls again and hits the steering wheel with the flat of her hand. A man in a red ute shouts at them through his opened window. Louisa starts the engine and accelerates, gripping the steering wheel, rigidly upright. Isla adjusts the air conditioning on the dashboard and lifts her T-shirt away from her skin.

'That would be a big help,' Louisa says, her voice tight. 'If you could take care of the party.' She changes gear. 'You're so good at that sort of thing.'

Isla drags her hand over her face, fighting the tired, grimy feeling and the lingering rage. 'Leave it to me. I love a good party.' It's true; she is good at bringing people together. It's also true that she hasn't been sober at a party since she was fifteen. She turns to the window, where the quiet suburban streets of

Agnes Bay have replaced the city landscape. There is not a soul in sight. Roller blinds are drawn at the windows; doors are shut. It could be a movie set: row after row of neat, empty shells.

'Things are still the same around here,' Louisa says, turning onto Bay Street.

Isla looks out at the street where she grew up. The houses crouch low under a huge sky, each with a tidy lawn at the front, manicured hedges; wide passages between one building and the next. The small, identical bungalows on the ocean side of Bay Street were built in the early sixties when her parents were newlyweds and property along the coast was affordable. Across the street the houses are newer, bigger and wider, with smart fences, red brick instead of weatherboard. Some even have a second storey over a garage. But the yards at the back of the newer houses are small squares of grass, fenced off on all sides. Isla must have been three years old the first time she visited the Walkers' house and encountered the fence that stood between their property and the people behind. She had believed until then that everyone had a beach at the end of their yard.

Louisa parks outside the house, yanks the handbrake. 'So,' she says. 'What do you think?'

Isla can't speak for a moment. She must have lived in this house almost twenty-five years without ever looking at it. She had no idea it was so ugly.

'It took your father all weekend to paint the woodwork,' Louisa says. 'As soon as you said you were coming home, he managed to find time for all the jobs he's been putting off.'

Isla can see now that the fencing around the verandah has been freshly painted. The hedge at the front of the house has been trimmed into a sharp oblong and hanging baskets have been suspended either side of the door, spilling over with something pink and purple. The weatherboard looks old next to the fresh paint and the baskets look foolish. Mutton dressed as lamb. Her throat tightens. 'I'd have walked past it.'

'You've been away too long.'

She manages a murmur of assent.

'That one,' Louisa says, pointing at the house next door, 'was Mandy's.'

Isla turns in her seat. Her mum is very still, holding her hands in her lap.

'Was it?'

'You don't remember?'

Isla looks from her mum to the neighbours' house and back. She remembers nothing. The sense of Mandy that she felt on the phone to her dad has gone. She only has the present: the exactness of the buildings, the gateposts, the hedges.

'You never mentioned her,' Isla says. 'I don't remember you ever saying her name before.'

'Why would I?'

'Weren't you friendly with her?'

'No, not really. I hadn't thought of her in a long time, before the police turned up.'

Isla suspects this isn't quite true. The car is hot without the air conditioning and there's a smell of melting plastic. She catches her mum's eye as she unfastens her seat belt and is surprised to see hurt in her face.

'She might be living quietly, somewhere remote,' Isla says. 'Isn't that the most likely thing?'

'I don't think so. People don't disappear without a trace these days.'

'But this was thirty years ago.'

'Thirty years without a trace is suspicious, Isla.'

'Says who?'

'Says the police.' She says it sharply. 'They seem to think something happened to her. I'd love to think they were wrong.'

This isn't quite true either, Isla thinks. This is a chance for her mum to air her discontent. Decades of it.

Isla gets out of the car, slams the door shut and pulls her bag from the boot.

'Let me take that,' Louisa says, reaching for Isla's bag. They have a brief, ill-tempered struggle over who will carry it: Isla refuses to let go and the strap starts to rip from the fabric of the case. She drops it and the weight surprises her mother, almost toppling her over.

'Sorry,' Isla says. She doesn't like herself in her mum's company. Ten years have changed nothing: they still bring out the worst in each other. Tiredness hits her and she wishes she were elsewhere. She longs for the dark chill of London, the damp paving slabs, the cool slant of the sun.

'I thought we might swim later,' Louisa says, swinging the bag onto her shoulder. 'Keep you in the right time zone!'

Isla follows her mother up to the house, stepping over the tiles with the cracks in them, two at a time.

7

Sydney, 1967

Mandy tipped the remains of Louisa's gin into her own glass, sat down at the table and waited for her hands to stop shaking. It was quiet; just the waves in the distance and the hum of the fridge. This was her favourite time of day, once the sun had moved around to the front of the house and the yard had cooled down a bit. Sometimes you got a cool breeze coming in off the ocean. Hard to enjoy it but, when her husband was crying out on the verandah, refusing to come inside.

She was out of her depth with all this. Nothing she said or did could help him when he came home inconsolable, when he cried at the end of the day. Lately it seemed to bring out the hard-hearted bitch in her; the woman she was trying not to be. The woman only the bottom of the gin glass knew about, who was disappointed her husband couldn't get on with his job and take the knocks like a man. Who was ashamed of his weakness, God help her. There it was.

Still quiet. She stood and put some fresh ice in her glass. Might as well sit out in the yard for a bit, try to get some pleasure from the afternoon. She put her cigarettes in the pocket of her sundress. A flower had blossomed that morning on the passionfruit vine, and a couple more were opening up. She put her glass down on the paving stones and held the opened flower to her nose, looked into the heart of the blossom, with its gaudy tendrils and its petals flung back. Big, hairy, purple thing it was, when you got close to it. With any luck they'd get fruit this year. They'd had nothing so far, despite a dozen or more flowers on the vine every summer. You don't get fruit if the flowers don't pollinate, Louisa had told her. No pollination, no fruit. Which pretty much summed things up around here.

She sat down in the striped garden chair and heard her front door slam. She took a cigarette from the pack and shunted the chair around, turning her back to the house. Her hand shook and it took her three goes to get the thing lit. This was ridiculous. She needed to get a grip.

'Mandy.'

She didn't reply. She was facing right into next door's line of shrubs and her eyes had fixed on Lou's roses. They were bright and full, opened up from a day in the sun. She couldn't bring herself to look away.

He was right behind her now. 'What are you doing out here? I was calling you.'

'Sorry. Just enjoying the quiet. Nice breeze.'

He stood next to her. His face was bloated from crying and

40

two purple veins had risen jaggedly at his temples. She reached
out for his hand and he gripped it tightly.

'Feeling any better?'

He nodded. 'Bit.'

Isla ran out her back door, turned several off-kilter cartwheels
on the grass and applauded herself loudly, scaring the cockatoos
in the trees. Steve's frown unfolded as he watched her. He was
soft over kids. Isla wasn't his biggest fan, mind. She'd seen and
heard too much of all this. The tears and the outbursts. Mandy
was used to it but she could see how a child might be put off.

'Look at my cartwheels, Daddy!' Isla called out to Joe, who
had walked out onto his deck. 'Look at me!'

Joe clapped his hands and cheered as Isla cartwheeled past.
He caught Mandy's eye and nodded, raising a hand in greeting.
God Almighty, she was looking straight at him. She waved
back, and shunted her chair to the right.

'You're home now, love,' Mandy said. 'Try to relax. There's
a few beers in the fridge.'

He shook his head. 'Thing is, Mandy—'

Joe sat down and undid his tie with both hands, tugged it
free of his collar and threw it down on the deck. Something
was different about him. He'd changed his hair, she thought.
Cut it much shorter. And he was wearing a suit, of course. That
must be it. He looked twice the man, somehow, in the crisp
white shirt and the suit pants. She felt blood rush to her face.

'I can't take much more of all this,' Steve was saying. 'I'm
not up to it, darl. It's a dirty job.'

Mandy moved her chair another few inches to the right,

clipping Steve's boot. 'You always feel this way afterwards. Give it a day or two and you'll be right.'

'I don't think so. Not this time.'

She caught the edge to his voice. It exhausted her, the way he needed her. She felt drained and guilty, both at once. She held her hands out and he lifted her to her feet. 'How bad was it?'

'It was bad. Like always.' He spoke into her ear. 'I don't like who I am sometimes.'

'Stop that.' She eased her hands free. 'Don't start all that now.'

'She cried herself hysterical,' he said. 'Begged us to take her back home. That can't be right, can it?'

Mandy smiled at him, kissed his cheek. He smelled of sweat, and the hot interior of his truck. 'Come on,' she said, letting the smile slip as she looked over his shoulder at Isla roaming around the back of her yard; the mob of cockatoos shifting about in the trees. Sweet Jesus, she thought, don't let him start up again, not here. 'Why don't you take a shower, Steve? Get yourself freshened up. That always helps.'

He looked down at himself. His police blues were creased and stained. 'You're right. Been wearing this getup for days.'

'Once you're changed I'll fix you something to eat. We can have a quiet evening. Get your head straight.'

'Righto.' He stayed where he was. 'Sorry, darl. I'm not sure I'll spring back from this one too quick.'

'You got the job done, love. That's it now, for a while.'

He nodded. 'Hope so.'

'Gotta take the rough with the smooth. Right?'

'Right.' He didn't look convinced. 'I'll take a shower.'

Mandy sat back down and tried to get settled again. Her gin had gone warm. She was still aware of Joe sitting out on his deck, smoking a cigarette. The curve of his spine, his neck, the back of his head.

She looked away. Joe Green had never caught her eye before. He had a knockout wife and a second baby on the way, for God's sake. What was with her today? She stood, picked up her glass and took a quick glance in Joe's direction. Louisa stared back at her. Brown, sad eyes. She was sitting at Joe's side, telling him something, and he was looking out at the yard, watching Isla run around in the trees.

Mandy's face burned up. Her skin flushed hot, then cold. She nodded at Louisa and turned her back, self-conscious in her crumpled sundress as she walked away. She felt caught out. Exposed. Which was daft, but she felt it all the same.

8

Sydney, 1967

'What's howdy?'

'It means hello in America.' Joe patted the seat beside him. 'Come and sit down. Watch the film with me till your mum gets home.'

Isla climbed onto the couch and sat in his lap. 'Howdy,' she said.

'Howdy, partner.'

She knelt on his thigh and ran her hands over his scalp. Since he'd had this buzzcut, she wanted to stroke his head whenever she could get close enough. She wasn't gentle about it. He moved his whisky tumbler so she couldn't knock it and tipped his head forward for her. Sometimes with Isla you had to give in and let her have her way. The same was true of her mother, although he didn't give in to her half as often. Isla was less complicated. She thought he was God on earth, and he was putty in her grubby little hands.

'Why don't they say hello?'

'Different places have different words, love. They think hello sounds funny.'

She moved her hands across his skull. 'Is that why Mummy talks funny?'

'She doesn't talk funny.' He smiled to himself. The head massage was helping, now she'd calmed it down a bit. He let his eyes close. 'Your mum's from England, like me.'

Isla climbed down from the couch. 'Pop to the loo,' she said, in a half decent English accent. She spread her hands and held her arms out. 'I think I'll just pop to the loo.'

He laughed. 'That's not bad.'

'Goodness me.' She lifted her chin, flared her nostrils. 'What a ghastly candelabra.'

'A ghastly what?'

She was bent double, laughing at herself. It was that time of night when she'd be in stitches one minute and crying her heart out the next. He shouldn't have let her stay up so late. But she was good company. Nobody else made him laugh these days.

'Where d'you get this stuff, Isla?'

'From the telly,' she said, sitting back down beside him. 'Mandy lets me watch her programmes with her when it's raining.'

'Does she now?' He smoothed her hair, which was stiff with seawater, and full of sand.

'Why don't you talk funny?' She yawned. 'Daddy?'

Because I've lived here six years, he thought, and I made the

45

effort to fit in. And I never had a plum in my mouth to start with.

'I don't know, Isla,' he said. 'I think it must be bedtime.'

'You said I could watch the film till Mummy got home.'

He laughed and she laughed back, pleased with herself. 'Did I say that?' He wrestled her a little bit, going easy so he didn't make her cry. 'You look sleepy,' he said, and she didn't deny it. 'Why don't I put you to bed?'

'I can sleep here with you.' She lay down with her head in his lap and pressed her face into his shirt.

'As long as you do sleep,' he said. 'I don't want you chatting to me all night, you hear?'

'I won't.'

He reached for his drink.

'What's a candelabra, Daddy?'

'I'll give you a candelabra if you don't go to sleep.'

She started laughing again. He was useless at this stuff. 'Come on,' he said. 'Don't play me up, love.'

He managed a sip of whisky while she stretched out and got herself comfortable. After a minute she went still and he tried to watch the film. He'd lost the thread of it a while back, but it was helping to numb his brain after working all day. That and the whisky. He was leaning on the grog a bit heavy, these past few weeks. He'd expected the promotion to be hard going, but there were days lately when he felt like he was in over his head. Nobody knew what they were doing and they were looking to him for decisions. Sometimes he wondered if he should have stayed where he was, supervising the site and the men, taking his tea breaks with the rest of them and knocking off early on a Friday. They'd all changed towards him the minute he'd turned up in a suit and tie. He'd expected it, of course, but it didn't make it any easier when they headed off to the bar without him, leaving him up to his neck in plans and drawings and problems. More problems than he could have imagined. Every day the newspapers were asking why Sydney needed an Opera House on Bennelong Point, and he was halfway inclined to think they were right.

But he'd decided to buy the Holden. The latest model. They had more than enough in the bank. It was a lot of money, and they'd have to step up the savings plan afterwards, but he needed something to make it all worthwhile, to balance out the long days and the stress. The thought of the car was keeping him going when he was dead on his feet at the end of the day. They'd be able to get out of town at weekends, see the places they'd read about when they were planning to move out here. Lou had liked the look of those spots up the coast – Byron Bay, Noosa – but they'd never got there. He wanted to take her out of Sydney, show her this country, make her see it the way he did.

Isla was asleep. He'd lift her into bed in a minute, so it all looked shipshape when Lou got back from Mandy's. She'd been gone a while, come to think of it. Still, it was good for her to have someone to talk to. Mandy was a nice woman. She'd known what to do when Louisa was low, back when Isla was a baby. They'd come to rely on her.

Joe picked Isla up and carried her through to her room. It

was going to be tough if Lou had another low patch with the new baby. He hadn't said so, but it had been his first thought when she'd told him she was pregnant again: what if you can't cope? What if you draw the curtains for six months and cry every time the baby cries?

He set Isla down on her bed and pulled the covers over her, found her Digby bear and tucked him in the crook of her arm. She'd be starting school before long, and if Lou got her driving licence, it would all start to come together. She'd be a busy mum, taking the kids to the beach, to the park, to school and back. She could stop working, stop relying on Mandy so much. Stop pining for home.

Isla turned in her sleep and kicked her covers off. She was the love of his life, this girl; this funny kid who came along before they were ready and knocked them sideways. The whisky was turning him soft, but still, it was a fact. He'd been mad about her from day one. He leaned down and kissed her forehead. Her hair and skin smelled sharply of the sea. He should have made her take a bath. Then again, it was outdoor dirt, the healthy kind of dirt that kids should smell of. He'd smelled of mildew and cabbages at her age, and had never seen the sea. He needed to remember that, whenever Louisa's moaning got to him. This was a better life for them all, by a long shot.

He left Isla's night light on and shut her door behind him. There was a shootout on the TV, filling the lounge room with gunfire and stampeding horses. It was almost ten o'clock. He took the whisky bottle through to the kitchen and topped up his glass. He'd make this his last one. Looking for matches in the second drawer down, among the elastic bands, coins from the old currency, reels of cotton and paperclips, he found a set of keys, held together with string and a cardboard tag that read *Steve and Mandy*. God help them if they ever needed their spare set; it was hopeless trying to find anything in this house. The thing you needed was never the thing that emerged from the chaos. He'd spent ages looking for the savings book earlier and hadn't found it. The mess, the clutter, drove him mad. He couldn't relax when the place was a tip. Louisa knew that. But she'd rather put up with mess than give in and do as he asked.

Joe sat down at the kitchen table and smoked a cigarette. He was sober enough – just – to know that his own voice, in his head, was starting to sound like his dad. Time to knock it on the head with the whisky and call it a night. He stood and tipped the dregs from his glass down the sink, ran the glass under the tap and drank some water. There was something his dad had never done in his life.

The credits were rolling on the TV. He was tired, but he didn't fancy the thought of the empty bed. He'd just close his eyes on the couch while he waited for Lou. She'd be home any minute. This wasn't what he was used to, was all. Usually she was the one at home on her own on a Friday night.

He woke to the sound of the back door slamming shut, movements in the kitchen. He tried to unfurl himself from the tense ball he'd slept in. His legs and neck were stiff, his mouth dry. 'Lou?' He sat up and listened. Nothing. He got himself up on his feet and called out to her again.

'I'm in here,' she said at last. She sounded strange.

'You ok?' He pushed the kitchen door open. She was sitting at the table with her head in her hands. He sat down beside her. 'What's wrong?'

'I need to tell you something.'

'What?' He pulled her hands away from her face. 'What is it?'

'I don't want a car.'

He waited, and when she didn't continue he laughed and rubbed her back. 'You had me worried there.'

'The money you want to spend on the car could get us home.' She turned her chair to face him. 'I don't want to be here, Joe.'

He groaned, and put his hands on her shoulders. He didn't have the energy for this. 'It'll get easier. Once we've got the car, we can—'

'Listen to me.' She twisted out of his grip. 'The car won't solve anything.'

'How do you know? You haven't given it a try.'

'I knew you'd say that. I knew this was pointless.'

He held her eye a few seconds. 'You've been talking to Mandy about this, haven't you?'

'I might have.'

'For Christ's sake.' He sat back and looked at the ceiling. 'What did you tell her?'

'Never mind about that.'

'I do mind. What did you tell her?'

'I told her I want to go home before the baby comes. She persuaded me to talk to you about it.'

'Some things are private, Louisa.' He felt his voice rise. 'Some things should stay between us.'

She stood, and her own voice rose to a shout. 'I knew you wouldn't listen. I knew you'd do this.'

'I've worked my backside off for the car.' He stabbed the air with his finger. 'Months of overtime. And now this promotion. Do you have any idea—?'

'I didn't ask you to.'

'What?'

'I didn't ask you to work so hard. I'd rather not have the extra money if you're going to spend it all on yourself.'

'The car is for us!'

'Rubbish. It's a status symbol.'

'That's not true!' He slammed his hand on the table. 'I want us to see the country, as a family. Start to enjoy being here.'

'I don't want to see the country.'

'You are the most ungrateful—'

'I can't be grateful for something I don't want!'

'You're unbelievable.'

'Am I? For wanting a say over how we live? Where we live?' She threw her arms up. 'Can't you see, I can never be happy in this country? Don't you care about that?'

'Do you really think you'd be happy if we went home?'

She stared at him. 'I was happy before we got here.'

'We weren't married long before we got here. Maybe it's us that's wrong. Maybe we'd be in trouble wherever we lived.'

He hadn't meant to say that. He hadn't known he even thought it until he heard himself say it. He lit another cigarette, just to occupy his hands, to avoid looking at her.

'Is that what you think?' She sounded hurt.

51

'I don't know. Maybe.'

'You think we're the problem? You and me?'

'I just meant.' He reached for the whisky bottle and poured himself a glass. 'I think we'd likely have the same set of problems if we went back home. Running home's not the answer.'

'You'd still drink too much in England, you mean?'

He drained the glass in one. 'Don't start.'

'You remind me of your father lately, you know that?'

'I said, don't start!'

She picked up the bottle, which was nearly empty, and held it up for him to see. 'That's gone down quick, Joe. Aren't you meant to be saving?'

He snatched the bottle from her – too hard, too rough – and slammed it down on the table. 'If I can't have a drink in my own home –'

'You're drunk.'

'Can you blame me?'

She started crying then. He was drunk, it was true, and he wanted her to leave him alone so he could finish the bottle in peace.

'Don't cry.' He stood beside her and reached for her hand. 'Come on. It's late, and we've both said things we shouldn't have.'

'I meant everything I said.' She was crying hard. 'Is there any chance, Joe? Any chance we could go home? Would you consider it, one more time?'

'No.' He held her by her arms. 'This is where we live. This place is home for us, for our family. We need to make the best of it.'

She pulled away from him, more forcefully than she needed to. 'I'm going to bed.'

Joe waited for the bedroom door to shut behind her and then he reached again for the whisky, drank it down from the bottle in quick, painful gulps. The kitchen turned dark. His head was full of things he wanted to say to her, now she was gone. He moved into the hallway and leaned against the wall next to the bedroom door. The bed shifted under her weight and he thought of her lying there, angry with him, thinking she was hard done by because he wouldn't let her go home to bloody England. She didn't know how lucky she was. She let him work himself into the ground and then she threw everything he did for her back in his face.

He pushed the bedroom door open and stood over her. 'I know you're not asleep,' he said.

She didn't respond. He reached down and pulled the covers away from her body. She opened her eyes then and stared back at him. 'Leave me alone, Joe.'

He held the headboard and leaned over her, his face close to hers. 'Do you know how lucky you are?' No reply. 'Do you?'

She rolled onto her back and pushed him, hitting his shoulders with the flats of her hands. 'Go and sleep on the couch.'

He grabbed her by the wrists. She shouted and struggled and he knew he would regret this, but it was too late and he had already gone too far. This rage between them, it was stronger than him. 'I've tried to make you happy,' he said. 'You're never happy, are you?'

She must have positioned her feet against his chest. The last thing he saw, before he flew backwards, was the look of fear in her face. She kicked him with all her strength and he landed flat on his back. He was out cold before his head hit the floor.

'Daddy?'

He didn't see Isla at the door, scared by the noise. He didn't hear her voice.

'Isla,' Louisa said. 'Did you wake up, darling?'

Isla looked up at her mother on the bed. She had seen her dad fly backwards. The force of the kick. Its energy was locked inside her, tightly.

'It's all right,' Louisa said, joining Isla at his side.

'Is he dead?'

'No!'

'Is he going to wake up?' Isla's voice was high-pitched, close to a scream.

Louisa looked guilty and afraid, an expression Isla hadn't seen before, that she would try to forget. Isla stifled a wail. Louisa knelt down and slapped at Joe's face.

9

Sydney, 1967

Isla stood on the verandah to eat her toast. It was shady out there and the street was quiet. The cement mixer was turning in the empty lot near the Walkers' place, next to a pile of bricks and sand which was going to be a new house. Mr Walker had already left in his car and Andrea was out on her bike, cycling up and down the street, ringing her bell each time she passed and lifting her arm to wave in that show-off way she had. She'd recently told Isla she was getting a kitten on her next birthday, when she turned ten. Isla had been trying ever since to be nicer to Andrea, who said she was too big to be Isla's friend, and who had so far refused to let Isla have a ride of her bike. Isla figured if she didn't get to hold the kitten she would give up being nice to her. There were a few months to go till Andrea's birthday and already she was wondering if she could keep it up.

She ate her toast and watched the windows opening in the

houses across the street; curtains being pulled back. Behind her, through the open front door, she could hear Daddy getting ready for work. Finding his wallet, his cigarettes; the papers for his briefcase. He was cranky because Mummy was not talking to him. She'd been ignoring him over the weekend. They hadn't made up since the bad thing that happened on Friday night, after Mummy went to Mandy's. Isla did not like thinking about the bad thing: Daddy on the floor, not asleep and not dead but something else. She'd found him asleep on the couch the next morning, his body cramped like a toy in a box, his head at the wrong angle.

Isla looked down at the steps leading to the front yard and tried to remember if she'd trodden on the wrong tile yesterday. Maybe she'd brushed a crack with the tip of her sandal. Her new sandals were too big and they made her feet heavy. She wished she had been more careful.

'There you are,' Daddy said, standing at the door behind her. He looked like something was hurting in his head. He crouched down and pinched her cheek. 'What's up?'

'Nothing,' she said.

'Good girl.'

She reached out and he tipped his head forward to let her move her hand across his short hair. She felt his soft skin and his hard bones.

'Got to run,' he said.

'Are you going to put the roof on today?'

He laughed. 'Maybe.'

'Hope it fits on right.'

'Me too.'

Daddy turned to wave at the gate, like always. She waited on the verandah till he turned the corner. Bay Street was very quiet now. She finished her toast and wiped her fingers on her pyjama shirt. Three doors down, Mr Blunt was out on the footpath with his shears, snipping at his hedge. He would have no hedge left before long, Mandy always said, and then he'd need a new way to stickybeak at all the neighbours. But you had to go easy on him because his wife was dead.

'Has he gone?' Mummy shouted from inside the house.

'Yes,' Isla shouted back.

'Good. Come inside.'

Isla found her mum in her bedroom, sitting on the edge of the bed. Her wet hair was loose down her back and her dress was only zipped up halfway. She was looking at an envelope full of money: different sizes and colours of notes.

'What's that for?'

Mummy patted the space next to her on the bed. 'We're going to do something together today.'

'I don't want to go shopping.'

'That's not it.' She patted the bed again. 'Why don't you come and sit down beside me?'

Isla did not move. She had a bad feeling, looking at Mummy on the bed.

'How would you like to go in an aeroplane?' Mummy smiled in a pretend way. 'What do you think?'

'Is Daddy coming?'

'No, darling. Just us.'

Isla tried to speak but the bad feeling was big in her neck. Her mum stood and reached around to pull her zipper up at the back, turning in front of the mirror to look at herself sideways. She wore her yellow sundress, patterned with daisies, the one Isla had always liked. Today the daisies were stretched wide over her belly.

'I picked out a dress for you to wear,' Mummy said. She helped Isla climb out of her pyjamas. 'A special dress for a special day.'

Isla lifted her arms up and her mum put the dress over her head, buttoned it at the back and stood her in front of the mirror. She knew this was one of the dresses that Andrea Walker had grown out of. It was red and white and it made her feel like Andrea was here in the room, showing off about school and her two-wheeler bike. She didn't like looking at herself in the dress. She wished her mum was going to work, so she could go to Mandy's for an ordinary day, wearing her swimmers and a hat.

Her mum was moving around in a busy, quick way, putting things into a bag that was open on the bed. 'Brush your hair,' she said as she left the room. 'Get all the knots out!'

Isla found the brush and followed her mum into the kitchen. She pulled the brush through her hair a couple of times, hoping she might get away with making just the hair you could see look tidy. There was a big, matted knot at the base of her neck which caught the bristles of the brush.

Mummy sat down at the table with a pen and paper. She picked the pen up and put it down again, picked it up and sucked the end, put it down. Isla kept brushing her hair as softly as she could. She could see her mum hadn't written anything on the page yet.

'Come here,' Mummy said, and pulled Isla onto her knee. 'Let me brush it.'

Isla tensed herself for pain, but her mum was careful, taking one strand at a time. Isla stayed still and hoped her mum might have forgotten about the aeroplane. Mummy sniffed and blew her nose a few times, but she didn't talk.

There was a knock at the door and Mummy put the brush down, turned Isla to face her and kissed her cheek. 'I need you to be good,' she said. 'Please be good, darling, all right?'

Isla nodded, and tried to be good, which meant not saying things out loud except for good manners. She tried not to think of the bad thing. Daddy on the floor, Mummy on the bed. It was clearer than before and she couldn't not think it. She sat very still on the chair in the kitchen, ankles together, and smiled at her mum. Mummy smiled back because she didn't know Isla could see her in her head with her legs stretched out, kicking Daddy backwards. Nobody knew except her. She was like the smooth, brushed hair with the very bad knot underneath.

Mummy ran to the bedroom and when she came out she was holding the bag that had been on the bed. Around her shoulders she wore a long, grey coat that Isla had never seen before. Isla got the bad feeling again, looking at the coat. Her mum rushed past to open the front door. When she came back inside, the coat and bag were gone.

'Oh God oh God.' Mummy leaned over the kitchen table, picked the pen up and wrote something, carefully, looked at it and shook her head. She put the pen down and walked towards Isla, holding her hand out. 'Let's go,' she said. 'I've packed you a bag.'

10

Sydney, 1967

Mandy stood on the back of the couch to reach the curtain rail with the duster. Funny what you saw from this angle. A dead fly on one of the blades of the ceiling fan; a layer of dust on top of the display cabinet. And a taxi, outside Louisa's house, waiting at the kerb.

She stood down onto the rug and gripped the duster. It was probably nothing. She pushed the fibres in the rug back and forth with her toe. Almost certainly nothing. She stood back up on the couch. The taxi was still there. Engine running, the boot standing open. She leaned against the window and kept her eye on the driver, who had his window down, elbow jutting out in the sun. He was looking expectantly up at Louisa's front door.

Louisa came into view, opening up her gate. She was holding a heavy-looking carpet bag, and she had a long, grey coat around her shoulders. A winter coat. It reached her ankles and had a look of gloom to it, like a hearse. She lifted her bag into the boot and threw the coat in after it.

Mandy held onto the curtain rail. She'd told Lou not to do this. She'd spent hours talking her out of it, persuading her to hold her bloody horses. Surely she wasn't really going through with it?

Louisa turned back up to her house, rushing, and reappeared moments later, leading Isla by the hand towards the car. Isla looked small and neat, in a red and white dress and bright, white socks up to her knees. Her hair was loose down her back, white-blonde at the tips from the sun. She was carrying a little red suitcase.

Mandy dropped her duster. By the time she got out onto her verandah, Isla was climbing into the taxi. 'Wait! Hold on!'

'Mandy!' Isla leaned out of the rear window, her face grave. 'I'm going in an aeroplane and Daddy isn't coming.'

'Are you?' Mandy reached for Isla's hand and breathed deeply, in and out. 'An aeroplane?'

Louisa was writing something down on the back of an envelope, leaning awkwardly on her knee. She had on her short, yellow sundress, patterned with daisies. She looked tired, the light gone from her. 'My mum's number,' she said, holding the envelope out. 'Take it.' She took Mandy's hand and closed her fingers around it. 'Please, Mandy.'

Mandy looked at the envelope, at the string of numbers reaching lopsidedly along the page. She didn't want it. She wanted to slow this down; to wind things back a bit.

'Lou. Are you –? You're going through with it?'

Louisa nodded. 'We're going to the airport.'

'Did you tell Joe you were leaving?' Mandy tried not to look at Isla, who was still holding her hand. She couldn't take the sight of her in that dress, her curls all brushed out and clean. 'Does he know?'

'Of course I didn't tell him.' Louisa lowered her voice. 'He wouldn't have let me take Isla. He'd have stopped me.'

'Did you try to talk to him?'

'Yes. It was pointless. I told you it would be pointless.'

The driver leaned across and opened the passenger door. 'Thought you were in a hurry,' he said. 'We should get a move on.'

Mandy gave Isla's hand a squeeze and turned her back on her. 'Lou,' she said. 'You can't do this to Joe. This is going to kill him.'

'God, Mandy. Don't say that.'

'He loves that child every bit as much as you do. He's her bloody father for Christ's sake.'

Louisa sat in the passenger seat and folded her long legs in front of her. Mandy could see she was crying from the way her body shook. The daisies on her dress shuddered.

'Louisa.' She knelt down beside the car and spoke softly. 'Please don't do this.'

Isla was staring wide-eyed at Mandy from the back seat. Her chin had puckered but she was managing not to cry.

'Are we going or not?' the driver wanted to know. 'If we're going we need to move it.'

Louisa reached out and touched Mandy on the arm. 'Let me

go,' she said. Her face was wet. 'Will you call me in a few days? Let me know if he's all right?'

'You'll be at your mum's?'

She nodded, and Mandy nodded back. She couldn't find any words. Isla was crying now and the driver was drumming his fingers on the steering wheel.

'Bye, sweetheart.' Mandy fixed a smile on her face, touched her fingers to her lips and reached past the hot vinyl seat to press them against Isla's cheek. 'You be a good girl for your mum.' She stood and pushed the car door shut.

The car pulled away sharply from the kerb, and Isla twisted round in the back seat. Her voice carried through the open window, 'I don't want to go!'

Mandy ran after them, stumbling and losing a house shoe in the gutter. Isla was a small, blonde dot in the back of the taxi, her hands pressed pale against the rear window. Mandy stood in the road and waved until she was gone.

She hobbled back to the footpath. The sun was scorching the back of her neck, and the bitumen had burned the sole of her one bare foot. David Walker was practising his violin, sending a sequence of flat, trembling notes across the street. The gate outside Louisa's house stood open. Mandy couldn't look at it. She found her missing house shoe and slammed her own gate shut behind her.

11

Sydney, 1997

Isla smooths a tablecloth over the trestle table she's assembled in the yard. She's been up since dawn, cooking and tidying, rinsing out tumblers and champagne flutes. The lamb has marinated overnight, the salads are prepared and ready to serve; the drinks are perfectly chilled in the ice bucket. She has arranged the glasses on the trestle table so they slope in order of height across its surface. Her sober self is quite the perfectionist, it seems. Her bad self wants her to have a drink, just one, to get away from this edgy, over-prepared, damp-pitted person she has become.

Her dad walks towards her across the grass. She's still shocked at the sight of him, three days in. He has circles under his eyes and deep, curved lines running from nose to mouth, more pronounced on one side. His hair is a wiry grey, swept back from his face. And there is something else; a change in his demeanour which troubles her. He looks like a man on the back foot, a man who has been caught out.

'Hope you're thirsty,' he says.

She looks down at the trestle table. 'Don't want to run out.'

'I don't know if anyone's going to turn up, love. I'm not flavour of the month round here.' He stands beside her and nods at the pastel-coloured bunting she's strung around the back of the house. 'It's enough just to have you home. I don't need all this fuss.'

She winces. 'Is it too much?'

'Tell me you haven't got a brass band tuning up in the lounge room.'

'No band,' she says.

He lights a cigarette. 'Thanks,' he says, and his smile takes a decade off him. 'This is great. Who cares if it's just us?'

Isla moves the ice bucket into the shade, beneath the table. She squats there a while and fixes a length of bunting which is coming loose from the underside. Her dad paces nervously on the grass in front of her. He'll enjoy the party once it's upon him. She knows this because she is absolutely his daughter. This is also how she knows he's had a drink already today; something to take the edge off, to get him in the mood. Maybe more than one.

'I met up with Scott yesterday,' she says, standing.

'Did you?'

'We had coffee across the road from his office. He didn't have long.'

'That sounds like Scott.'

'He said he'll come along later.'

Joe coughs into his fist, turning from her until the spasm

passes. He's perspiring when he faces her again. 'I haven't seen your brother in a while,' he says. 'Must be six months at least. You wouldn't know he lived in the same city.'

'He promised me he'd come.'

'Did he?' He coughs again, beating his chest.

'Are you all right, Dad?'

He finds an ashtray over by the barbecue and crushes his cigarette out. 'Never better.'

A breeze blows in from the ocean, lifting the bunting. Isla catches the scent of eucalyptus from the tree next door and she sees Mandy in a rich slice of memory, folding laundry into a basket. A blonde woman, on the plump side of curvy, with a conspiratorial smile. Fine, fair hair that she holds back from her face with a scarf. So different to her mother that to love her had felt like betrayal.

'Does your mum know Scott's coming today?' Her dad stands at the trestle table, toying with the wine glasses. He picks up a champagne flute and returns it.

Isla is still in Mandy's backyard with a handful of clothes pegs and grass beneath her bare feet. She had been safe with Mandy. She had breathed easily in her company. She is flooded with loss, inexplicably, for this woman she barely remembers.

'Does she know?' her dad repeats.

'Yes.' She smiles at him. 'Yes, Mum's excited to see Scott.'

He turns from her. They hear laughter and voices in the kitchen. Someone squeals in excitement. 'Looks like we'll have to share the grog, after all,' he says.

A small boy in a cowboy outfit runs out the back door,

followed by tall, athletic Andrea Walker and her short, stocky husband in his loud Hawaiian shirt.

'What's his name?' Joe asks, in a low voice. 'Andrea's husband?'

'Ben,' Isla says. 'He does something with computers.'

Joe strides across the grass in Ben's direction. 'Ben!' He claps his back like an old friend. 'How's the world wide web?'

Isla pours a glass of wine for Andrea. 'Thanks for coming.'

'Wouldn't have missed it.' Andrea smiles, exposing straight, white teeth. 'Ben and I moved back to Agnes Bay. We're a ten-minute drive from here.'

'So I heard! My mum gives me all your news.'

Andrea raises her glass. 'Aren't you joining me?'

'I don't drink these days.'

'Since when?'

'Not long.'

'You're not pregnant?' Andrea mouths the words, nudging her.

'No!' Isla laughs loudly, and across the yard her mother turns her head. 'Maybe one day,' she says, smiling at the little cowboy as he runs past. She wonders, in a panic, if she's going to cry.

The weather holds. The day heats up and everyone spills out into the yard. Isla runs in and out of the kitchen with plates and glasses, refilling the ice bucket, greeting people she hasn't seen in a decade, repeating herself. Yes, she's been in London ten years now. She works in television, in post-production, editing programmes. No, she's not married. No, there's nobody waiting at home for her. She makes her excuses when their faces look dismayed: she needs to fetch the mustard; she thinks she can hear the door.

There's a lull once everyone has eaten. It's quiet in the kitchen and Isla decides to let the tap run over the greasy plates, stop a while and watch from the window. It's not a bad turnout. Her mum's swimming club friends are all here, laughing at one another's anecdotes in a huddle on the patio. Most of the neighbours have shown up. The men are grouped around the barbecue, supervising the sausages, which is all that's left of the food. The atmosphere feels strained, she thinks, but that could be in her head. Her parents are keeping to separate sides of the yard, separate conversations. Her dad has that apologetic look to him, and her mum looks like she wants him out of her hair. Once or twice Isla has caught people talking in low voices, glancing in her dad's direction. They stop talking when they see her. It's hard to relax and ignore it. She is too alert, too watchful. She wouldn't invite herself to a party.

'There you are!' Carol Taylor from next door taps Isla on the shoulder, smiling tipsily.

'Thanks for coming,' Isla says, crouching down to let Carol hug her. She gets a waft of sunscreen and lipstick. In all the years Carol has lived next door, Isla has never seen her without lipstick, often a vibrant pink. She still has the same shade of hair, despite the passage of time: a pale brown, the same colour as her skin. Even her eyes are the colour of milky tea. If it weren't for the lipstick she would be entirely beige.

'I love what you did to your hair. Kind of punky,' Carol says, reaching up to touch a strand and thinking better of it.

Isla wishes her sober self could return the compliment. 'Thanks,' she says, stiffly.

'I can't believe you're really single. Are you?'

'I broke up with someone. A few months back.'

'Did he mess you around?'

'He wasn't good for me.' The lie is like metal against her teeth. 'I wanted kids and he didn't,' she says, which is at least partly true. He didn't want kids with me, would have been closer to the whole truth. He didn't want kids with me because I was a train wreck.

Carol is pouting at her sympathetically. 'Time to come home?'

'I don't think so.'

'I know your mum and dad would love to have you closer.'

'I don't think so, Carol.'

A glass breaks on the patio outside and someone swears and then apologises. Farther away, a woman laughs a high, shrieking laugh. *You are awful*, the woman says. Isla moves to get the dustpan and brush from the cupboard, but Carol is holding her hands.

'You got a dustpan and brush?' Douglas Blunt joins them in the kitchen, holding the fractured stem of a wineglass. 'We had a breakage.'

Isla leaves Carol and Doug in the kitchen as she sweeps up the glass. She takes her time over it, brushing every last shard into the pan, along with some cigarette ash and a few stray pine nuts from the salad. In the kitchen she hears Doug telling Carol that Isla sounds like a stuck-up Pom with a rod up her arse. He has the sort of voice that carries.

'I didn't go much on the lamb,' Doug says. 'Some sort of fancy marinade.'

When she looks up from the dustpan, Isla sees her brother standing by the barbecue with the other men. She didn't notice him arrive. He's holding a bottle of beer, talking to Roger Walker. Their dad is standing next to Roger, at the edge of the conversation, looking down at his feet. Scott looks older today, without his suit and tie. The weekend-wear hugs his belly. Somehow she thought he would have aged better, what with the money he makes, the size of his house in Bellevue Hill. He earns a living buying up land and building houses bigger than the one he grew up in, with pools in their yards and open-plan kitchen-diners. He was one of the first to predict that people would start moving back into the city from the western suburbs; that the harbour and the coast would skyrocket. Still better value than London, he'd insisted yesterday, over coffee. The apartment on Sinclair Road had shrunk in her mind as she'd described it to him.

She nods at Scott as she stands and he raises a hand. Ruby, his wife, is holding court over at the drinks table, pouring champagne. Isla wonders again if one drink would be such a big deal. Just to go and join in the toast, to celebrate her dad's birthday.

But then, what is the point of one drink?

In the kitchen, Doug is standing at the table with Carol, recalling the early years living on Bay Street, back when the houses were newly built, when Agnes Bay was still being settled out of bushland and you could get all the way across Sydney by tram. Isla listens as she empties the broken glass into the bin.

'Joe and Louisa took the last house on the coastal side,' Doug says, gesturing out at the yard. 'The rest of the suburb was developed a few years later. They didn't pave the streets until 1964. I remember the bulldozers.'

Carol drains her glass of wine. 'I had no idea you'd lived here so long.'

'First couple to buy a house on Bay Street,' Doug says. 'For a few months it was just us, until the Mallories moved in.' He trails off. 'Lovely grub, Isla,' he says, turning red under his sun hat.

Isla returns the dustpan to the cupboard. The kitchen is quiet. Carol clears her throat and presses her thumb against the crumbs on the cake board.

'Did you say the Mallories?' Isla steps closer to Doug. She has a familiar feeling, that her heart is too big for her chest. 'Did I hear you right?'

Carol licks her thumb and shakes her head, looking at Doug for help.

'The Mallories lived in Carol and Dave's house before them,' Doug says, offsetting awkwardness with volume. 'Nice people. A policeman and his wife.'

'They lived next door?'

'That's right.'

'What were their names?' She raises her voice. 'I might remember them.'

'I doubt you'd remember,' Doug says. 'You were only –'

'Try me.'

Doug hitches his shorts up. 'Steve and Mandy,' he says. 'The Mallories.'

Carol takes a bottle of wine from the table and tips the dregs into her glass.

'Mandy. Isn't that the woman who's gone missing?' Isla looks from Carol to Doug.

'That's right.' Doug is perspiring though his shirt. 'Her brother was asking around, looking for her. She inherited their father's estate.'

'No record of her death,' Isla says. 'I'm sure I heard that.'

'That's right,' Doug says. 'No record of her at all. She disappeared.'

'Sounds suspicious to me.'

Doug is silent. He shrugs and blows air from his cheeks.

'She might have been killed. Murdered.' She gets a heady thrill from the word. 'What do you think?'

'I wouldn't like to say.'

'Wouldn't you?' She is high on anger, outside of herself at last. 'I think you would, but you don't have the guts to say it in front of me.'

'Isla, look. I don't want to spoil a nice afternoon.' Doug nods towards the door. 'Maybe it's about time I was off.'

'What about you, Carol? What's it like living in the house of a woman who's missing, presumed dead?'

Carol runs her tongue over her teeth. 'I didn't know her, darl.'

'Do you think my dad might have buried her under your paving stones?'

Carol shakes her head, signalling her to stop.

'Is that what you think?' She turns to Doug. 'Is that what you've been telling people?'

'Give it a rest, Isla,' he booms. 'I don't have to take this.'

Isla laughs, shocked at herself but still high, not yet sorry. Doug pushes past her, meeting Scott at the back door with a stack of dirty plates. Doug makes his way to the back of the yard, Isla notices. She thinks she sees him talking to Andrea's husband, Ben. Gesturing and pointing.

'I think I'll get going,' Carol says. She puts her glass down on the kitchen table. 'It's been a lovely party.'

'Sorry, Carol.'

'It must be difficult.' Carol gives Isla's arm a squeeze. 'Maybe she doesn't want to be found, this Mandy. Maybe she's happy where she is.'

'Maybe,' Isla says, as Carol makes her exit.

The kitchen is cluttered and airless, reeking of warm wine and cigarette ends. Isla thinks of Dom, shaking his head at her, reproachful, unforgiving. She'd thought it was drink that made her this way. She wants to crawl into a hole.

'What was that about?' Scott puts the plates down on the counter.

'How much did you catch?'

'Most of it.' He turns to the door, checking they are alone. 'Who the hell is Mandy?'

'A neighbour from years back. Before Dave and Carol moved in.'

'And what was that about Dad?'

'I lost my rag. I shouldn't have said that to Carol.'

He opens the door into the hallway, pulling her along by the hand. In the lounge room he holds her by the shoulders, scrutinising her face. 'What's he done?' he says.

She breaks free of his grip and sits down on the couch. 'The police have been asking around, that's all. They seem to think Dad was the last person to see Mandy before she went missing.'

He shakes his head at her. 'When did she go missing?'

'Thirty years ago, they think.'

'Thirty years?'

She nods. 'Must have been the year you were born.'

'Was Dad questioned at the time?'

'Nobody reported her missing at the time.'

He pinches his temples. 'Why not?'

'I guess nobody missed her till now. Her brother started trying to trace her when their dad died. He's the one who contacted the police.'

Scott sits down in the armchair across from her. The sun is going down behind the houses across the street, giving the room a pink glow. He leans forward with his elbows on his knees, his hands in his hair.

'What does Dad say about it?'

'Not much. It's kind of a touchy subject.'

'Do they think she's dead, this Mandy?'

'Seems that way.' She stares out at the street. 'This neighbourhood certainly thinks so.'

'Christ, Isla. You should have told me.'

'I know. I meant to.'

'Did it slip your mind?'

She stares back at him. 'I thought you'd assume the worst of him, like you always do. I thought you wouldn't come to the party.'

'You'd have been right.'

She thumps the couch. 'Don't do this, Scott.'

'I'm not doing anything.'

'You think he's capable of—' She can't say it. 'Don't you?'

'I think you should come back with me and Ruby, is what I think.'

'I can't do that.'

'I don't want you here, with him.'

'He needs me.'

'And what if it turns into a murder case? What then?'

'Then he'll need me even more.'

He groans at her. They are back in their trenches: Scott firing shots at their dad, Isla taking the bullets for him. It's been this way since she can remember. She has always known, without it ever being spoken, that her father had no one if he didn't have her.

'He doesn't deserve your loyalty,' Scott says.

'Yes, he does.'

'You're being naive.'

'I don't think so.'

'Wake up, Isla.'

She looks past him. In this light, the patch of plaster on the wall next to the dresser stands out, although it's been painted over. She can see the brushstrokes.

'Thanks for the offer,' she says.

There are voices in the kitchen, too quiet to make out. Isla listens as they move into the hallway. A child's voice, footsteps running ahead. Ben and Andrea, she thinks, with the little cowboy. Ben is still talking, saying something about databases, computer searches.

'She'd be on the electoral roll if she was alive,' Ben says. 'The police have access to all that data.'

They let themselves out onto the street, shutting the door behind them. The sun drops behind the houses opposite and the room falls into darkness. Scott stands and pulls her to her feet. Her head meets his shoulder and he rocks her side to side a few times, gripping her tight against him. It throws her. She returns the hug hesitantly, scared she might sob into his polo shirt.

'Call me,' he says, 'if you don't feel safe. I can be here in half an hour.'

12

Sydney, 1967

Joe put his keys down on the kitchen table, which was exactly as he'd left it that morning. The ashtray was full. The toast he hadn't eaten was still on the plate. The note Louisa had left – if you could call it that – was folded, face down, under a dirty coffee cup.

He sat, pushed the toast away. Tried to think straight. She'd been gone around twenty-four hours, he figured; she couldn't have gone far. He'd checked her wardrobe; she'd barely taken anything. Isla's Digby bear was still in her room, and so were most of her clothes. She must have gone to stay with some friend he didn't know about, someone from work who could put her up for a bit. She was sulking; waiting long enough to scare him. He wasn't going to play her games. But he had to admit, he was getting worried. The thing he hadn't done, that he would have to do now, was call Hordern & Sons to see if she'd gone in to work. And if she wasn't there, if they didn't know where she was, he'd have to call the police. A sweat crept up his back at the thought of it.

The note was what worried him. Just one word – sorry – written neatly, at the top of the page. There was no anger in it, nothing to suggest she'd written it hastily. Sorry was a considered word. Nobody apologised in advance unless they were going to do something serious, something permanent.

He'd had too much to drink last Friday while Louisa was out at Mandy's. He'd found the empty bottle of whisky in the bin the next day but he didn't remember putting it there. He remembered leaning over Louisa in bed, the two of them struggling, her face close to his in the dark. Nothing after that. She'd said nothing about it the next day. He'd woken on the couch but that was nothing new. He'd wondered if he'd dreamt it, but it felt real, and he had a guilty feeling in his gut, like he'd crossed a line. But blackouts always left him feeling like a monster. Surely she'd have said something if he'd hurt her. She'd have given him hell for it.

It made him want a drink, the thought of it. He stood and looked out the back door, tried to distract himself. Mandy's laundry was hanging across the length of her yard, propped in the centre with a wooden post. Sheets and towels, strung out like bunting in the sun. She was out there, he could see her, over by the eucalyptus where the grass was longer. The pale pink of the scarf she wore around her head and the yellow-blonde of her hair. She was gathering flowers to bring inside, by the look of it. He watched her for a minute or two, snipping flowers at the base of the stem and draping them over the crook of her arm.

Mandy knew where Louisa was. The thought brought the blood back to his head, stopped his heart racing. He'd seen her skipping back inside when he went out into the yard this morning; it made perfect sense now. She'd promised Louisa not to tell him, most likely.

He waited for Mandy to turn back towards the house before he walked out onto the deck. She looked straight at him, nodded, and put the flowers down on the garden chair in the shade of the vine.

'Mandy!' he called out, as loud as he dared without sounding rude.

She straightened up, wiped her hands on the apron around her waist. It was roasting hot. She looked flushed in the face; reluctant. For a moment he thought she might turn away. He raised his hand: a hesitant half-wave. He tried to smile, and found he couldn't.

'Can I have a word?' He stood at the line of shrubs that separated his yard from hers. Louisa's roses were a bright, cheery pink. The sky was blue, cloudless. Beach weather. The salty air, the colours, all of it filled him with a nameless terror.

'Afternoon.' Mandy moved closer, a few feet back from the shrubs. 'Humid today. I'd give anything for a southerly.'

Joe got as close to the shrubs as he could; one foot in the dirt. 'Mandy, did Louisa say she was thinking of going away for a bit? Anything like that?'

Mandy pushed her hands into the pockets of her apron. 'She said she was leaving. She told me when she came over on Friday night. I'm sorry, Joe. I tried to talk her out of it.'

'She said she was *leaving*?'

'That's right.'

'She used that word?' Joe had a sick, scared feeling. The cicadas were loud in his ears. When had they started that noise? He could barely hear himself think. 'Are you sure?'

'She promised me she'd go home and talk to you.' She was squeezing the tip of her finger with a clothes peg she'd brought out of her apron pocket. 'I really thought I'd changed her mind.'

Joe didn't like the words Mandy was using. He didn't like her tone of voice; her sorry smile. As if this were a situation he might just accept. As if it were definite.

'Where are they, Mandy?'

She dropped the clothes peg. Stared at it, lying in the grass. 'You don't know where they are? She didn't leave you a note, or—?'

'No.' His shirt was stuck to his back. 'No idea.'

Mandy's eyes moved over his face. 'You must be worried sick.'

'She wrote one word on a piece of paper. *Sorry*. That's all.' He gave Louisa's rose bush a kick, making the petals shake. 'Which doesn't help me much.'

Mandy bent and picked up the clothes peg. Her shoulders were red; he saw a pale stripe as the strap of her dress slipped down her arm. 'They went to England,' she said, as she stood. She put the peg in her pocket. 'They left the country, Joe.'

Joe shook his head. The cicadas screamed. 'They can't have.'

'I'm sorry. Louisa should have told you herself.' She looked away. 'I can't believe she's left me to tell you this.'

'They can't have gone to England.' He felt exasperation wash through him. 'That's not possible, Mandy. She couldn't just go to England.'

Mandy smiled apologetically, and he despised her for pitying him, for telling him what he didn't want to know. 'I saw them go in a taxi. She asked me not to tell you right away.'

He kicked the rose bush a second time, sending petals into the air. For a couple of seconds the cicadas fell quiet. He kicked it again, harder.

'I'm sorry, Joe.'

He turned his back to her, facing his house. His empty house. Jesus, the note. The guilty, final-sounding note.

'If there's anything I can do, Joe.' Mandy sounded nervous. 'Anything at all.'

He turned around. She'd stepped back a couple of paces. 'Why didn't you tell me she was going to do this? I could have stopped her!' It felt good to shout. 'I'd have stopped her if I'd known she was thinking this way. You should have said! You should have told me!'

Mandy threw her hands in the air. 'Do you think I like being wrapped up in your business? Do you think I like being the one to tell you where your wife and daughter are? I wish I'd never tried to help her.' She turned on her heel, back towards the chair where she'd left her flowers. She picked them up, held them in her arms: purple, with bright yellow stamens.

'Mandy.' He called out to her as she reached the paving stones. 'Mandy, I'm sorry. I just. I can't make sense of this.'

82

She looked down at the flowers, which were wilting in her arms. 'Drop by if you need to talk, Joe. Any time.'

He crossed the grass and fell into the house, sat down at the kitchen table, beside the stale toast and the coffee and the note. Pink rose petals were pressed into the soles of his shoes; he'd trodden them through the house. Louisa's beloved roses. He pulled a shoe off and threw it with all his strength across the room.

13

Sydney, 1967

Mandy stubbed her cigarette out and tipped the butt into the bin. Cigarettes were all she could think about since she'd told Steve she was going to pack them in. It would have been easier to put up with him complaining. She pushed the packet back under the serviettes in the drawer and opened the back door to let the smoke out. Another thing to lie about, was all it was.

The front door opened. Steve was singing something to himself, a nameless song that might have begun this morning as something he heard on the radio and had ended up here, hours later, with a whole new set of words and the tune pretty much gone. It was a good sign, but. He'd pulled himself together. She knew where she was with this version of her husband: upbeat, noisy, tone deaf. Long may it last.

She pulled the back door open and shut a few times to let out the last of the smoke.

'There you are, darl.' He dropped his lunchbox and flask on the kitchen table. 'What you cooking?'

'Made a stew. You hungry?'

'Bloody starved.' He opened the fridge and looked inside, shut it again and lifted the lid on the stew. 'Is that ready?'

She slapped him on the arm. 'Get out of there.'

'Just seen Joe out the front.' He opened the fridge and took out a beer. 'Poor bastard. Didn't know what to say.'

'Nothing you can say, is there?'

Mandy drank the last of the gin from her glass. She had a guilty feeling over Joe; it had been there all afternoon. She kept recalling the sight of him when she'd told him where they were.

'Still can't believe it, can you?' Steve sat down at the table and unbuttoned his shirt. 'Lovely girl like that walking out without a word. I'd never have thought Louisa would do that.' He let his beer rest against the sloping shelf of his stomach. 'He says you told him she'd gone back to England.'

Mandy turned to the stove, took the lid off the stew and gave it a stir. 'That's right.'

'Why?' He suppressed a belch. 'What's she want to do that for?'

'She wanted to go home, Steve.' She wished he'd leave it alone. 'Louisa was homesick. She was never happy in this country. Couldn't settle.'

Steve put the bottle down hard on the table. 'What's Louisa got to be homesick about? This country's given her everything she could want.' He gestured out at the yard, where the laundry was strung out, just visible in the fading light. 'Lovely home for her family. Good standard of living. You'd think she'd be grateful.'

She heard the drink in his voice and turned back to the stove. One beer and he was half cut. She gripped the spoon she was stirring with, tried to be patient. He'd only been home five minutes.

'It doesn't work that way, Steve. It's not as simple as that.'

'Sounds to me like she doesn't know when she's lucky.'

'She's been through a hard time. She didn't know if she could cope with the new baby, what with her family so far away.' She tapped the spoon against the side of the pot and did her best not to think about cigarettes. She had one left in the pack. 'Joe never understood any of that. What else could she do?'

There was a long pause. She could see his face without needing to look round at him. He was gawping at her, building up to an outburst.

'A woman shouldn't do that to a man!' He thumped the table, rocking the orchids in the vase beside him. 'She took his little girl! He came back to an empty house. Imagine that.'

'I know.' She spooned a portion of stew onto a plate. 'I know what she did.'

'She left him high and dry. Poor bastard.' He looked down at his plate and picked up his fork. 'Lovely girl like that. You wouldn't get over her in a hurry.'

Mandy gave Steve a look, on principle, although she knew he thought Louisa attractive and didn't mind it particularly. There'd be something wrong with him if he hadn't noticed. She had legs up to her ears. And that thick, dark hair she swung about every time she moved. She was a beauty, in her awkward, British way. She pictured Joe's hand gripping Louisa by the hair as he kissed her neck, her shoulders, her collarbone.

'This is tasty, Mand. Very nice.'

She let go of the image. 'There's plenty more. Made enough for a few days.'

'Did Louisa say anything to you before she left?'

He wasn't going to drop the subject. The room was warm and close and she was irritable now from the thought of what she'd done, holding out on Joe like that when she could have told him right away. She took a cigarette out of the pack and lit it up.

'Thought you were giving them up?'

'This is my last one,' she said, shaking the empty pack at him. 'Let me enjoy it.'

He watched her inhale. 'Did Louisa tell you she might do this?'

'She told me she'd drawn the money out of the savings account. To pay for the flights.' She moved closer to the ashtray on the windowsill.

'Flights?' His face was shocked, open-mouthed, in the corner of her eye. 'What is she, the bloody Queen?'

'I know. There must have been a lot of money in that account.'

He put his knife and fork down. 'How did she get hold of the money?'

'It was a joint account. Joe gave her access.'

'I bet he regrets that now.' He stood and took a second beer from the fridge. 'She cleared out the lot, did she?'

'Think so.'

She felt his outrage as he opened the bottle and drank. She shouldn't have mentioned the money. They'd end up rowing if he kept raking it over. The last fight they'd had was over money. And there was no chance of her clearing out the bank account and leaving him; she didn't even have a chequebook. She'd get as far as Manly on the housekeeping he gave her each month.

'I was shocked when she went,' she said. The yard was dark now and she hadn't brought the washing in. 'I still can't believe it.'

'Neither can I.' He put his empty bottle alongside the rest of his empties, next to the bread bin. 'I always had her down as a lovely girl. Shows how wrong you can be.'

'No, it doesn't.' She opened the back door and stood there with her cigarette. 'It's not easy, this country. Not if you weren't raised here. It's hard to be so far from home.'

'Now you sound like your mother. Rest her soul.'

'Don't say that.' She spun around to face him. 'Don't you compare me to her.'

'All right.' He raised his eyebrows. 'Don't get cranky with me.'

Mandy blew smoke out into the yard. A light came on in Joe's kitchen and she watched him moving around, opening cupboards and shutting them. Looking for something, maybe. 'I'm going to bring the washing in.'

'You not eating?' He looked dismayed. 'Why don't you sit down?'

'I won't be a minute,' she said, closing the back door behind her.

She stepped into the warm, clear night; the sky full of stars. A bright half-moon had risen behind the tea trees that ran along the backyards on the coastal side of Bay Street. The cicadas were still calling their high-frequency note. The air got fresher with each step away from the house, and the boom of the ocean got bigger in her ears until finally she felt her head stop churning. She closed her eyes, leaned against the eucalyptus and breathed.

Minutes passed. She looked back at the house. Steve was framed by a square of light in the back door, bent over the stove, spooning a second helping of stew onto his plate. She didn't love him. The thought shocked her but she couldn't dismiss it. He loved her as much as he always had, she knew this. But it wasn't the same for her. She'd had an idea of him and the life he would give her, and it was different to the reality.

The bedsheets were stiff with salt from the ocean. She unpegged them and folded them into her arms, held them up to her face. She didn't love him. She spoke it aloud into the sheets, quietly at first, and then louder. It was like watching someone fall from a cliff.

'Mandy.' Joe was standing on his deck, still in his work clothes. He held a whisky tumbler in his hand, and he wasn't quite steady on his feet.

She ducked under the washing line and walked towards him. 'Beautiful evening,' she said.

'Sorry about earlier.' He met her at the shrubbery. 'It's been a shock, all this. I'm still taking it in.'

'That's understandable.'

'I shouldn't have spoken to you that way. I took it out on you.'

'I was in a difficult spot, Joe.'

'I know. I'm sorry.'

She stood there a while, looking back at him. She liked his height and his build, his lean frame. His arms. He made as if to turn towards the house and she spoke just to keep him there.

'I was thinking you might need a hand with the housework,' she said. 'I could get the place straightened out for you, while you're at work. Give it a tidy. It'd be no trouble.'

He passed his glass from one hand to the other, considering. 'That's very kind.'

'I'd be happy to. Think nothing of it.'

'That would be a help. If you really don't mind.' He nodded and stepped away. 'Thank you, Mandy.'

She took her time unpegging the rest of the laundry, shaking out the creases, folding it into the basket. She'd iron the bedding tomorrow and change the sheets. They'd smell the ocean in the cotton as they slept.

Joe's kitchen light switched off and his yard fell into darkness. Steve was right, in a way. Louisa didn't know when she was lucky. The homesick part you could understand, but leaving a man like Joe Green was nothing short of madness.

She picked up the basket and walked back to the house.

14

Sydney, 1997

It must have rained all night. Isla stands on the deck with her coffee. A breeze blows in from the ocean, sending a shiver through next door's eucalyptus. The sun is low behind the tea trees. Winter's coming. It's beautiful, she realises. Despite the drab remains of the party, the damp bunting and the upturned ice bucket, it's a beautiful day.

'Coffee?'

Isla turns to see her dad holding the coffee jug, offering it up to her. He looks like death. His blue eyes are ghostly pale against his grey skin.

'Thanks.' She stands at the door and takes a mug from him. 'You're up early.'

'Couldn't sleep. Might as well get to work.'

He puts the radio on and sips his coffee. His singlet hangs loosely from his collarbones. She wants to ask him when he started to look so ill. If he's scared, since the police called to see him. If he's told her everything.

'I'll make some breakfast,' she says, instead.

Joe nods, distracted by the radio. 'Not for me, thanks, love. I'll get something later.'

She steps into the kitchen. A government minister is being interviewed on the radio. It's the same story she's been hearing since she arrived: Prime Minister John Howard won't apologise to Aboriginal people for the forced removal of their children. People back then thought they were doing the right thing, the minister says. It was a different time.

'Bet this didn't make the news in England,' Joe says.

'No. You wouldn't know any of this was going on.'

'Typical.'

'There's been an election in the UK, to be fair. A new government.'

'That's right.' He snorts. 'Cool Britannia. Not so cool from where I'm standing.'

They sip their coffee and listen. It wouldn't hurt to say sorry, the interviewer says.

'Tell Tony Blair to come here and apologise.' Joe glares at the radio. 'Tell him we're the bloody great continent with the kangaroos and the boomerangs.'

It would be healing, says the interviewer.

'It all comes back to the British.' He points a finger at nothing in particular. 'Everywhere you look, in this country and in most of the world. If there's a conflict, you can bet it dates back to a time when the British charged in and put their flag in it.'

Isla knows better than to defend the British from her British
father. He's never come to terms with her moving to England,
the country he left. She finds some eggs and cracks them into
a bowl.

'Sooner we become a republic, the better,' Joe says.

It was a long time ago, the minister says, repeating himself.
Most Australians were unaware this was going on.

Joe puts his coffee down and lights a cigarette. 'Wasn't that
long ago,' he says. 'I remember it.'

'Do you?'

'That bastard next door was up to his neck in it.'

Isla pours the eggs into a pan. She looks up at her dad, who
is staring out at next door's yard. 'Dave Taylor? He's an archi-
tect, isn't he?'

Joe keeps his voice low. 'Steve Mallory,' he says.

She lifts the edges of the omelette with a spatula. Her movements feel slow and heavy. 'Mandy's husband?'

He nods.

A sweat springs up on her forehead. She flips the omelette,
although her appetite is gone.

'He was a policeman,' Joe says.

'Did he drive a truck? A dark green truck. Always dirty.'

'That's right. You remember that?'

The sweat spreads across her body. 'I was scared of him.'

'Kids can tell when someone's no good.' Joe rests his cigarette
in the ashtray and drains his coffee. 'He put on a good show,
mind you. People liked him round here.'

'Did you?'

'No. Can't say I did.'

'How did you stand by and let it happen?'

He frowns. 'What d'you mean?'

'If you knew what he was doing. Taking kids away. Couldn't you have done something?'

Joe stops with his cigarette halfway to his mouth. He takes a while to reply. 'It wasn't that easy.'

'Did you try?'

'I did,' he says. 'It didn't go anywhere. I should have pushed it harder, in hindsight.'

Isla slides her omelette onto a plate and sits down. Steve Mallory is a throb behind her eyes, threatening to surface. She can see the clean, orderly rooms that he lived in next door. The smell of ironing and carbolic soap. Mandy standing at the window, watching him park his truck, her shoulders tense.

She picks up her fork. 'So nobody did anything. You let it go on right under your noses, for years.'

'Steve was a copper, love. He was on the right side of the law.'

'All those families lost their kids.'

He is staring intently at his cigarette. 'I didn't know how bad it was at the time.'

'What did Mandy think of it?'

'I don't know.' He turns from her and looks out at the yard. 'If she talked about it I don't remember. Long time ago.'

Isla pushes her plate aside and stands beside him at the back door. The sun has risen over the tips of the tea trees, brightening the grass.

'How can someone be missing for thirty years and no one notice?'

'We thought she'd moved away,' he says, after a pause. 'Her and Steve. They sold the house and moved away, down to Victoria, as I recall. Didn't see any reason to question it.'

She can't catch his eye. 'Wouldn't that mean Steve was the last one to see her?'

'I'd have thought so.'

'Why do the police think it was you, then?'

He is perfectly still beside her, holding smoke in his mouth. 'I guess Steve has a different take on it,' he says, eventually. He puts his cigarette out. The radio is playing music now, something upbeat, and he crosses the room to turn it off.

'Why did nobody report her missing?' Isla stands in the door frame with the sun at her back. 'What about Steve? He was a cop. Why didn't he organise a search?'

'I don't know, love. You'd need to ask Steve that question.'

'What about her family?'

'I think she'd lost touch with them.'

'Her dad left her his estate. He must have loved her.'

'I'm sure he did.' Joe's hands tremble as he pours more coffee from the jug. 'Families are complicated, Isla.'

'That's true.'

Isla turns away so she doesn't have to watch him mop up the spilled coffee from the counter. The sun has gone in. The wind lifts the bunting around the trestle table.

'You must be counting the days till you can get out of here.'

'No.' She turns back to face him. 'I'm glad I'm here, Dad.'

'I'll be all right, you know.' He rubs at a spot on his singlet where he has dripped coffee. 'This will all blow over.'

He finds his cigarettes and puts them in his pocket. Isla hears him move around the house, from the bathroom to the bedroom, and then the room that was Scott's when he lived at home. Her dad keeps his vodka in there; she found it on her second morning, looking for Scott's CDs. Three large bottles at the back of a filing cabinet. There will be more, dotted around the house. It's always been this way, but she is stupidly surprised at how it's taken its toll on him. She's only just cottoned on that this is why he looks unwell, why he trembles and stumbles; why he no longer drives the car. Why he seems defeated.

She tips the last of the coffee into her mug, puts the radio back on and scrapes her breakfast into the bin.

96

15

Sydney, 1967

Mandy smiled at the sound of Joe's key in the door. She'd spent the best part of the day cleaning his house and it looked good, if she did say so herself. It looked like the sort of house she liked to walk into. Clean, tidy, decluttered. She unplugged the vacuum and wound the flex up, hooking it on her thumb and down around her elbow. It was a job well done, and she'd enjoyed it. Made a change from her own house, which was so clean she'd erase it one of these days.

She wheeled the vacuum back to the kitchen, took a few deep breaths and tried to look nonchalant. Men often didn't notice a clean house, or understand the work that went into it. Not that Joe was accustomed to a clean house, mind. Louisa never did keep on top of the housework. She'd seemed over-whelmed by it, always pushing clutter into cupboards and leaving dishes in the sink. But then, none of us is perfect,

Mandy thought. Lou might not be house-proud but she always looked fantastic.

She quickly pushed her hair back under her scarf as Joe came through the door.

'What the?' He dropped his keys on the coffee table. 'What the hell?'

She saw him before he saw her. In the instant before he knew she was there, she knew she'd made a mistake. He looked shocked, and not in a good way. He looked like he'd been punched in the stomach.

'Joe, I—' She moved forward, and he saw her.

'Christ, Mandy!'

'Did you forget I was coming?' She walked through to the living room. The carpet was damp under her feet where she'd shampooed it. 'We did agree I'd come today.'

He passed his hand over his face. 'What have you done? Where is everything?'

'I put a few things away in drawers and cupboards.' She followed his gaze, taking in the shine of the windows and the pictures she'd straightened and wiped; the clean face of his sunburst wall clock. 'Then I dusted and polished. What did you expect?'

He pulled a few drawers open and shut them again. 'I've never seen the house like this. I don't recognise the place.'

'I thought you'd be pleased. I like a tidy house.'

He sat down on the couch and ran his hand over the crown of his head. 'I can see that.'

'If there's something you can't find, something you'd rather I hadn't moved—'

'Christ.' He dropped his head into his hands and said nothing for a while. 'I can't find my wife, Mandy.'

'Oh.' She curled her toes into the damp carpet. 'I thought—'

'Or my daughter.' He looked around him in fresh surprise. 'They were here. Their mess, the things they left behind. The smell of them.'

'You wanted me to leave the mess?'

'I thought you were going to empty the ashtrays. Maybe wash the dishes.'

'I didn't realise.'

'Did you—?' He stood up and walked quickly out of the room, his face white.

Mandy stood for a while in the living room, which looked too bright and bare, now she saw it through his eyes. It looked like no one lived here.

The house had fallen very quiet. She hesitantly checked each room and found Joe in the small bedroom at the end of the hall, sitting on a circular mat next to the bed. Two of Isla's dolls lay abandoned on the carpet, half dressed. Digby bear was slumped in the small chair in the corner, just visible under a pile of laundry.

'I didn't clean the bedrooms,' she said.

'No.' He rested his hand on the mattress. The top sheets were crumpled at the foot of the bed. Isla's pyjamas were folded on the pillow. 'Please don't come in here, Mandy. Just leave this room, please.'

'All right.' She backed out into the hall. 'I'd best be off, anyway. Steve'll be home any time now.'

In the kitchen she left Joe's spare key on the table. She was smarting with the shock of it, of how wrong she'd been. To think she'd half expected him to ask her to come back and clean again; maybe even cook a meal now and then. She untied the apron she'd borrowed and hung it back on its hook. God, the shame. She must have been out of her mind.

She was letting herself out through the back door when she heard Joe's voice behind her.

'Forgive me,' he said.

She turned to face him. 'I went overboard. Totally overboard. I'm so sorry.'

'Sit down.' He pulled a chair out and nodded for her to sit. 'It's my fault. How were you to know?'

She sat and looked at the soapsuds drying on the table top; the circles she'd made with the cloth. 'I can be insensitive. I don't mean to be. Steve's always on at me about it.'

Joe held the kettle under the tap. 'Tea?'

'Lovely. Thanks.'

'That makes two of us,' he said. 'Insensitive.'

Mandy watched him struggle with the tap. His right hand was red raw across the knuckles and swollen as far as his wrist. 'Says who?'

'My wife.' He put the kettle down and used his left hand to turn the tap off.

'Did you two have a big fight, then?'

He studied his reflection in the kettle. 'I think so.'

'You think so?'

He looked up at her. 'That night she was at yours. She came back late. I'm a bit hazy on the details but I think we argued. I think it got pretty heated.'

Mandy nodded. 'You blacked out?'

'Must have.' He unbuttoned his collar. 'Did she say anything to you about it?'

'No, she didn't mention anything. She had Isla with her whenever I saw her, mind you.'

'Right. I wish I could remember.'

'You didn't really want me to clean your house, did you, Joe?'

He looked at her and smiled. He had quite a smile. 'Not really. I wanted to talk to you.'

'Talk away.' She felt better for clearing that up. 'You should've said.'

He took two mugs from the row of hooks on the wall. 'I phoned around all the docks. All the shipping companies. There's no record of them getting on a boat to England or anywhere else. They must still be in the country, Mandy.' He smiled again. 'They're still in Australia.'

'I don't think so.' She spoke softly, carefully. 'I don't think they went by boat, Joe.'

He took a long time to reply. The kettle whistled. 'They went by plane?'

'They did.'

'They can't have.' He opened the cupboard over the basin and closed it again; tried a few drawers and slammed them shut. 'Where did you put all the ashtrays?'

101

'Should be a few in here.' She leaned behind her and opened the drawer next to the stove just as he reached for it, and both their hands closed around its metal handle. 'I washed them all out,' she said, sitting back into her chair. She put her hands in her lap and held them between her knees. 'You had ashtrays everywhere. Spilling out over the surfaces.'

'I know.' The cigarette in his mouth jerked as he spoke. He sat, and offered her the pack. His movements were rushed, nervy. 'They can't have flown back to England, Mandy. It costs a lot of money to fly to England.'

Mandy lit her own cigarette and let him be for a minute or two. He was quiet, in a restless way, taking in what she'd said. She figured he'd check the savings account soon enough, once the shock had worn off. She didn't want to give him any more bad news. After a while she stood and poured tea into two mugs, found some milk and set it all down on the table. He didn't appear to notice.

'I can't get used to them being gone.' His right leg was leaping in a quick, jerky rhythm. 'I keep thinking she's in the next room. I think of something I want to tell her and when I go to speak I remember.' He stared into the steaming mug. 'She must have been planning it. She must have made her mind up a long time ago.'

'I think you're probably right.'

'Not even a proper note.' He thumped the table, and winced. He held his swollen fingers in his good hand. 'I thought she was doing better,' he said, more to himself than to her. 'I really thought so.'

Mandy sat back in her chair and drank her tea. Joe held the cup with his hand wrapped around the base, his thumb hooked through the handle. He was miles away, working it all through, trying not to believe it. It was hard to watch.

'Do you miss England?' she asked.

'No.' He looked up at her. 'I never have. Not for a minute.'

'You like it here?'

'I love this country. I loved it from the minute we got here. The extremes of it. The heat off the sun; the space between one place and the next. The sky. I'd never seen so much sky.'

'What about the green English pastures?' She put on her English accent. 'The countryside?'

He snorted. 'None of that where I come from. My England was a cold, crowded sort of place. Everyone on top of each other in concrete boxes. Rats in the gutters. I lived in the bit of England they don't put on postcards.'

'You don't ever want to go back?'

'No. No, I don't. I hate England, to tell you the truth. People like me don't stand a chance over there. They like to keep us in our place. Born poor, die poor.'

She sipped her tea. 'What if Louisa won't come back?'

He stood and went to the sink, tipped the rest of his tea down the drain. 'I can't think about that, Mandy.'

'Sorry.' She shouldn't have said that. He was staring hopelessly into the sink.

'I've worked so hard for all this,' he said. 'Louisa knows how hard I've worked to build a life for us here.'

She crushed her cigarette in the ashtray and stood. It was getting late. 'I'd better go. I need to get Steve's dinner on.'

'Right. Of course. Thanks for everything. The cleaning, and—'

'Don't mention it.'

He followed her to the door. 'Thank you for trying to stop her, Mandy.'

'I think she's made a mistake.' She reached out and touched his arm, just above the swelling. They looked at each other in surprise. 'You been punching walls?'

He held his arm still. 'You noticed?'

''Course I noticed. There's a hole in the wall, Joe.' She nodded towards the lounge room, where she'd picked plaster out of the carpet. 'You should put ice on that hand.'

'I'll do that.' He stared down at his swollen knuckles. 'I need to watch myself on the drink.'

'Don't we all.' She took her hand away and clamped it under her left arm before she did something else she hadn't planned to do. 'Thanks for the tea.'

'Mandy?' He followed her out onto the deck. 'Did you find a savings book?'

'Yes.' The yard was in shade. It was later than she'd thought. 'I did. I put it in the dresser drawer in the lounge room.'

'Thanks. Where was it?'

'Under the bed.' She called out to him over her shoulder as she walked towards her own house. 'Pushed quite a long way under. I sucked it out with the vacuum cleaner.'

16

Sydney, 1967

Mandy stood at the back of the house while the kitchen floor dried. It wouldn't take a minute in this heat, but it was an excuse for a cigarette, a pause. She was getting through the housework too quick these past few days and the afternoons were long and empty. No Isla to distract her, was why. No one to drag her down to the beach once the washing was hung out.

It hurt Mandy more than she wanted to let on, that Lou had taken off to England without a thought for her. It was only by chance she'd seen them out the window that morning. She hadn't been able to say goodbye, not properly, in that hot taxi with the meter running. The thought of it made her eyes fill and she dug at them with her knuckles, told herself to buck up for God's sake. She had no right feeling this way about somebody else's kid. She knew what Steve would say: a child of our own will keep you busy. Which was true enough.

She stared out at the yard. She needed to trim the long grass over by the eucalyptus. Water the plants. There wasn't much laundry but it wouldn't hurt to wash the towels and dishcloths again, in the name of hygiene. She wondered if she was the only woman on earth to consider starting a family just to generate more laundry. The only woman to feel a growing panic at the idea, to reach for another cigarette.

'Where are you, Mand?'

She pushed the cigarette back into the packet, her hands clumsy with shock. 'What are you doing home?' She just managed to put the packet back in the drawer and push it shut before Steve came in. 'It's not even lunchtime.'

Steve sat down at the table with his boots on and rubbed his eyes. 'Ray wants me to drive back out to Ivanhoe.'

'What, now? Weren't you there a few weeks back?'

'I was.'

He was staring out the window at nothing, looking hot and tired. She ran the tap and put a glass of water on the table for him. When he didn't look up, she pulled out the chair beside him and sat down.

'Ray should've told you if there was more than one child needed removing out that way. Save you making two trips.'

'He did.'

'Did he?'

He swallowed half the water down and wiped his mouth with the back of his hand. 'I was meant to remove another child last time I was there. A little boy.'

She pulled the chair up closer. 'You were meant to take two kiddies the last time?'

'That's right.'

'Was there trouble?'

He was looking right at her but his eyes were blank. She heard his stomach churn the water around.

'No,' he said. 'There wasn't any trouble that time.'

'Then why didn't you—?'

'There was no trouble because I didn't take him. I went into the house and saw him there with his grandpa. And I couldn't do it. So I left without him.'

'What do you mean, you couldn't do it?'

'I mean, I couldn't do it. He was just a baby, Mandy. It never sits right with me to take a baby. He looked to me like he was perfectly fine right where he was.' He pulled his boots off as he spoke, left them lying on their sides on the clean lino. 'And the place he'd end up, if I took him, would likely be a whole lot worse.'

Mandy picked his boots up and took them to the back door, stood them out on the paving stones. She took a few deep breaths, caught the sound of waves down on the beach, a peal of laughter. She'd never felt more reluctant to turn back into a room with her husband in it.

He was staring at his hands.

'You didn't tell me about this.' She picked up a few bits of dirt that had dropped from the tread of his boots. 'That you'd left a child behind. You didn't say.'

'No. I put it out of my mind.'

'Have you done that before?'

'No. First time.'

'And now Ray wants you to go back and get him, does he?'

'That's right. He was none too pleased I came back without him the last time.' He trod across the lino in his socks, looking out at the yard. 'I can't face going back out there, Mand. Think I've come to the end of the road with this business.'

She filled the kettle at the tap, put it onto the hob and lit the flame beneath it. She considered her words, her tone. 'You know,' she said, keeping her back to him, 'you're taking it all too much to heart. Letting it get to you again. You need to remember this is about the best interests of these kids. Making sure they get a decent start in life.'

'Now you sound like Ray.'

She turned to face him. 'Ray might have a point. You don't know what's really going on in these families. Just because you don't see anything wrong, doesn't mean there's nothing wrong. You might have left that child to get neglected.'

'You might be right, Amanda.' He looked down at his feet. 'But you might be wrong. That's the trouble.' He was sweating through his uniform, dark rings forming under his arms. 'I went into this thinking I was the good guy. But over the years it's turned itself around on me. I think maybe I'm the bad guy.'

'Don't say that.' A kookaburra laughed at the back of the yard, making her jump. She wished he wouldn't talk this way. 'Of course you're not the bad guy. I know who you are. You don't have a bad bone in your body.'

'You don't understand.'

'You're a decent man doing a good job. Don't talk daft.'

He crossed the room and reached for the drawer where her cigarette packet was lying open. Only two left in the pack. He drew them both out and handed her one.

'I'm not doing so well at packing them in,' she said, leaning forward gratefully as he lit a match.

'I know. I'm not stupid, Mandy. I can smell 'em on you.'

'Right.' She inhaled deeply.

'I want us to be straight with each other. Honest.'

She stood next to him and leaned back against the counter top. 'So do I, love.'

'I need you to hear what I'm saying. Try to understand.'

'I do understand.'

'Do you?' He crushed the empty packet and lit his own cigarette. He wasn't much of a smoker. Cigarettes looked thin in his hands, and he rarely took more than a few puffs, which was wasteful in Mandy's view.

'Look, it's not up to you if a child gets taken or not, is it?' She rinsed out the ashtray and put it down on the counter top. 'It's not your fault if there's a mistake.'

'They should look at some of the Homes if they want to see neglect.' He pointed north, out through Joe's house and beyond. 'They ought to go look at the places I take those kids to. Neglect's the least of it.'

Mandy looked around at her half-clean kitchen, the bright sunlight in the yard, the mess of her interrupted morning. She was going to have to hear him out. He was right; she didn't understand, not really. She'd thought he was taking kids into care, where they'd have a better life. She'd thought she'd married a policeman and he'd be brave and uncomplicated.

'Is it that bad,' she said, 'in the Homes?'

'They shouldn't call 'em Homes.' He puffed on his cigarette, barely inhaling. 'They're not homes, they're institutions.'

'It's got to be better than leaving them where they are, hasn't it? I remember you saying they live in dirty conditions, these people. Kids looking after themselves, not enough to eat. I remember you were shocked by it.'

'That's true.' He closed his eyes against the smoke. 'There's a time I was shocked by that kind of thing.'

'It's not good for children, growing up dirty and hungry, but.'

'People who live that way still love their kids, Mandy. Once you understand that, you start to have your doubts about all of it.'

The kettle rumbled and she reached into the cupboard for two cups. 'He's a baby, is he, this boy you're meant to go back for?'

He nodded. 'Few months old, I think.'

'Why do they want him removed?'

He shrugged a shoulder. 'The family unit's not regular. The dad doesn't have anything to do with 'em. Mum's just a kid herself. The grandpa seems to keep the family going but there's not much money to go round.'

'Maybe it'll be better for the boy then, Steve. Getting taken out of there so young. He won't know anything else. Won't remember his family.'

He stood up straight and thumped the counter top with his fist. Smoke streamed from his nostrils. 'Christ, Mandy. Haven't you heard me?'

'Yes, I heard you. I'm trying to make you see sense, is all.'

'You're the one who needs to see sense. It's not right, this business. Do you understand?'

'I understand you're a good man.' She said it softly. 'That's what I understand.'

'How can I be? I'm on the wrong side.' He shook his head. 'I'm through with this. I can't do it any more. I'm going to tell Ray I'm done with it. He can find someone else to do the job.'

'What's he going to say to that?'

'I don't know.'

'Ray's been good to you. Understanding.'

'I know.' He nodded, and she thought he might have calmed down a bit. He ground out his cigarette and wiped sweat from his neck with the palm of his hand. 'I'd have walked away years ago if it weren't for Ray. That and the thought of my old man. I'm ashamed to think what he'd say if he could hear me.'

'You have nothing to be ashamed of.'

'That's where you're wrong.' He pulled her tight against him. He smelled of smoke, sweat and dust, and a heat came off him like a stove. 'I have so much to be ashamed of, darl.'

She leaned against him a while and rubbed his back. She didn't want to look at him in case she saw what she feared she might see. That something was unravelling in him, quite rapidly, like an untethered rope from a harbour wall.

'I think you should finish this job,' she said. 'Don't end on a bad note.'

'I can't, Mandy.'

'I think you can. Leave after you've done it if you still feel the same.' She held his face in her hands. 'Walk away with dignity once you've done what he's asked you to do.'

His chest rose and fell. 'I need to think about it.'

'You do that, love.'

She went back to the kettle, poured water into the pot and swilled it around. In the corner of her eye he brought his hands to his face. She went to the fridge for milk and stood there a while with the door angled so she couldn't see him.

17

Leeds, 1967

Isla sat on a wooden chair in the kitchen wearing a sweater that was much too big. The windows were steamed up and it was dark outside, like always. You couldn't go outside in that perishing cold. The kitchen was the only room that wasn't perishing, because of the stove, but it wasn't warm in here either. It wasn't warm anywhere in England. You had to wear a vest and socks and a sweater inside the house and you could catch your death in the bathroom: there were icicles at the window and it was best not to sit down for too long on the toilet seat. Grandma had a pot under her bed that she used in the night because she did not want to catch her death and one of these days she would get the chill on her chest and that would be the end of it.

Grandma was tidying up the kitchen, wiping the crumbs from the bread board into the sink with the flat of her hand. Isla could tell Grandma was nice but she didn't like her. England made her hate everything, even nice things. The worst thing about England was, it was a bit the same as Australia, but everything was a bit wrong. Isla did not like the way English houses were tall. She did not like stairs. She liked flat, wide houses, with just the roof on top. English people thought they had it right about houses, this was the thing that made Isla want to cry. They thought their way was right and nobody cared what she thought.

'You not eating your toast?' Grandma stood next to her. She was looking at Isla and Isla was looking at the toast. 'Why don't you try it? You must be starved.'

'It's not Vegemite,' Isla said.

'I think it's the same thing.' Grandma showed her the jar, which was brown and curved, with a yellow lid. 'It's your mum's favourite.'

Isla shook her head.

'You might like it if you try it.'

'It's not the same.' Isla hated Grandma for not understanding this. 'And I don't like it burnt as well.'

Grandma took the plate away and tipped the toast into the bin. 'I don't blame you, lovey,' she said. 'Horrible stuff.'

Isla decided she would wait until she got back to Australia before she ate anything else. She didn't want to eat anything English.

'How does your mum do your toast?' Grandma took the bread knife and balanced it on the loaf.

'Mandy makes it for me how I like it.'

'Mandy?' Grandma said her name funny. 'Who's Mandy when she's at home?'

Isla didn't know how to answer this question. She swung her feet under the table until she wasn't thinking about Mandy saying goodbye.

'Will I toast it lightly with a bit of cheese?'

Isla looked down at her hands and shrugged one shoulder. She liked cheese on toast but was not ready to break her fast.

From the hallway the telephone rang. Grandma went to answer it but Mummy ran down the stairs and got it first.

'Someone's awake,' Grandma said.

Isla listened to her mum on the phone. She was talking loud, the way she did at home when she called England. 'Hello,' Mummy said. 'Yes, it's me.'

Grandma was listening too. She stopped sawing at the bread and tipped her head towards the door.

'It's great to be home,' Mummy said. 'Really lovely. Bit cold!'

Isla knew her mum wasn't talking to Daddy. It was her pretend voice. Grandma went back to slicing the bread.

'Have you spoken to him?' Mummy said. There was a long pause, then, 'I'm so sorry, I wasn't thinking straight.'

'Are you sure you won't have a bit of Marmite on this toast?' Grandma said.

'No, thanks,' Isla replied.

'You sure now?' Grandma was doing a face. It was quite a good one. She could do her eyes crossed and one eyebrow up higher than the other.

In the hall, Mummy put the phone down. She said something to herself that Isla couldn't hear.

'Grandma?'

'Yes, lovey?' Grandma stopped doing the face.

'Why are we here?'

Grandma reached up and turned the grill off. She wiped her hands on her apron and held out her arms. 'C'mere,' she said.

Isla climbed down from the chair.

18

Sydney, 1967

Mandy put the phone down. England was great, was it? Jesus. She was seeing another side to Louisa, just lately. It was a shock, in all honesty, to hear her sound so happy with herself.

'Who were you talking to?'

Mandy swung around. 'You scared me. How long have you been standing there?'

'Sorry, Mand.' Steve lumbered into the kitchen in his pyjamas, barely awake. 'I thought I heard you talking to someone. Were you on the phone?'

'It's nearly midnight, Steve. You must have been dreaming.'

'I'm sure I heard you say something. Bloody nerve, I thought you said.'

'I didn't say that. You were dreaming.' Mandy twisted the watch on her wrist, tried to stop it pinching. She didn't know why she'd lied to him. She could have told him she'd called

Louisa. They could have talked it over, sat down and laughed about it, like the old days. Why had she flat out denied it?

'What are you doing up?' Steve asked.

'Couldn't sleep. Too hot.'

Steve yawned into his hands. 'I'm not right in myself, Mandy. Turning things over.' He passed his hand through his hair, making it stand on end, and stared into the dark room. 'I've decided I'm going to go and remove that kiddie up in Ivanhoe. I'll go today.'

He looked sad, she thought, and older than his years. 'You sure? I thought you'd decided you couldn't do it.'

'I know. But it doesn't sit right with me that I haven't seen it through. Don't want Ray thinking I've shirked on a duty.'

She stood next to him and smoothed his hair. 'You've always been a proud man. You want to be able to hold your head up.'

'That's it.'

'We should've talked about all this a long time ago. I should've tried harder to understand.'

He rubbed his nose with the palm of his hand. 'I started to dread coming home to you. I couldn't stand the way you looked at me when I was in a bad way.'

'I'm sorry.' She leaned into him. 'You should've said something sooner.'

'I want us to be honest from now on. All right? It's the only way, Mand.'

She reached for his hand. She knew he was right. She'd got in the habit of holding him at bay. 'There is something. Maybe I haven't been straight with you about it.'

'Go on, darl.' He blinked.

'I don't want to get pregnant, Steve.' The words were out before she could think it over. She almost laughed with the relief of it.

'You don't—?'

She shook her head.

'I thought you were coming round to the idea.'

'I'm sorry, love. It's not what I want.' His hand was heavy in hers. 'I can't pretend any more.'

He didn't speak for a long time. The second hand on her watch moved briskly around the dial and the relief died back in her.

Steve dropped her hand and sat down at the table. 'You were starting to come round to it,' he said. 'Weren't you?'

'I did try, Steve. But the more I tried, the more I knew I didn't want it.'

'You don't think you'll change your mind?'

'No. I'm sorry.'

'That's a blow, Mandy.' He stared down at his feet. 'I've been wanting a child a long time. It's what I want more than anything.'

'I'm so sorry.'

He stood and walked through to the bathroom, hitching up his pyjamas at the back where the elastic had gone.

'Steve, don't go. Come back and talk about it.'

'Might as well make an early start.' He switched the bathroom light on. 'Get it over with.'

'It's the middle of the night. Don't be daft.'

119

He pulled the bathroom door shut behind him. Mandy looked in the drawer for cigarettes and found the pack was empty. She stood by the open back door and looked out at the dark yard. Her dad came into her mind. The best man she ever knew. Proud, solid and decent, broken by the woman he loved.

19

Sydney, 1997

Isla stirs in the night and reaches out for Dom, certain of his weight in the bed beside her, the heat and the smell of him. She feels his mouth against hers. He is drowsy at first and then insistent. She lets him touch her, keeping still so he works harder. He's good at it. Responsive and generous, never needy. She pulls his shorts down to his knees. He rolls her onto her back and she resists him. Not yet. She doesn't say it, she can't seem to open her mouth. He speaks into her ear but his voice is thick with sleep and she can't hear him. His mouth is wet, dripping. He tastes of blood.

She opens her eyes. He stares down at her, eyes dark and bruised, mouth formless, bubbling red as he speaks. 'Not again,' he says.

Isla sits up. The room is black and he is not there. She is drenched in sweat. She pulls the covers back, reaches around in the single bed. It wasn't real, of course. A phantom, made from fear and shame.

She switches the bedside lamp on. It glows a soft pink, the thin cotton shade patterned with roses. Her childhood furniture sits alongside boxes of coat hangers, boxes of shoes, boxes with smaller boxes inside. An industrial-sized carton of laundry detergent is now stored on top of the desk she once sat at to do her homework. She feels outsized in this room. A disappointment to the younger, hopeful self who lived here.

She lies back down, shuts her eyes, but Dom is still there, clean-cut and smiling, the way he was when she first met him, when her boss introduced him to the team. He'd blushed at the sight of her and it had taken all her strength not to stride across the office and kiss him hard on the mouth.

For the first few months she didn't drink in front of him. She drank orange juice in the pub after work and filled the fridge at home with cans of full-strength lager. It got harder when he moved in. At some point he'd rumbled her, caught her drinking vodka neat from the bottle when she'd thought he was asleep. She'd played it down, promised to change. He'd believed her. He'd talked about marriage as she'd thought about the bottle he hadn't found in the pannier of her bike. And later, years down the line, he'd become the enemy, the person she hid from, the person who forced her to look at herself. The one she took it out on when she hated what she saw.

She misses him like he'd just left.

The clock beside the bed shows it's still early, not quite eleven. She changes into a dry T-shirt. She needs water and fresh air, her new clean-living staples. A light is on in the lounge room and the door is ajar, the television turned down low: British accents, canned laughter.

Isla makes for the kitchen, treading lightly. She stops, hearing her mother's voice.

'Get rid of it, then,' Louisa says. 'If it means nothing.'

Her dad's reply is inaudible. A grunt. A shifting of weight on the couch.

'Why not, Joe? Why keep something like that?'

'Will you shut up about it?'

'Can't you see how it would look?'

'Can't you shut up for God's sake? What do I have to do to make you drop it?'

Isla pulls her bedroom door shut with deliberate force. Her parents fall quiet. She waits in the hallway, listening, aware they know she's there. If there's a scuffle or a cry she'll go in, if there isn't she'll go back to bed and listen out for noises, sleeping lightly, scared for them both. How many times has she done this? Her dad says something and she tenses, ready to go in and hold him by the arms, stand between them, make them stop. She will scream if she has to. She will prise them apart. She remembers beating her fists against her father's back, the solidity of him. Her mother crying. His remorse, his regret and the calm it brought with it. Scott crying.

It's not one memory. She knows there must be more, packaged inside. Like boxes in boxes in boxes.

'It's getting late,' her dad says, and his voice is warm, reasonable.

'I'm going to read a while,' Louisa says. 'Don't wait for me.'

Isla turns back down the hall towards the kitchen. Her dad glances up at her as he pushes open the bathroom door, pulls the cord for the light. A potent stare, brief but malign. She steps away from him, into the dark of the kitchen.

20

Sydney, 1967

The heat showed no sign of breaking. Mandy stood at the top of the coastal path and looked out to the horizon. The sky was a rich blue. The ocean was still; just the odd fleck of foam on its surface, a small fringe of white at the water's edge. This weather would hold a while yet, she thought. Weeks of this ahead of us. Months, even.

Isla would have wanted to swim today. She'd have taken her snorkel out to look at the fish. Might have collected some shells too, in her bucket; had a poke around in the rock pools to see what she could find among the coral and seaweed. Always in hope of an octopus, that girl. Or a shark. Down on the beach, a small boy and his mum were kicking around a slightly deflated beach ball. An older man came striding out of the water, shaking himself off like a dog: Mr Harper from the chemist on Bridge Street, it looked like, taking his regular lunch-hour swim. A few older kids were climbing around on the flat boulders at the edge of the bay, jumping in and out of the shallow pools. They were laughing but she could barely hear them from up here. She hadn't been down to the beach at all in the fortnight since Isla left. Hadn't felt like it. It did look good down there, but.

She felt the sun high over her head as she began the walk down the coastal path. The ocean was more inviting the closer she got. She rarely swam – didn't like the thought of what might be out there – but on days like this you could see the appeal. She threw her straw hat onto the sand and kicked off her sandals. The sand was baking and there was almost no breeze. She rolled her jeans up and wet her feet in the shallows. The water was so cool and calm. She walked in past her knees, leaned over, splashed her face and arms, ran her fingers through her hair, pushing it back from her face, away from her neck. Her jeans were wet now so she went deeper, lifting her blouse to keep it dry. The sand dipped away beneath her feet and she was soaked up to her waist before she knew it. She laughed. What the hell.

'Nice day for a swim.'

She turned to see Joe standing at the shoreline in his work clothes. His shirt gaped open at the neck. The hems of his suit pants were dragging in the sand. She felt ridiculous, suddenly. She waded towards him.

'The water's lovely.' She smiled at him but he didn't respond. He might have been scowling at her, or he might have been squinting in the sun. 'Why aren't you at work?'

'Couldn't face it. Got halfway there and came back.'

She stood beside him. 'Forgot my swimmers,' she said, looking down at her wet jeans.

'I followed you down,' he said. 'Saw you from my place.'

She sat on the sand, stretched her arms out behind her and turned her face to the sun. Joe pulled off his shoes and socks, left them on the dry sand and sat beside her with his feet in the shallows. His right hand was bandaged, tightly wrapped around his knuckles and fastened at the wrist with a safety pin. She wondered if he'd done it himself or if he'd seen a doctor. If he'd made the hole in his lounge room wall any bigger.

'How you going?'

He swallowed, and frowned at the horizon. 'She cleaned out the savings account. The whole lot.'

Mandy dragged her heels through the wet sand and watched the two shallow channels fill back up with water. 'I guess it costs a lot of money to fly to England.'

The sagging beach ball landed heavily at her side. She threw it back to the child and noticed, as she drew her arm back, that she'd worn her watch in the water. The delicate second hand had stopped ticking. It showed twelve-thirty, just gone. She held it to her ear. Silence.

'I couldn't even follow them over there if I wanted to,' he said. 'Not without selling the house.' He ran his hands over his face, grains of sand mixing with sweat and dirt. 'She left her job, too. Gave them notice.'

'I know.' She glanced at him. 'Sorry. I didn't want to say.'

'Have you heard from her, since she left?'

Mandy nodded. 'Just a quick call. She wasn't on long. Bad connection.'

He stared hard at the side of her face. 'What did she say, then?' He threw a small rock into the shallows. 'Did you call her?'

'I did. I called her at her mum's.'

'And—?'

She kept her eyes on the horizon. He was dying beside her and she didn't want to see it. 'She said it was great to be back in England, Joe. That's what she said. I'm sorry.'

The tide was coming in. A wave broke over their feet and soaked them both up to the knees. Neither of them moved. She felt the heat of the sun on the back of her neck. Her hair was dry now and her skin was tight from the salt.

'I'm going to head back up to the house,' she said. 'Fix myself a drink and something to eat.'

When he didn't reply she stood and picked her hat up off the sand.

'Steve's away,' she said, and she waited for him to turn around. 'He'll be gone a day or two.'

Joe stood, clumsily, and brushed the sand from his clothes.

In the bedroom, Mandy drew the curtains against the afternoon sun. She'd left Joe by himself in the kitchen with a beer. He wasn't too good with his own company right now, but still she sat down on the bed and lit a cigarette. The thing she'd wanted to happen was happening. It had a weighted feel to it, like water flowing downstream. She exhaled slowly and watched the smoke thicken and descend.

Her jeans were almost dry but they were stiff with salt and she was sore where they'd rubbed against her skin. She stepped out of them into a clean pair, turned in front of the mirror to check she looked nice but not too nice, so he wouldn't think she'd made an effort for him. On the dresser a framed photograph of her dad looked back at her. She turned it to face the wall.

From the kitchen she heard Joe shift in his chair, put his beer bottle down on the table, clear his throat. Her heart was going at a quick, nervy gallop. She almost wanted to back out of this, to send him home. But the stronger want was to let it happen, to know that pleasure with him. She couldn't think beyond it.

He looked up at her as she walked through to the kitchen and put the ashtray down on the table.

'Another beer?' she asked.

'Thanks.'

She took one for herself, as an afterthought. Joe looked a wreck in his damp, sandy work clothes. His face was sunburned around the hairline and his eyes were bloodshot. He'd barely spoken since they left the beach. She pushed the cigarette packet across the table and he took one, lit it and sat back in his chair.

'I trusted her,' he said, lifting the bottle to his mouth. 'Trusted her totally.'

''Course you did. Why wouldn't you?'

'I wish I hadn't.' He tugged at his tie and pulled it over his head, throwing it down on the table. 'I might have seen this coming. Might have stopped it coming to this.'

'You can't go back and change what's happened, Joe.'

He crushed his cigarette out. 'The car was for her. I'd arranged for her to have driving lessons. It was going to be a surprise. I was hoping she'd pass her test before the baby came. And this is how she repays me.'

She reached her leg out under the table and rested her bare foot against his knee, holding it there until he was still. 'You don't deserve this,' she said. 'The way she's treated you. It's not right.'

For a moment he didn't react. Mandy had never made a pass at a man in her life. If he rejected her she would die.

Slowly, he wrapped his good hand around her foot and pulled it into his lap. He moved his thumb between her toes. The pleasure of it passed through her. She gripped the chair.

'Can I ask you something, Mandy?'

She swallowed. 'What is it?'

'Do you think she's left me?' He moved his thumb over her instep, up and down. 'I mean, has she really left me? Or is she trying to hurt me?'

'I don't know.' She moved to the edge of her seat to let him run his hand over her calf. 'Both, maybe.'

'That's what I thought.'

'You deserve better, Joe.'

He looked up at her. 'Are you sure, Mandy? About this?'

She pulled her foot away. He reached across the table to hold her hand. He'd taken his wedding ring off, she noticed. A white stripe crossed his finger where it had been. 'No one's going to get hurt.' She smiled at him and wondered if this was another lie; if this would be the lie that blew the whole thing apart.

He took both her hands and pulled her from her chair.

21

Ivanhoe, 1967

Steve's back ached as he climbed out of the truck. He slammed the door and the kids down by the creek scattered, into the bush and gone, quick as rabbits. The dog was tied up this time, but it watched him, stretching its leash and snarling as he knocked on the door. He stared it down and it sat, bared its teeth.

'You remember me, don't you?' he said to the dog. His voice sounded hollow. He hadn't spoken all day. 'You remember me,' he repeated, and it growled from the base of its throat.

He was giving the dog stinkeye when the door opened. A young woman peered out from inside and he almost didn't turn quick enough to stop her closing it in his face. He jammed his boot in the door. She pushed against him from the inside and rammed the door with her shoulder, calling him every name she could think of, telling him to go to hell, get off her property, leave her alone. The dog barked, pulling hard on its leash. Inside the house, the baby cried.

He held the door steady with one hand and pushed against her weight. It gave easily and she took a few steps back, stood there looking at him with real fear in her face. He'd seen it before. He was her worst nightmare come to life.

'Sorry,' he said. 'You're going to have to let me in.'

She turned to look at the child. 'Please don't take him.' The fight had gone out of her. 'Please. I beg of you.'

He noticed then, she was younger than he'd thought. Sixteen, maybe. 'You his mum?'

She nodded. 'My grandpa said you'd be back. He warned me, after you came for Dora.'

'The boy will be looked after,' he said, and the words sickened him. 'He'll get a good start in life.'

'That's a lie.' She pointed her finger at his face. 'My auntie was taken as a kid. She told me what it's like.'

The baby's cries lifted as he shut the door behind him. She picked the child up, held him tight, cried silently with her face pressed against his. This was the one that would break him, he thought; he'd known it since he first set eyes on that child. This one would finish him.

'It won't be like that,' he told her.

She turned from him and her body shook uncontrollably; her cries became a moan. He stepped closer and summoned the poison for the last time. The last time.

'I promise you, it won't be like that. I'll see to it,' he said, and he reached for the boy.

22

Leeds, 1967

Isla had a sore throat and her nose was stuffed up. She had been sent to bed because she was sick. It was cold in this bed and she suspected it wasn't bedtime. It was hard to tell because it was always dark in England. The blankets were thin and she didn't like the touch of them. They were making her more sick. She had left her Digby bear behind in Australia, and she was starting to think she might never get to hold Andrea Walker's kitten. She had been nice to Andrea all those weeks for no reason.

Someone put a light on in the hall. The flowers in the wallpaper bloomed, big and ugly, yellow and brown. When Isla shut her eyes the flowers were still there, growing big and close then shrinking back. Isla watched with her eyes shut to see if the yellow flowers would push the brown ones away, but new colours started growing, green and then pink, with fat petals like tongues. There was a brick inside the bones of her head.

She couldn't move because the brick was heavy and hurting. She lay still. From outside she could hear Grandma's voice, 'Didn't I try to tell you?'

'Did you?' Mummy said.

'You'd have a degree by now. A career.'

'I know.'

'I said at the time, he's no good.'

'You don't know him, Mum.'

Grandma snorted. 'I'll knock the bejesus out of him, so I will.'

Grandma's words repeated in Isla's head without meaning. She liked Grandma because she was from somewhere called Island. Grandma did not like England much either. And she liked you even when she was shouting. She was only cranky in her voice. If you made a face she would laugh and make a face back.

'He's not all bad,' Mummy said. 'He can be wonderful.'

'Sure, can't they all,' Grandma said.

Isla sat up and the brick in her head banged against her bones. 'Mum!'

The flowers were turning, their petals growing fat and leathery. She didn't know if her eyes were shut or not. It was hot in this bed, very hot, making her skin wet. The brick was broken. It had smashed into bits and all the pieces of brick were sharp in her head, her neck, her back. Isla sat on the edge of the bed and maybe she was dreaming again. It was hard to tell. The flowers poked their tongues at her. 'Mum!'

The door opened.

'Mandy?' She knew it couldn't be Mandy but her name was in her mouth. 'Mandy?'

'It's me, darling. It's Mummy.'

Isla tried not to cry. 'I'm hot.'

She lay back down and her mum put her hand on her forehead. Her mum could tell about the brick. She pushed the
covers away and her hands were quick.

'Oh God, you're burning up.'

Mandy always smiled when you made a face, and she made
faces back. She did good faces and she didn't shout much. When
Isla tried to see Mandy's face she saw huge flowers with tongues
lolling, green and pink, yellow and brown.

23

Sydney, 1997

It's raining again by the time Isla reaches the back of the yard. The ocean below is grey and heaving. She stands under the tea trees and decides she won't swim, after all. She feels cold, although the air is warm. Her shoes are letting in water. She's about to turn back to the house when she sees a woman on the beach, wading out of the sea, tall and upright despite the waves crashing against her. Older than her, Isla thinks, but in better shape. The woman picks her towel up from the sand and dries herself off, shaking the water from her hair. Isla recognises the floral-patterned beach towel and then she recognises her mother: the new short hairstyle and the plain black costume, the good posture. Her admiration drops away and she is filled with hate, so cold and quick it turns her stomach. She wants to kick her across a room.

She stays where she is, watching her mum walk over the sand with the towel over one shoulder, scaling the path without pausing to check her footing. She sees her face as she draws closer: preoccupied, frowning. Isla raises a hand and waves. She doesn't truly hate her, does she? Maybe she does. Maybe she always has.

'Hey,' Louisa calls out. 'Are you going to swim?'

'No. Looks cold.'

'It's not too bad. Warmer than this rain.' She's barefoot and her skin is damp. Despite the climb from the beach, she is barely out of breath.

'I think I'll leave it,' Isla says.

They stand together under the trees, looking out at the yard. The bunting droops low across the back of the house.

'Not like the British rain,' Louisa says. 'The British rain got under your skin. I don't think I dried out till I'd been here a year.'

'Do you miss it?'

'England?' Louisa laughs. 'Not any more. I can't imagine why I ever wanted to go back.'

They watch the rain fall. Isla has heard the story many times of how her mum, overcome with homesickness, ran back to England with Isla when she was small. Only to find when she got there that it wasn't home any more. That she'd made an awful mistake. And Joe had begged her to come home, saying he couldn't live without her. So the story goes. Isla's memories of her time in her grandmother's house are of snow drifts and frozen pipes; wind blowing down the chimneys, filling the rooms with smoke. Missing her dad.

'How did you do it?' Isla asks. 'The time we went to England.'

The ocean roars behind them. 'What do you mean?'

'How did you pay for the flights? You can't have earned much back then.'

Her mum bristles beside her and Isla looks down at her feet, the water seeping into her old canvas shoes. This is not the correct version of the story. This is its dark underbelly; the chapter that was scrapped.

'I withdrew all the savings,' Louisa says. 'There was a lot of money in the account. Your dad had been saving for a car.'

'And he didn't try to stop you?'

'I hid the savings book. By the time he found it we were gone.'

Isla stares at the rain. 'I can't believe you did that.'

'I felt like I had no choice.' She is quiet for a while. 'I don't suppose you can imagine what it's like, to be dependent on a man for money.'

'I guess not.'

'I remember your dad had to write a letter, giving his permission to name me on the account. So I could pay money in from my wages,' Louisa says. 'It was unusual back then. Bank accounts were for men, not their wives.'

Isla keeps her eyes on the back of the house. Next door, Carol Taylor slams her kitchen window shut.

'I betrayed his trust,' Louisa says, rubbing briskly at her hair with her towel. 'He's never quite forgiven me.'

'When did he start pushing you around?'

Louisa swings around to face her. Her towel falls to the ground.

'Is that why you left him?'

She picks up the towel and shakes it vigorously. 'He's never been an easy man.'

'I know that.'

She shakes the towel again. Dirt and wet sand cling to it. 'I gave as good as I got,' she says.

'Did you?'

Louisa looks at her and nods. 'I fought back. For a long time he was stronger.'

Not any more, Isla thinks. She wonders when the power tipped. If her dad is nervous, in the house with a woman who harbours a grudge. She thinks of Dom tipping vodka down the sink, his back to her.

'There were happy times, weren't there?' Louisa says.

You're never happy, Isla thinks, and she wonders where that came from. 'Of course there were,' she says. 'But the bad times were really bad.'

The rain falls harder, the house barely visible. Isla watches her mum's face, the stiffened tendons in her neck. She knows her mother won't apologise, or express her regret. It's not her way. Isla spent her teenage years enraged over this: her mum would never bend or concede that she might be wrong. It had driven her ever closer to her dad; neither of them were ever in the right about anything.

'Do you believe him, Mum?'

'Believe who?'

'Dad. Do you believe his story, about Mandy?'

Louisa steps backwards into the rain. She is immediately

drenched, her hair flattened. 'Do you want to see something?'

Isla can barely see her mother's face. 'Do I want to see what?'

'Something you ought to know about.'

Isla follows her mum across the grass, keeping her head down. She leaves her shoes on the mat. Louisa walks straight through to the main bedroom, throwing her towel over a chair. 'Come on,' she says. 'In here.'

Isla sits down on the bed. Rainwater drips down her neck. The room is warm, the window misted up. The ironing is piled high on a chair in one corner, the laundry basket overflowing beside it. A bunch of roses, long dead, droop from a vase on the dresser.

Louisa reaches around in the back of a drawer. 'I found this a few months ago. Your father keeps it at the back of his sock drawer with the vodka we pretend I don't know about.'

Isla pushes her wet hair out of her eyes. She has a suspended feeling, of curiosity meeting dread. 'What is it?'

'It was Mandy's.' Louisa holds a watch by its strap. 'I recognised it the moment I saw it.'

Isla stands and looks at the watch. It's long and narrow, gold-plated, with a thin, oblong face and notches instead of numbers. The time has stopped just after twelve-thirty.

'Your father didn't bother denying it was hers,' Louisa continues. 'I told him to get rid of it but he refused.'

Isla turns away from the watch. The rain is heavy against the window. She has a trapped feeling in the airless room.

'I always had a suspicion about him and Mandy,' Louisa says. 'You can tell, can't you, when a man's head is turned.'

'It doesn't mean.' Isla can't finish the sentence.

'She was an attractive woman,' Louisa says.

'It doesn't mean anything.'

'For God's sake.'

'You're jumping to conclusions.'

'He's admitted he was infatuated with her. Nothing serious, he claims.' Louisa closes her hand around the watch. 'This was a while ago of course, before the police turned up.'

Isla feels the shock in her body, the heat of it in her skin. 'So he was infatuated with her and he kept her watch. So what?'

'He's lying, Isla. He's hiding something.'

'You don't know that.'

'I can tell when he's lying. He's on edge. He's drinking more. Something's eating at him.'

'What are you saying?' Isla shouts it, to hide her fear. 'Are you saying Dad killed her?'

'I didn't say that.'

'But that's what you think?'

'I do think it's possible. Yes.'

Isla turns to face her mother. They are feet apart and the room feels small, the air stifling. 'Do you want to know what I think?'

'Sure.' She wraps the watch around her fingers.

'I think you'd like to see him arrested.'

'That's not true!'

'He had an affair with your friend.'

Louisa puts a hand through her hair and holds her arm there, elbow jutting sideways. She shuts her eyes.

'She *was* your friend, wasn't she?'

Louisa nods. 'I thought so.'

'You're taking it out on him, but they both hurt you.'

'That's not what this is about.'

'When did you find out they'd had an affair?'

'Will you stop saying that?' She is red in the face, her body tense.

'Is that why you left him? Did you take all the savings and go to England because you found out –?'

'No!' She screams it. 'No. I started to suspect it when we got home from England. I think it must have started while we were away.'

Isla steps back. She has always feared her mum's temper. They have learned over the years to tread carefully around each other, to avoid clashing.

'You must have been angry with her,' Isla says.

Louisa's eyes drop to the ground, where the ironing has fallen from the chair.

'When did you last see Mandy?'

Louisa raises her head. 'I haven't seen her in thirty years.'

'When exactly?'

'Before you and I went to England.'

'Are you sure?'

'Of course I'm sure.' Her mum stares levelly back at her. A bird calls out from the yard, a familiar cry.

Louisa turns and puts the watch back in the drawer. Her

shoulder blades jut out as she lifts out socks and replaces them, pushes the drawer shut when she's done. 'Don't mention this to your father,' she says. She keeps her back to Isla, watching the rain against the window.

24

Sydney, 1967

'When are you expecting Steve back?'

Joe stood in Mandy's kitchen drinking coffee, dressed in his creased shirt and suit pants. The sun was only just up. No colour in the backyard yet. Mandy knew he'd leave soon. She wished he'd get on with it. At the same time, she had to admit, she wished he'd stay.

'He went out to Ivanhoe,' she said. 'Takes the best part of a day to drive it.'

Joe cut short a yawn. 'He could be back any time, then.'

'Relax.' She poured her own coffee and gave it a stir. 'He'll be back tomorrow at the earliest.'

'Mandy, I—' He put his coffee down on the counter top. 'What if he cuts the trip short?'

'He won't.' She sat down at the kitchen table. 'He's got to drive out to one of the children's Homes with this kid. Last time he was gone a week.'

He frowned back at her. 'Is it a regular thing, then? Removing these kids?'

'It's more regular than he'd like it to be. It's been getting to him, lately. These families take it hard.'

'Do they?'

'He says they love their kids the same as the rest of us. And he reckons the Homes he takes them to are no good either.'

Joe's eyebrows lifted. 'So he's not even solving the problem.'

'No.' She shifted in her chair. 'He's got to thinking he *is* the problem.'

'Why doesn't he leave? Do something else for a living?'

'I think he might. It's not easy for him, but. He comes from a long line of policemen, going back generations. He knew what he was taking on and he thought he was up to the job.'

'I didn't realise,' he said. 'I mean. I didn't know it was that bad.'

'He doesn't talk about it much.' She thought of Steve crying out in front of the house. 'Louisa knows all about it. I'm surprised she didn't tell you.'

He dropped his eyes and she wished she hadn't mentioned Louisa. 'Sorry,' she said.

'No. It's all right.'

He drained his coffee and went back into the lounge room. She heard the rattle of his belt buckle and the armchair being shifted around as he looked for his shoes.

When he came back his shirt was tucked in, his belt buckled. The bandage was unravelling from his arm. 'Can I ask you something?'

'Go ahead.' She smiled. From his face she thought he might want to know where he stood with her, if he could see her again.

'Did Louisa mention me, when you spoke to her on the phone?'

She picked his shoes up from the floor and handed them to him, smarting a little. 'She asked how you were. How you'd taken it.'

'Did she?'

'I told her she had a nerve, leaving me to tell you where she'd gone.'

He pushed his feet into his shoes. 'Did she say anything else?'

'Just that it was good to be back in England. Like I said.'

She sat back down. Joe tightened the bandage, flexing his fingers, making a fist with his good hand. Maybe she shouldn't have told him what Louisa said on the phone. He had a way of stoking himself up about things, she'd noticed. Like prodding at a bad tooth.

'My mum was from London,' she said, more to distract him than anything else. 'Lou reminds me of her in a way. Just that she was homesick the whole time.'

'I didn't know that.'

'She emigrated before I was born and she spent the rest of her life griping about this country. The flies, the heat; the spiders. She never did get to like it here.'

'Did she ever go back to England?'

'No.' She took a cigarette from the pack on the table. 'She ran off with the window cleaner when I was eleven. He was a Pom. Sorry. British, I mean.'

146

He leaned forward for a light. 'He was her way of being closer to home, was he?'

She smiled. 'Except he lived up the road in Pyrmont and drank schooners at the bar with the rest of them.'

'Well. A man's got to fit in.'

Mandy hadn't thought about Mikey Benson in a long time. He'd liked Mandy a bit more than she'd wanted him to like her. Wandering hands. Her mum had noticed and said nothing. Married the dirty bastard and wondered why Mandy never visited.

'Did your mum take you with her? When she left?'

'God, no.' She downed her coffee. 'No. It was us kids she was running from.'

He visibly swallowed his shock. Disapproval too; just a hint of it. She looked away.

'My mother had four kids before she was twenty-five. Three boys and then me.' She heard herself defending her, as she always did. 'She stuck with it as long as she could.'

'I'm sure you weren't that bad.'

'I was the nail in the coffin.' She had an edgy feeling from the coffee. Out in the yard the cicadas were off-key. 'My dad never let her back in the house. He took all her things to the op shop. And he cleaned his own windows after that.'

'I bet he did.'

There was the disapproval again. 'None of us is perfect. I don't blame her really.'

'Is she still with the window cleaning bloke?'

'She died a few years ago. Cancer.'

'God. Sorry.'

'It's all right.' She hadn't meant to get into this. 'The whole family's scattered, since she went. My brothers don't keep in touch. Last time I tried calling my dad the number had been disconnected.'

Joe sat down across the table from her and tapped his cigarette over the ashtray. 'Can I ask you something else?'

She nodded. 'Just so long as it's not about your wife or my mother.'

'You don't have to answer. It's just.'

She sat forward. 'Go on.'

'Have you done this before?'

It took her a moment to get his meaning. She shook her head. 'Steve's the only other man I ever went with.'

'Right.' He cleared his throat. 'Same here. I mean, I've never. Not since I met –'

'It's all right.' She didn't want him to say her name. 'I know what you mean.' She ran her bare foot over the lino, then spoke before she thought better of it. 'It was never like that. With Steve.'

He looked up at her. 'No?'

'No.'

They smiled at each other, and the room filled with light as the sun broke through the tea trees. Mandy wondered if she could ever forget what she'd done with Joe Green on her kitchen floor.

'You'd better get off home.'

He held his good hand out and she took it, stood up and

leaned in against him. She liked the way his chin met the top of her head. The gait of him, loose and upright. She liked that he was not her husband.

He kissed her and turned for the door. She didn't watch him go.

25

Sydney, 1997

Isla is lost in thought when the police car passes her on her way back from town. She looks right at it, watches it make its way up Bay Street, but she doesn't see it. She looks into the gardens of her neighbours and sees Douglas Blunt crouched on his lawn, dead-heading his roses. He has a concentrated look which tells her he has seen her and is not planning to say hello. She pauses beside his gate.

'Mr Blunt.' She coughs. 'I wanted to apologise.'

He takes a moment to shift his gaze in her direction. His face is blank.

'I shouldn't have spoken to you that way. At the party. I was out of line.'

'You were.'

'I'm sorry.'

He points his secateurs at her parents' place, where the police car has stopped. 'Looks like you got company.'

A uniformed policeman gets out of the car and slams the door. Isla watches him open the gate and climb the steps to the verandah. She tries not to run. Her dad is out, he won't be home for hours. If they wanted to arrest him they would have come later in the day. They know where he works. The door shuts behind the cop and she stops, holds onto a fence post in a spike of fear. The watch. She tries to think. Behind her, Doug snips at his roses.

She lets herself into the house and stands in the hallway. The door to the kitchen stands open and the house is bright, flooded with sunlight. She hears the cop talking to her mum.

'I came as soon as I could,' he says. 'If it's not a good time, I could come back later.'

'No,' Louisa says. 'Don't do that.'

There is a pause, a scraping of chairs. The kettle starts to boil. Isla steps quietly into her parents' bedroom. She opens the drawer where she saw her mum hide the watch and reaches around inside. It's not there. She checks twice, lifting out the quarter bottle of vodka and the balled up pairs of socks. It's gone. Sweat runs under her arms. She tries the other drawers, quickly, shaking out T-shirts and shorts, checking the pockets. She checks the laundry basket, the base of the wardrobe, under the mattress. Nothing.

From the kitchen, her mum's voice reaches her: nervy, polite small talk. Isla creeps from the room. The cop's boots are visible from the hallway, and the edge of his jacket, hanging from the back of his chair.

'You mentioned an item when you called,' the cop says. 'Something that might help our enquiries.'

151

'That's right,' Louisa replies.

Isla stops where she is. Shock passes through her: a band of heat that moves along her limbs.

'We appreciate your help, Mrs Green. It all helps to build up a picture.'

'Of course,' Louisa says.

'Perhaps you could repeat what you told me on the phone. And you could show me the item you mentioned.'

Isla pushes the kitchen door open. The room is a white box of light, two faces turned towards her, open-mouthed. Her mother drops her teacup on the floor at her feet.

'Isla. Dear God.' Louisa stands among the shards of china with her hand at her throat. 'I didn't know you were home.'

'I got back early,' Isla says. Her voice is crisp in the bright room. 'Just a moment ago.'

The cop looks from Isla to Louisa and back. 'Everything all right, ladies?'

'This is my daughter,' Louisa says.

Isla throws the cop a smile. He is tall and stooped, grey-haired, with a dense, white moustache. Behind his glasses his eyes are small and hard. Isla takes in the three stars on each of his shoulders and the radio at his belt. 'Isla Green,' she says, shaking his hand.

'Inspector Perry,' the cop replies, taking his seat at the table. 'Are you happy to continue, Mrs Green?'

Louisa stands by the sink, holding the pieces of her broken cup in her hands.

'Go ahead, Mum,' Isla says, sitting down. 'I'm fully in the picture,' she says to Inspector Perry. 'Don't mind me.'

He hesitates. 'We could continue this down at the station, if you'd rather—'

'It's all right,' Louisa says, without turning around. She drops the shattered cup into the bin. 'Let's carry on.' She takes another teacup from the cupboard. They wait for her in silence. The Inspector takes a notebook from his breast pocket and opens it to a blank page. From his belt, his radio blurts wordless noise.

'Now, Mrs Green.' He removes his glasses to look at Louisa. She puts her tea down on the table and sits. 'Could you repeat what you told me on the phone, if you would be so kind.'

Louisa clasps her hands in front of her. 'I have reason to believe . . .' She looks down at her hands. 'That my husband had an affair with Amanda Mallory, thirty years ago, while my daughter and I were in England.'

He digs at his eyes and puts his glasses back on. 'Can you remind me of when you were in England?'

'The first three months of 1967. Between January and March.'

He writes this down in his notebook. Isla watches her mother, who is nervously turning the gold stud in her ear.

'And your husband was alone, here in Sydney, for that whole period?'

'That's right.'

'When you got back to Australia, did you see or hear from Mrs Mallory?'

Louisa shakes her head. 'Their house was empty when we got back. They'd moved to Victoria, I think.'

153

'What makes you think they moved?'

'That's what Joe told me at the time.'

'I see.' He pinches the knot of his tie. 'So the last time you saw Mrs Mallory was January 1967?'

'That's right.' Louisa watches him write it down, turning her earring at double speed.

'Has Mr Green admitted to this affair?'

'Not in so many words.'

'What makes you think he had relations with Mrs Mallory?'

'He kept something that belonged to her.' Louisa reaches down beside her, into her handbag. 'He admitted this belonged to Mandy.'

The cop turns a page in his notebook. There is an eagerness in his face as he looks up, a suggestion of a smile. Isla wants to turn the table over. She grips the underside of the chair until her fingers hurt.

'I found it a few months ago,' Louisa says. She glances at Isla for the first time as she sets the watch down on the table. She has the bright-eyed look of the tattletale, the teacher's pet. 'Joe kept it hidden at the back of a drawer.'

'And you're sure this belonged to Mrs Mallory?' He looks over his glasses at the watch.

'Quite sure,' Louisa says. She sips her tea. 'I remember Steve – her husband – gave it to her for Christmas, shortly before we went to England.'

He writes this down, taking his time. 'This is very helpful, Mrs Green.' He takes a plastic glove from his pocket and uses it to put the watch into a specimen bag. 'I'll need to take this with me, of course.'

Louisa nods. The colour has gone from her face. 'I don't suppose you can prove it belonged to Mandy,' she says.

Inspector Perry removes his glasses, leaving deep grooves in the side of his head. 'You might be surprised. A lot of cases are being reopened from twenty or thirty years ago, now that DNA profiling has moved on. All it takes it a strand of hair, or the residue of sweat.' He nods at the specimen bag. 'Or a drop of blood.'

Louisa covers her mouth with her hand.

'There's no evidence that my dad and Mandy had an affair,' Isla says. The Inspector looks at her in surprise. 'My dad hasn't admitted to that.'

'I think I've taken up enough of your time.' He goes to stand.

'What about Steve Mallory? Mandy's husband.'

The Inspector pauses, half out of his chair. 'What about him?'

'Have you questioned him?'

'I can't tell you that, I'm afraid.' He puts his glasses back on. 'I need to get going.'

'Is he still with the police?'

Her mother stares at her. The Inspector's radio hisses at his belt.

Isla stands. 'Do you know him? He was a cop when he lived next door to us.'

'Mr Mallory no longer works for the police force,' the cop says.

Louisa puts her hands flat on the table and goes to stand. 'I'll show you out,' she says.

'One more thing.' Isla stands in the doorway, blocking his path. 'Why is an Inspector involved in a missing person's case?'

He looks down at Isla with huge impatience. 'Mrs Mallory's case is not straightforward.'

'Is this a murder enquiry?'

'We have a large number of records on file in New South Wales. Deceased persons who have never been identified, some of whom died in suspicious circumstances. It's possible one of them is Mrs Mallory.'

'Are you looking outside of New South Wales? If Mandy moved to Victoria—'

'I suggest you leave the police work to me, Miss Green.'

'But if she moved away—'

'It seems she did not.' He glares at her, rattled. 'Steve Mallory claims his wife didn't go with him when he sold the house and moved away.'

'So you did question him.'

He moves to push past her. In the corner of her eye, Isla sees her mother shake her head.

'Do you think Mandy's alive?'

He shuts his eyes. 'I hope so.'

'But you think it's unlikely?'

'I think thirty years is a long time to live with no record at all.'

Isla waits in the hall while her mum shows the Inspector out, shuts the door behind him and stays there, watching through the peephole. They hear the chink of the gate.

'Did you have to do that?' Louisa turns her back to the door. 'Did you have to cross-examine him?'

'Someone had to fight Dad's corner.' Isla shuts the kitchen door behind her, darkening the hallway. She steps closer to her mother, pausing at the door of her parents' bedroom, where the laundry basket is disturbed and the drawers stand open. 'Sorry to spoil your plan.'

'I don't have a plan,' Louisa says.

'Oh, really? It looked to me like you were planning to land Dad in jail.'

'I thought it might be important. The watch. After I showed it to you I started thinking—'

'What?' She is just about keeping her voice steady. 'What did you think?'

'I'd have been withholding evidence,' she says.

'We could have got rid of it.'

'I thought they should know.'

'You thought it might make Dad look like he was obsessed with her,' Isla says. 'Like he killed her and kept a memento.'

'It *does* look like that, doesn't it?'

'Not to me.' She feels a swell of rage and she is glad of it, its familiar heat. 'I think you're deflecting attention from yourself.'

She laughs. 'Don't be absurd, Isla.'

'I don't think it's absurd. Mandy betrayed you. I think you're sucking up to the cops so they don't look too closely at you.'

'I would never—'

'I think you would,' Isla says.

157

The house is still and quiet. Isla hears her mum breathing; her own breath and her blood in her ears.

'I haven't told you much about Mandy, have I?'

'No,' Isla says. 'Maybe you should.'

Louisa meets her at the bedroom door. She eyes Isla apprehensively. 'Mandy saved me when you were a baby,' she says. 'She was the only person who understood I wasn't coping. I didn't have to tell her, she took one look at me and she knew. She helped me with you. When you wouldn't settle she picked you up and calmed you down. She took you out in the pram so I could have a break. She stopped me going under.'

Isla finds she is mirroring her mother, her stance and the tilt of her head. She stands up straighter. 'Go on.'

'I came to rely on her. She looked after you when I went back to work. I took her for granted, although it took me a while to realise that.' She turns into the bedroom and squats down by the bed. 'The Mallories' house was empty for months after we got back from England. Your father was working long hours and I had no help with Scott when he came along. I've never been so lonely.'

'Sounds tough.'

'That's one word for it.' Louisa reaches under the bed and pulls out a suitcase. 'If Mandy had walked through the door back then, I'd have forgiven her anything. I'd have fallen at her feet and begged her to help me.'

Isla sits down on the bed. The rage has passed. She feels a prickle of shame, of foolishness. 'Why didn't you ever talk about her?'

'It was easier not to.' Louisa takes clothes from their hangers and throws them into the case. 'Your father jumped out of his skin when I mentioned her name. I tried to put her out of my mind.'

She's leaving, Isla thinks, as her mum takes sweaters and T-shirts from the drawers, barely pausing to look at them. She folds them briskly, and Isla remembers her in a yellow dress, patterned with daisies. A hot day and a taxi with vinyl seats that burned the backs of her legs.

'I can't protect your father any more,' Louisa says. 'I know you love him.' She takes her nightdress from under the pillow. 'I know you don't want to believe it.'

'I don't believe it.' She shakes her head.

'He was the last one to see Mandy alive.' Louisa nods towards the kitchen, as if the cop were still there with his notebook and his radio. 'Steve Mallory left without her.'

'It's Steve's word against Dad's as far as I can tell. And Steve was a cop. They're bound to believe him.'

Louisa tuts, and throws a hairbrush into the case, followed by a framed photograph of Isla and Scott, taken by the school photographer: Scott with a neat row of baby teeth, Isla with her hair teased into plaits.

'Steve was one of the cops who carried out the forced removals. The Aboriginal kids who were taken from their families.'

Louisa stares at Isla. A cloud passes over the sun and the light flattens. 'How did you know about that?'

'Dad told me.'

She snaps the suitcase shut. 'I don't see how it's relevant.'

'A job like that could send a man off the rails.'

'You're clutching at straws.' She lifts the case from the bed. 'Steve adored Mandy.'

'You're ready to think well of a man who was involved in that? But not your own husband?'

'You seem ready to suspect anyone but your father.'

'That's not true.'

'I think it is, darling. I think you want to lay blame on anyone but him.' The sun comes out. Louisa stands in a slant of light from the window, lit up with dust motes. 'Come with me, Isla.'

She finds she is crying. 'Where are you going?'

'Scott and Ruby's.'

She thinks of the taxi, the hot seats, the hurriedly packed suitcase. She feels captured, complicit again in a huge betrayal. 'I'll stay here,' she says.

'There's plenty of space at Scott's.'

'Is he expecting you?'

'Yes.'

'You planned this?'

Louisa looks at her feet. 'Yes.'

Isla wipes her face with her sleeve. 'I'm not going anywhere.'

'I can't force you.'

'No, you can't.'

A bird screeches, a rasping cackle, close to the window. Isla stands, and Louisa steps backwards, flinching.

'Are you scared of me?'

'Of course not.'

'You look scared.'

Louisa picks up the case. 'It's just you remind me of your father sometimes.'

She waits for Isla to step aside before she leaves the room.

26

Sydney, 1967

Mandy put her shopping down and took a breather. She wished she'd got the bus instead of walking home under this hard, hot sun. She'd only made it worse for herself. Now she'd have to face Steve with a headache on top of a guilty conscience. The shopping was hardly essential. She could have gone later, once she'd given him a bit of a welcome home. Bit of grub and a cup of tea. That would have been the right thing to do.

'G'day, Mandy. How's it going?'

Douglas Blunt was smiling at her from beneath his sun hat, holding a pair of garden shears. She nodded hello. 'Not too bad,' she said. 'Bit hot.'

'Roasting,' he agreed, nodding at his veggie patch. 'Me tomatoes have cooked in their flamin' skins. Didn't get 'em under the shadecloth in time.'

He looked like a big baked tomato, she thought, with his hat pulled down low over his hot face. Poor Doug. They'd laid him off at the port and his wife died a few months later. He didn't know what to do with himself.

'You should get yourself in the shade, Doug.'

He pointed his shears at her house, where Steve's truck was parked up on the kerb. 'Saw Steve drive past a while back.'

She managed a tight smile, which made her head throb. 'I was hoping he'd be home already. I never know when to expect him.'

'Haven't seen Louisa lately.' He leaned backwards, better to see her under his hat. 'Or the little girl.'

'No. Me neither.'

'Gone back to England, I reckon.' He snipped a few leaves from his hedge. 'Didn't settle.'

'No. It's a shame. We were fond of them.'

Doug stepped away from a bottlebrush that shuddered with bees near his shoulder. 'Lovely girl, Louisa. Have you heard from her?'

'Can't say I have.' She picked up her shopping. 'Cheerio, then.'

She took two steps and stopped. The sound of a baby's cry met the pain in her head, sending fingers of shock down her back. She dropped her shopping; heard the eggs crunch as they hit the footpath.

'That child's been bawling for hours.' Doug stared accusingly up the street. 'Somebody needs to put a plug in it.'

It was the strangest feeling: shock without surprise. As if it were right that she should hear a baby crying from the direction of her house. As if she should have known.

'The Walkers are expecting,' she said. 'Their baby must have come early.'

Doug shook his head. 'Saw Abigail not ten minutes ago. Still the size of a house.'

Mandy swallowed. Must be thirst, putting strange thoughts in her head.

'Sounds like a kiddie that's getting its teeth, Abigail reckons.' Doug went back to pruning his hedge. 'Got some lungs on it.'

Andrea Walker shot past on her bicycle, rang her bell as she reached the end of Bay Street and turned out of sight.

Mandy's limbs were heavy as she climbed the stairs of her verandah. Behind the closed curtains of her living room she could hear the uneasy whine of a baby not quite asleep. She let the shopping fall at her feet and stood for a minute in the shade with the key in her hand.

27

Sydney, 1967

Joe opened his eyes and shut them again. He hadn't closed the curtains properly last night and now they were letting in the sun. The room was hot and bright and he was a dirty grub, a waste of space, lying in bed half the day, hiding from work when there was nothing wrong with him except the usual blinding hangover and the mess of his life. He turned in the bed and the pain rolled around the base of his skull, darkening. He held onto it, let it fill his head.

No matter how much he drank, he woke up knowing that Louisa had left him and taken his daughter. The hangover curdled it in his head, turned it bad before he had a chance to make any sense of it. It doubled his agony. Of course it did. He knew that, and he drank anyway, because his old man was winning. His dad was always right, in the end.

He forced himself to sit up, to swing his legs over the side of the bed. God, his throat was rough, he must have smoked most of a pack last night. His fingers were yellow, brown in places. He reached into the top drawer of the bedside table for his headache pills and crunched two, dry-mouthed. Nausea passed through him and he closed his eyes against it, let it pass. He thought of Louisa then, with a towel wrapped around her head, holding a plate of toast, asking if he wanted any. He had to watch himself, getting sentimental over her. She hadn't made him toast in years. She spent the mornings running around after Isla, trying to find something clean to wear for work.

The phone started ringing as he got in the shower. He let it go. If he didn't answer, he could imagine it was her, calling to apologise. To explain. He could think of her waiting for him to pick up, nervous and hopeful. She could ring as long as she liked; he wasn't giving in that easy. He lathered up the soap. Let her sweat. The ringing stopped and he washed the soap from his face, holding his breath as water streamed from his nose. That wasn't her on the phone. It was the middle of the night in England. If she was going to call, she'd wait till it was evening here, morning there. Around nine.

He was always drunk by nine.

The towel stank. He threw it to the ground and walked naked into the lounge room; stood on the carpet, dripping. He'd shrunk all his shirts in the washing machine the day before and wasn't about to try it again. The machine must be faulty, or else he didn't have the setting right. He'd never used it before. He suspected Mandy might know how it worked, but the thought of asking her made the sweat prickle in his hair. It was humiliating, this whole situation. He'd rather drip dry naked than let Mandy come round and see his smalls on the floor and his whisky tumblers in the sink.

He'd have to be careful with Mandy. She was taking the edge off, helping him through a dark time, nothing more. She wasn't even his type. Maybe that was the attraction. She was an antidote to Louisa: fair-haired, curvy, knowing. She'd been there at the edge of his vision for years, of course she had, and he'd never expected to do more than wonder about her. Knowing she was next door, catching sight of her sometimes, was distracting, a bit of an itch. But she was married. And life was complicated enough.

The stink in the kitchen was horrible. Stale smoke and something rotting somewhere, a blocked drain maybe. He opened the back door and straight away heard a baby crying, loud and close. It still got to him, that sound. Hard to ignore it when a baby was crying like that, the way Isla used to when she was tiny.

Christ. He shut the door and lit a cigarette, unsteady with the lighter, sending it black down the side. He turned the radio on. *Another battalion to Vietnam before the end of the year.* He reached for the dial, turned it quickly, looking for something to calm his head. He found another news channel; Harold Holt was saying he wanted to drop the word 'British' from Australian passports. About time. He found himself half listening. His mind wandered to Mandy on the beach, walking into the water with all her clothes on, wading deeper with her arms up high.

In the bedroom he pulled yesterday's clothes onto his damp skin and tugged the covers over the sheets. Louisa's clothes were slung over the chair on her side of the bed. The book she'd been reading was still there where she'd left it, pages splayed open against the bedside table, spine up. *The Bell Jar*. He picked it up, scanned a few lines and put it down again, losing her place. His head throbbed. He picked the book up again, put it in the drawer and slammed it shut. He lifted her clothes from the chair, opened the wardrobe and threw them into the cluttered space at the bottom where she kept her shoes. The door wouldn't shut so he knelt down and pushed her clothes further back, aware of her blouses and dresses hanging above him, grazing the back of his head. He leaned against the wardrobe until it closed. He was sweating. His shirt was drenched.

He ought to open a window but if that baby was still crying he didn't want to hear it. Might be better to get out of the house. Go and buy some coffee and more headache pills. Maybe he'd go as far as Bridge Street and get himself a couple of new shirts. If he could stay off the grog tonight he'd go into work tomorrow.

The phone rang again as he was lacing his shoes. He didn't bother kidding himself it was Louisa this time. It would be Stan calling from work, wanting to know where the hell he was. He'd told him he had a bug. First excuse to come into his head. If he'd thought harder he might have invented something that would last a few weeks. He couldn't face the office, the stack of papers on his desk, the meetings about meetings, the internal politics. It had been bad enough before his wife left him.

The little girl across the street cycled past. The Walker kid, what was her name? Isla had been so jealous of her on that bike. He'd planned to get her a bike of her own, once the pay rise came through. But he'd put the money in the savings account instead, and Louisa had taken every last cent of it to fly back to England.

He stood and leaned in against the wall, felt his arm draw back and his fist slam against the plaster, once, twice, three times. It was broken already, he was sure of it. The agony made his legs weak. He swallowed the bile in his mouth.

The phone stopped ringing. He sat down on the couch and kicked off his shoes.

28

Sydney, 1997

Isla stands in the hallway and dials the London number. Her parents' framed photographs look up at her from the hall table. Her younger self holding a gymnastics trophy, posing for the local press in a leotard, surly with embarrassment. ('Couldn't you have smiled?' her mother had said.) School photos, graduation photos. Her parents outside the house when it was newly built, the sun in their eyes, holding each other at the waist. A happy family, trimmed of its backstory. Isla stares them down.

The phone rings distantly in London.

'Hello? It's Isla Green, regarding the first-floor apartment on Sinclair Road.'

A British accent replies, saying he's glad she called. The vendors of the apartment have had to raise the price. The chain will fall through, he tells her, if she doesn't up her offer. Isla calmly agrees to another £20,000. The property will appreciate in value, he tells her, in clipped vowels. She can't lose.

'One more thing,' she says. 'I'm going to stay in Sydney a bit longer than expected. Something came up.'

The estate agent takes her parents' number. She walks from room to room, picking up her dad's overflowing ashtrays and taking them into the kitchen to empty them. Her mother doesn't allow him to smoke anywhere but the kitchen, at the back door, and he is breaking this rule angrily; pointlessly, since Louisa is not there to notice. She has been gone three days and her absentminded mess has been swallowed up.

In the kitchen Isla stacks the dirty plates next to the sink, runs the tap and adds soap to the water. Dave Taylor is mowing his lawn next door, pacing up and down, leaving long, green stripes in his wake. A cockatoo lands on the arched trellis of his passionfruit vine. Mandy used to sit under there, Isla thinks. A striped chair, white and green. She pushes the image away. She's been trying not to think of Mandy these past few days. She doesn't want to imagine the last time her mother walked out, leaving her dad hurt and angry; hitting the bottle. Mandy just next door.

It's Steve Mallory she remembers. Not his physical appearance or the things he said. She remembers how it was to be in his home. Days spent in his backyard watering plants, digging for worms, always wondering if he'd pull up out the front in his truck. A current of fear beneath warm colours. She rinses a plate, sets it down on the drying rack and looks out at Dave Taylor and his mower, trimming around the eucalyptus. It's still there, this shadow of Steve at the edge of her vision, the threat she'd picked up on as a child.

She takes another plate and submerges it. She was so young, back then. She is remembering through the filter of her adult self, knowing all that she knows. The child removals are all over the news. The stolen generation, they're calling it. Aboriginal people talking about being removed from loving homes, taken to institutions where they were trained to work for white people. Stories of abuse, cruelty, inhumanity. It's no wonder she can't think of Steve without this edge of menace.

She leaves the plates in the water and returns to the phone in the hallway. She finds Scott's office number in the address book. His secretary puts her through.

'Isla?' His voice is loud in her ear. 'Are you ok?'

'I'm fine,' she says. 'I need to ask a favour.'

'Ask away.'

'Do you have a computer?'

'I do.' She hears him sit down, the creak of a chair. 'What's this about?'

'I need you to help me find somebody.'

A pause. She feels his impatience. 'Isla, the police will have searched for Mandy more thoroughly than you or I could. They'll have her dental records, medical records, birth certificate. There's no point me punching her name into AltaVista.'

She stretches the telephone cable into the lounge room, where the fog of cigarette smoke hangs low in the morning sun. Under the armchair, the neck of a bottle of vodka protrudes, instantly familiar. She moves to pick it up, to hide it. She is halfway across the room when she remembers she doesn't drink these days. She leaves it where it is.

Isla lifts the phone up from the carpet. 'It's not Mandy I want to find,' she says. 'It's Steve Mallory. Her husband.'

29

Sydney, 1967

The smell of baby reached Mandy's nose before she'd shut the door. Formula milk, and the foul, slightly sweet smell of soiled nappies. The heat had intensified the stink. She ran down the hall to the kitchen with her hand clamped over her mouth and nose. There were babies' bottles in the sink, and she leaned over them, dry heaving, as she ran the tap and let the water splash against her face. She managed to take a few mouthfuls of water and hold them down. Small dots passed before her eyes. She slid onto the lino and sat with her legs apart, her head between her knees. Colour seeped back into the room. The baby's cries rose and fell.

She went through to the hall and nudged the door open with her foot, throwing sunlight into the darkened lounge room. She saw cushions on the floor, the couch pushed back against the wall, the coffee table at an angle; a cloth nappy wrapped loosely around itself on the rug. A baby's bottle lay on its side on the couch, empty.

Mandy stepped into the room and pulled the door closed behind her, shutting out the sun. Steve was whispering to the baby, shushing it in a sugary tone she'd never heard before. 'There, now. There, now.' He'd pulled the curtains in his clumsy way, leaving a gap in the centre where the light bled through. As her eyes adjusted she made out his hunched shape, rocking from side to side. Mandy was sure he knew she was there. He'd have heard her. He'd have been expecting her for hours.

The room was hot and airless. Her head ached but the half-darkness helped, and slowly the cries became softer. Steve turned his body towards her, keeping his eyes locked on the baby, and sat down on the couch. Mandy waited for him to look up. He fussed with the towel the baby was wrapped in, got it positioned right in his lap, stared at it for a long while. She couldn't make out the baby's face, but she could hear its steady breathing, the occasional shudder on the in-breath. When Steve finally looked up at her, he was smiling. A proud smile that expected her to smile back. She reeled away from him. His eyes, sunken with lack of sleep, were backlit with surprised, overwhelming joy.

'Come and look at him, Mand.'

She stepped over the discarded cushions and crouched down beside him. He held the baby towards her and raised both eyebrows, still smiling. She leaned across and looked at the child. He was compact and solid looking, with round cheeks, a broad nose and a small, full mouth. In the dark room his skin was close to black.

Mandy slumped down onto the carpet, her back against the couch. Dots swam before her eyes, bigger than before, darker.

'Steve, what have you done?'

'Shh!' He shook his head. 'You'll wake him. Keep your voice down.'

She mouthed the words silently, 'What have you done?'

'I drove halfway to Nowra with him but I couldn't face leaving him there. I turned back.'

It was hard to break through the calming fog he'd built up around himself and the child. 'Ray's going to have a blue fit when he finds out you've taken a child home with you.'

'Will you give it a rest?' He moved the baby closer to his chest. 'It's taken me all day to get him off to sleep.' He adjusted the towel around the baby's shoulders. The sun scorched through the curtains, giving a honeyed thickness to the hot room. 'I promised his mother he'd be looked after, Mandy. I couldn't take him to the Home, not after I'd promised her.'

It was as bad as she'd feared, then. Her head thumped. 'Steve, you can't keep him. You'll be fired, apart from anything else.'

'I was going to resign, anyway.' He hugged the baby to his chest and patted his back. 'I know you don't want to get pregnant,' he said, after a pause. 'I understand you feeling that way.'

'Steve, this is not the way to fix things. This is –'

'But we could still bring a child up.' His hand closed gently around the boy's thigh. 'Bring him up as our own.'

'This is crazy talk.' She sat down next to him on the couch. 'What are you thinking? You can't bring a black baby home and stick him in a pram, expect people to think he's our child.'

176

'Keep your voice down, Mandy, for God's sake.' The baby sighed in his sleep, turned his head away and back again. 'It doesn't work like that. We don't need to pretend he's ours. We could adopt him.'

'Adopt him?'

'Why not?'

Mandy put her head in her hands. This felt like a retribution. She should have given him babies like he wanted. Out on the street she heard the tick tick tick of Andrea Walker's bicycle.

'I'm sure Ray could arrange it for us.' Steve smiled his new, peaceful smile. 'Why don't you think it over?'

'I don't need to think it over.' She stood, and the waft of the nappy met her, making her gag. 'I don't want to adopt a baby. Have you lost your mind?'

The baby stirred and Steve shunted him higher up his chest. 'I promised his mother, Mandy.'

'Take him back to his mother, then.' She flung the window wide and opened the curtain an inch or two. The child sighed softly in his sleep. 'If she made you promise her, she must love him. She must be breaking her heart, wanting him back.'

Steve shook his head. 'Ray wants him removed. You know that. I can't take him back.'

'Find another family for him, then.'

Steve closed his eyes and let his head fall back against the couch. 'You know how much I want a child, Mandy. You know it's what I want more than anything.'

She watched him with the boy, the way he held him in his arms. The gentle strength in him. Behind her, through the opened window, she heard Andrea slow up across the street and lift the bicycle onto her verandah; the dull chime of the bell as the front wheel rolled over the steps.

'He can't stay here,' she said, pulling the window shut. 'That's final.'

30

Sydney, 1967

At dawn the baby's cries grew loud enough for Mandy to admit defeat and get out of bed. She could sleep through almost anything, but this was something else. It wasn't just the noise, it was the fact of this baby being here at all. She splashed her face in the bathroom. She had a stale, grubby feeling in her skin and a pain behind her eyes which had been there for days.

From the room down the hall she heard Steve trying again and again to put the baby down. He was useless, God help him. She moved closer, watched him a while in the dark: leaning against the mattress, inching the boy down and slowly, silently standing back up. She could see his fear and confusion. The crushing loss of hope as the baby lifted his head and bawled: a long, upward curling sound.

'Steve.' She'd told him he was on his own with this. She'd

stuck to her guns until now, but in the name of sanity she was going to have to step in.

'I don't know what to do.' He picked the child up and turned to face her. The baby was wailing in his arms. 'I've been up half the night with him. He won't—'

'You need to feed him.'

'What?'

She raised her voice above the noise. 'Feed him. He needs his bottle.'

He frowned. 'D'you think?'

She turned back down the hall. He called after her but she kept going to the kitchen, felt around in the dark for the light switch. By the time he followed her in there she'd got his bottle made up.

'I should have thought of that.' The baby was screaming, leaning backwards in rage, fists clenched.

She held the bottle out for him to take it.

'Could you—?' He held him towards her. 'I need the bathroom, Mandy. Please?'

She gave him a long look. 'We agreed I wouldn't have to do this.'

'I'll be a couple of minutes, darl. Please.'

She held her arms out, weakened by the noise. 'Two minutes,' she said.

The child was beside himself, howling and thrashing, his body hot and rigid. She almost dropped him in the struggle to bring the bottle to his mouth, and when she tried again he turned his head away, angry, scared by the tension in her.

'Come on.' The teat brushed his lips and he turned his face

to it; his breathing quickened. She shifted his position and tried again. 'Come on now. That's it.'

He began to gulp as soon as the milk was flowing and his body relaxed against her.

'Good boy,' she said. The relief was huge, like a storm passing. 'That's a good lad.'

Steve smiled at her from the kitchen door. His face was pale. 'Well done,' he said.

She ignored him. The baby was drinking steadily, the milk inching down inside the bottle.

'You're a natural,' he said.

'No, I'm not. I remember this from when Isla was a baby, that's all. I know what a hungry baby sounds like.'

She heard him draw breath to reply, then a pause as he thought better of it.

'Have you spoken to Ray about quitting?'

Steve nodded. 'I called him yesterday. He didn't take it too well. Tried to persuade me to stay in the job.'

'Does he know?' She gestured at the baby with her head.

'Not yet. No.'

The boy's eyes were closing. She put the bottle down on the counter top.

'He'll find out,' she said. 'If you don't take him to the Home soon, he'll get a call from them, won't he?'

He nodded again, deflated. The child sighed in Mandy's arms. She rubbed his back and moved him up to her shoulder.

'I think we should consider adoption,' he said. 'I'm sure Ray would arrange it if I asked.'

'For God's sake, haven't I already told you no? Haven't I been crystal clear about that?'

'I won't take him to the Home. I won't do it.'

'We've been over this!' She swayed with the child, patting his backside. 'He's not ours, Steve. I can tell he wants his mum. I can feel it in him.'

He rubbed his hands up and down over his face. 'If I take him back to his mother, they'll just send some other bastard back to get him.'

She passed the baby to Steve. 'We can't keep him.'

'We could, darl. It'd be the best thing for him.'

She walked over to the back door. The sky was turning violet where the sun was coming up. It brought to mind Joe Green, standing where she was now, in his shirtsleeves, drinking coffee. It was an effort not to remember the rest of it, not to run through it again in her head. More than a week had passed and still the memory was fresh and shocking. It had been greedy and abandoned and revelatory. She didn't know what would happen if she saw him again. She might not be able to help herself.

At the same time, she knew it wasn't love. It was a physical thing entirely, a call of the flesh that would burn out soon enough. And what she had with Steve, next to that, felt closer to love. Faded and damaged and disappointing at times, but maybe that's what love came to look like after a while.

Steve stood beside her with the baby in his arms. 'I don't think I can give him up, Mandy.'

'And I don't think I can be his mother.'

'Couldn't you give it a try for a while? If it doesn't work out I'll get in touch with Ray.'

The sky was almost blue now behind the tea trees. She breathed in and out, slow and steady. She could feel the hope in him. He had too much love to give, this was the trouble. He needed more in return than she could offer.

'I'll give it a short while,' she said. 'Two weeks at the most. I mean it.'

He threw his head back in relief.

'We'll need to keep him inside, out of sight. Keep him quiet. We don't want people talking.'

He kissed the baby's head. 'We can manage that, can't we, William?'

She froze. 'What did you call him?'

'William,' he said, as if this were reasonable. 'I named him William, after my old man.'

'You named him –?'

'Why not? He needs a name.'

'Doesn't he have a name already?'

'I wanted to name him myself. I always wanted a son called William.'

'He's not your son!'

'I know that.' He kissed him again. 'Might be the closest I get, but.'

She shook her head at him but he was looking at the baby, smiling in that absorbed way. 'You need to slow down.'

The cicadas reached them through the window. She had the sense again, just briefly, of a rope unravelling. The rapid slip into a place beyond reason. She looked away.

'Why don't you go back to bed, Mand? I can manage now.'

She left him there, rocking the baby, looking out at the yard as the sun lit the sky.

31

New South Wales, 1997

'This was all prime real estate, twenty-odd years ago.' Scott changes gear and overtakes a truck, gliding past it noiselessly and pulling back in again. 'Back in the seventies, it cost more to live out this way than it would have to live in Darlinghurst.'

Isla looks out the window of Scott's low-slung Honda. A disused railway line runs alongside the road. The tracks are overgrown with grass and strewn with empty bottles. An Aboriginal man sits on the platform of what must once have been a train station, holding a bottle in a brown paper bag.

'Thanks for the ride,' she says.

Scott taps his fingers against the steering wheel to the beat of the song on the radio. 'Couldn't have you driving all the way out here on your own.'

'You mean you don't want me driving your car.'

'There is that.' He reaches for the dial on the radio and turns it off. 'And I wanted to see you again, before you go back to the dark side.'

'Sorry I've been bad at keeping in touch. It's hard, with the time difference, and—'

'Are you still drinking?'

She turns to him, surprised. 'I've been on the wagon a couple of months.'

He nods. 'How's that going?'

'Great.' She squirms in the soft leather of his car seat. 'Why d'you ask?'

'You were pretty wild before you left.'

'I was twenty-five.'

'You were off the scale, Isla. I was there, some of the time. Nobody could keep up with you.'

'I know.'

'I thought you might crash and burn in London.'

She puts her hands through the coarse mess of her hair. 'I did, in the end.'

He overtakes again, checking the mirror and holding his speed within the limit. Her sensible, careful brother, who studied hard and married young, who can remember his twenties. Who can remember her twenties, more to the point.

'You're right,' she says. 'It became a problem. The drink.'

'It's good to hear you say that.'

'I've got it under control. As much as you can, you know.'

'What does that mean?'

'It means I'm an alcoholic.'

He looks across at her and she looks away. She has never

said those words out loud before. The day is too bright, the sky too clear. The car is too smooth and silent. She sinks down into the seat and wipes her palms on her jeans.

'Are you going to meetings?'

'I don't want to talk about it.'

'It's meant to help. People say—'

'Would you give it up? I know what people say.'

'All right. I was trying to help.'

Her heart will not slow down. 'I was about to start going to meetings in London,' she says, just to test if her voice is working. 'It wasn't the best time for me to come out here.'

'You're doing pretty good, considering,' he says. 'Still got your temper.'

She laughs, because she knows he expects her to laugh.

'Personally, I hardly touch the stuff,' Scott says.

'Well, aren't you fucking perfect?' She looks pointedly out the window, at the long grass and the stripped down cars at the side of the road.

'Not really,' he says. 'And I'll leave you out there with the roadkill if you're going to be like that.'

'Sorry.' She looks back at him. 'I haven't told anyone else, that's all.'

'I care about you, Isla. You know?'

'Yeah, I know that. I do.' She shuts her eyes against the sun. 'I think I started drinking so I could be closer to Dad. I didn't want to disapprove of him. It made it easier to be on his side.'

'That makes sense,' Scott says.

'Does it?'

'Sure.' He glares at a white ute that flies past them in the fast lane. 'You were the only one who could calm him down. Can't have been easy on you.' He glances at her. 'D'you remember?'

'Some of it. The hardest thing about sobriety is remembering things I'd rather forget.'

'Do you remember when he broke all the fingers in Mum's hand?'

'No.' She thinks about it. 'No, that was an accident. He slammed her hand in the door of the car.'

He makes a growl of disagreement in his throat. 'He might have told you that.'

'It was an accident. I remember he drove her to the hospital.' She hears how this sounds. Her voice has a childish whine.

'There were no accidents in our house,' he says.

Isla sinks further into her seat. 'You always think the worst of him.'

'Jesus, Isla.' He slows his speed at the Ropes Crossing turnoff. 'I was the one who drove her to hospital when Dad was too far gone. One time he dislocated her shoulder. Another time he broke her ribs.'

She turns back to the window, stares out at the western suburbs. Street after street of fibro houses with steel fences. 'I didn't know that.'

'I could go on,' he says. 'But I don't want to knock you off the wagon.'

The sun is in their eyes as they head west. The road narrows. Isla wonders if her brother is as right as he thinks he is. If she has always been wrong. Her heart pounds.

'How did you turn out so normal, anyway?'

He smiles and taps the steering wheel. 'Therapy,' he says. 'Years of therapy. I recommend it.'

She waits, sensing there's more.

'I work hard. Too hard, Ruby would say. I'm not good with too much time on my hands.'

'Me neither,' she says.

'Ruby knows I don't want kids.' He turns to her with a sad half smile. 'I'm not going to risk it. In case I have the bullying arsehole gene.'

'That's a shame.' She sits up straight. Don't cry. 'I think you'd be a good dad.'

The sky has turned a deep blue. The buildings are low and makeshift; corrugated iron roofs and chickenwire fences.

'Have you thought about what you're going to say to this Steve bloke?' Scott says, after a while. 'How are you going to play it if he's not happy to see you?'

'I'm not going to lose my rag if that's what you mean.'

'That's a good start.'

'I know you think this is a bad idea.'

He keeps his eyes on the road. 'If I were him, I'd stick to my story, that's all. If I'd told the police I'd moved away and left my wife behind, I'd tell you the same exact thing.'

'I want to look him in the eye,' she says. 'I want to see his face when he says he moved away without her.'

The road turns and Scott drops his speed. They pull up outside a smart, new community centre with steps leading up to glass double doors. The doors part and an elderly man leaves the building, stepping aside for a younger woman with a baby on her hip.

'I'll come in with you,' Scott says.

'You sure this is where he works?'

Scott turns off the ignition. 'He's listed as a manager here. And he's on a few local committees operating out of this address. Neighbourhood development projects, that sort of thing.'

'Pillar of the community,' Isla says. They sit for a moment in the sealed capsule of his car. 'Maybe we should have made an appointment.'

She swings the car door open. Scott checks the car is locked before he follows her into the building. The doors open straight onto a small waiting area, where a ceiling fan rotates slowly and several people wait on plastic chairs.

An Aboriginal woman stands behind the front desk. She has close-cropped, bleach-blonde hair and a heavy-set jaw. 'Can I help you?' she says, looking doubtful.

'I'm here to see Steve Mallory,' Isla says.

'Do you have an appointment?'

'Yes,' she says, before Scott can reply. She smiles. 'He's expecting me.'

'We don't speak to journos.'

'I'm not a journalist. My name's Isla Green.'

'I don't have you in the book.' She taps the diary which lies open on the desk. 'I don't think we can help you, Miss Green.'

'There must be a mistake, then.' Isla steps away from Scott, who has gripped her by the elbow.

'I don't think so. Mr Mallory runs the Connect service on

Fridays. He's helping people find their families. People whose kids were taken. Or who were taken themselves, brought up by white folk. Stolen kids.'

Isla nods and smiles, lost for words. She thinks of her dad in the kitchen, listening to the radio: *that bastard next door was up to his neck in it.* Beside her, Scott fidgets uncomfortably.

'I can fix you a time in a couple of weeks,' the receptionist says. 'If it's the Connect service you need.'

'That's not why I'm here,' Isla says.

'No.' The woman glances at the window, where Scott's gunmetal grey Honda is visible out on the street. 'I didn't think so.'

'Could you pass my details on? I'm a family friend.' Isla takes a leaflet from a stack on the desk and writes down her name in the top corner. She adds her parents' address on Bay Street and underlines it. 'I've come from London to see him,' she says. 'I have to go back next week.'

The woman snatches at the leaflet and leaves through the double doors at the back of the room, letting them slam behind her. A fly circles the room, passing close to Isla's face. She swats it and it falls silent. In the waiting area behind them, a baby screams.

'I think we're the only white people in this place,' Scott says, in her ear.

'So what?'

'It's a service for Aboriginal people. We just charged in like we own the joint.'

She leans against the reception desk. 'I thought I'd catch him off guard,' she says, weakly.

191

'All he has to do is say no.'

'I think he'll come out,' she says. 'You wait.' She watches the double doors with a childish fear in her chest. The fly sets off again, louder than before, its circuit tightened.

'He's with someone,' the receptionist says, cheerfully efficient. She slaps her palms down on the desk. 'Sorry. Who's next?'

Scott steers Isla back through the glass doors and onto the street. He points his keyring at the Honda, unlocking it with a small, electronic bleep. 'That was a waste of time,' he says.

Isla slumps into the passenger seat. 'I know. Sorry.' She looks up at the building. The glass doors open and a man in a blue checked shirt stands behind them, his face hidden.

'He's doing some good work, this Steve Mallory.' Scott fastens his seat belt and turns the ignition. 'Doesn't sound to me like the bogeyman you had in mind.'

'Guilty conscience,' she says. 'He was the one who removed half those kids in the first place.'

'What makes you think that?'

'Dad told me.'

'Right.' Scott nods.

'What's that meant to mean?'

'I didn't say anything.'

'Just because Dad said it you think it's not true.'

'I didn't say that.'

She turns from him as he swings the car around. The man in the blue shirt walks out onto the footpath and watches them. He is short in the legs, broad in the chest, and Isla knows him as if thirty years had not passed, as if she were four years old and he had just walked through the door of the house on Bay Street.

'Stop.' She sits forward in her seat. 'That's him. That's Steve.'

Scott brakes. Steve crosses the street, holding up the leaflet that Isla wrote her name on. He leans forward to tap on the passenger window and they hear his voice through the glass. 'You wanted to see me?'

Isla lowers the window. He has ruddy skin and watering eyes and he looks genuinely moved at the sight of her.

'Isla Green,' he says. 'I came out as soon as I clocked your name.'

Isla climbs from the car and meets him on the footpath. She towers over him. He stands with his feet apart, shoulders back, and runs his hand over the bald pate of his head.

'Thanks for coming outside,' she says. 'I know you're busy.'

He's not as familiar now she's in front of him. His physical presence – gentler than she remembered – is in the way. She has a pang of doubt.

'Christ almighty,' he says. 'Isla Green. I remember you as a tiny thing. Always running around the yard looking for bugs and spiders.'

'The police have been to see my dad.' She blurts it, and his expression changes.

'I imagine they have.'

'They seem to think he was the last person to see Mandy before she went missing.'

He curls the leaflet with her name on it and taps it against the palm of his hand. 'That sounds about right.'

'My dad says Mandy left with you. He says she went with you to Victoria.'

'He's a liar. Sorry to have to tell you that.'

He moves the palm of his hand over his face, pulling at the skin beneath his eyes. He's almost crying, Isla thinks. He's only just containing a bank of emotion. This is what scared her as a kid: it comes to her as she stands before him. His surface layer is paper thin and behind it he is utterly broken.

'Mandy was soft on you,' he says. 'Do you know that? Do you remember?'

'Not really.'

'She would have made a good mother. We could have raised a family.'

Behind him, a woman leaves the building and turns onto the footpath. The baby on her hip wakes, lifts its head and cries out, a long wail of protest. Steve spins around in alarm. The woman takes a minute to settle the child, patting its back.

'My dad's going to take the blame,' Isla says. 'If they can't find Mandy.'

Steve turns back to face her. 'Your father took her from me,' he says.

'What do you mean?'

'I left her behind in Sydney with Joe Green.'

'He denies that.'

'There were witnesses, love. It was broad daylight when I left. People saw what happened.' Tears stand in his eyes. 'It's the biggest mistake of my life.'

She hears Scott climbing from the car, slamming the door. He stands beside her, his arm on her shoulder.

'I never remarried,' Steve says. 'I miss her every day.'

'Do you think she's alive?'

'No,' he says, fighting the tears. 'I know they're treating her as missing. But she wasn't the sort of woman to disappear without a trace. She was the sort of person you noticed.'

Scott taps Isla's shoulder. 'We should get going,' he says.

'We'd be a family now,' Steve continues. 'That's the hardest thing. It was what Mandy wanted more than anything. She was a natural with kids. We'd have had a brood of our own, if we'd had the chance. I never thought I'd be on my own at this time of life.' He wipes his face. 'Do you have a family, Isla?'

'No,' she says. 'Not yet.'

'There's still time for you.'

'I'm sorry.' She doesn't know why she says it.

'What good is that?' he shouts at her. 'Do you think that's any bloody use?'

'No. I just—'

'It's your father who should be sorry. Why isn't he the one standing here? Where the hell is he?'

'We should go,' Scott says. 'We've taken up enough of your time.'

Steve holds his arm up to block the sun. 'You are the image of your mother,' he says to Scott.

'We've got a long drive.' Scott steps closer to the car. 'Thanks again for—'

'How is Louisa?'

'Not so good,' Scott says. 'It's been difficult for her, with our dad being under suspicion. The police asking questions.'

'Sorry to hear that.' He looks bereft. 'She was always a cut above, was Louisa.'

'You're right there,' Scott says.

Steve considers Scott, lowers his arm. 'Send her my regards, would you?' he says, stepping backwards into the street. 'I hope she finds a way through this.'

He stands at the glass doors and watches them get into the car. Isla feels his eyes on her until they turn the corner. She waits in anxious silence for Scott to speak.

'I don't think he was lying, Isla.'

She looks out at the long grass and the telegraph poles.

'He left Mandy behind in Sydney, with Dad.' Scott changes gear and pulls into the fast lane. 'You heard the man.'

The telegraph poles fly by. 'He's volatile,' she says. 'He was always like that. I was scared of him as a kid.'

'You said they moved away before I was born.'

'They did.' She glares at him. 'I remember them. Mandy and Steve. I spent a lot of time with her.'

'You can't possibly –'

'I do!' She looks away from his sensible, doubtful face. 'I remember being scared,' she says.

'I remember that too.' He says it softly. 'I remember being scared all the time.'

She doesn't reply. Her certainty is slipping and she can think of no comfort besides alcohol. The landscape has no distractions.

196

Mile after mile of dry scrub. Stark, white ghost gums lit up against the blue sky.

'Will you come and stay with us? There's plenty of space.' He accelerates. 'I can come back to Bay Street with you now to collect your things.'

She shakes her head. 'No, thanks.'

'For God's sake, Isla. I'm scared for you, alone in the house with him.'

'Don't be. He'd never hurt me.'

He checks the mirror and pulls back into the middle lane. 'We all have a blind spot,' he says. 'And he's yours.'

32

Sydney, 1967

Mandy found Joe on the doorstep, smiling nervously.

'I noticed Steve's truck was gone,' he said.

His words took several seconds to make sense. She was shot through with desire at the sight of him. 'He's out.' She checked her watch, with its stopped hands. 'Not sure when he'll be back. Sorry.'

'Any chance of a cold beer? It's hot as hell out here.'

'You'd best come in, then.' She allowed herself to smile as she turned her back. She'd had him in her head all day. 'How have you been?'

'Not so good. Haven't made it into work for a day or two.'

'What you been doing with yourself?'

He shrugged. 'Trying not to hit the whisky before lunch. Going round the bend. That's about it.'

In the kitchen she took the top off a bottle of beer and handed it to him. 'How far round the bend did you get?'

'All the way round.' He drank from the bottle. 'I keep thinking I can hear a baby crying.'

Her stomach lurched. The baby often slept for a couple of hours at this time of day, but still, she ought not to have let him in. 'Must be Abigail Walker's little one you can hear.' She sat down at the table. She was pretty sure Abigail hadn't brought the new baby home yet, but Joe didn't question it. He pulled a chair out and sat with his legs crossed, his foot resting on his knee.

'Abigail had a boy,' she said, which was true: Roger Walker had told her the news just yesterday. She'd kept him out on the street, kept the conversation short, but he'd looked curious, like he suspected something. It was harder than she'd thought to keep a baby hidden.

Joe threw his head back and drained half the bottle. She really should send him on his way. It was good to see him, but. He was thinking what she was thinking and it was hard to care about much else.

'You look great,' he said. 'What's happening with you?'

'Nothing much.' She lit a cigarette and passed it to him. 'Too hot to get anything done.'

Joe's eyes followed the length of her legs to the hem of her denim skirt, which stopped a few inches short of her knees. She let him take his time. The cigarette burned down in his fingers.

'That's true,' he said.

She stood and opened a window, turned back to face him and leaned against the counter top. She unbuttoned her blouse.

He went to stand but she held him in his seat by the shoulders and let him kiss her stomach, open-mouthed, while she sipped from his beer bottle and watched a cockatoo land on the prop that held up the washing line.

'Been much too hot for weeks now,' she said, as he lifted her skirt. She closed her eyes and gripped his collar.

A kookaburra cackled throatily from the back of the yard and then fell silent.

'Get the fuck out of my house.'

Steve stood in the kitchen doorway with a shopping bag in each hand. His skin was slick with sweat, the hair on his arms darkened with moisture. He was gripping the bags as if they weighed five tons each.

'Jesus.' Joe stood up. 'Jesus, Steve, I didn't hear you come in. I didn't know you were there. I didn't think—'

Steve dropped the shopping. A child's dummy fell from one of the bags and rolled across the lino. Mandy hurriedly buttoned her blouse, pulled her skirt down. She was angry before she was shocked or ashamed. She resented Steve for intruding on this moment. She met his gaze and let him see the remains of her desire, her defiance.

'Don't just stand there,' she said to Joe. He gaped back at her. 'For God's sake, go home!'

Steve strode towards Joe, who had backed his way almost to the door, and thrust the palm of his hand into Joe's chest. 'On second thoughts, mate, how about you stay right where you are, and I send you straight through the wall. How about that? How's that sound?'

'Steve, look, I'm sorry.' Joe stepped closer to the door. 'I've been in a bad way lately. It's no excuse, I know that.'

'You've been in a bad way?' Steve threw Joe against the door, which slammed shut behind him. 'Pardon me if my heart isn't breaking, mate. Pardon me if I'm not surprised you can't hold onto your own wife.'

Mandy stepped around the kitchen table, reaching for Steve. She felt dirty, now the pleasure had left her. She was horrified at what he'd seen.

'Steve. Why don't we—?'

'Shut up, Mandy!' Steve held his hand up to silence her. 'Keep your whoring mouth shut and don't come near me until I tell you to.'

Mandy stood still. She hadn't known Steve was capable of speaking to her that way. She didn't recognise him. She'd altered him, she'd sent everything bad.

'Did you think you'd cheer yourself up by creeping round here?' He slammed his palms into Joe's chest again. The glass shook in the door behind him. 'Is that what you thought? Get her feeling sorry for you and see how long it takes before she lets you lift her skirt? How long did it take? An hour? Ten minutes? Five?'

'Like I said, it's no excuse.' Joe leaned away from Steve, holding his bandaged hand up. 'I can't defend it.'

'How about I fix your face so she doesn't like the look of you so much.' He grabbed Joe by his shirt and flung him backwards with greater force than before. 'How about that?'

'Do what you like to my face.' Joe looked down at Steve,

who was panting and fuming, his face barely level with Joe's shoulder. 'I deserve it. Go ahead.'

'Don't!' Mandy gripped Steve by the arm. 'It wasn't him who started it. I did. It was me who led him on.'

Steve looked at her with disdain. 'Are you sticking up for him now? Are you trying to save his bacon?'

'It's true. You know things haven't been right between us. Let's sort this out without him. Let him go.'

Steve turned to her, gripping Joe's shirt in his fist. 'Don't talk to me about sorting things out. Don't even think about that.'

A thin, discordant wail reached them from the hall. Joe tensed, looked around the room, tried to pinpoint the noise.

'Bloody hell.' Steve clenched his teeth. 'That's all we need.'

'I'll get him.' Mandy ran from the room. She heard a scuffle as she rushed down the hall to where the baby slept. A cry of pain sounded behind her. She picked the boy up from his bed and stood a moment, panicked at the shouts and blows from the kitchen. What had she done? Why had she let that happen? She shushed the baby, gave him his dummy, and to her surprise he quietened in her arms. The warmth of him calmed her.

'I messed up.' She stood with him in the dark and tried to think what to do. 'I really messed up this time.'

The baby was calm and still against her chest and she walked up and down with him, passing his hair through her fingers. From the kitchen she heard another shout, a thud, a chair falling to the floor. Then quiet. She opened the bedroom door and listened, took a few steps closer to the kitchen. The only noise was a small gasping sound.

She opened the kitchen door. Steve looked up at her from the floor. He sat astride Joe's chest with his hand at Joe's throat. Joe was choking, his eyes bulging, legs flailing.

Mandy screamed, 'Steve! You're going to kill him! Let him go! For God's sake, Steve!'

Steve looked down at Joe and considered him for a beat before he eased his grip on his throat. 'Get out of here.' Steve stood and Joe rolled away from him, retching. 'Get out of my sight!'

Mandy locked eyes with her husband. His lip was cut and his nose was dripping blood. 'You'd have killed him,' she said.

'Get William out of here, would you?' He wiped his nose on his sleeve. 'What did you bring him in here for?'

She clutched the baby to her, half aware that he was howling in her arms. At the back door, Joe pulled himself to his feet. He glanced across at her, taking in the baby, and she tried to show in her face that she was sorry.

'Why are you still here?' Steve shouted at Joe. 'Get out of my house! And keep away from my wife!'

Joe stayed where he was. He looked from Mandy to the baby and back. Steve ran at him, sending him into the yard, and he walked backwards towards his own house, coughing and spitting. Steve kicked the door shut behind him. A long, diagonal crack appeared in the glass, fracturing the pane.

Mandy sat down at the kitchen table with the baby in her lap, soothing him as best she could, glad of the distraction, the noise. Steve stood at the door a while with his back to her. She had no idea what he would do or say now. She'd believed, until today, that Steve would never physically hurt anyone, not deliberately.

She spoke before he could say anything. 'I've been unhappy for a while. It's not your fault.'

He crossed the room and leaned over her, his hand flat on the kitchen table. Blood oozed from his bottom lip. 'A while?' he said. 'What do you mean, a while?'

'Since we started trying for a baby. I never really wanted it.'

William sucked rhythmically on his dummy. Mandy let him take her finger in his hot, damp hand and shifted his position in her lap. She could feel the fright in his body.

'I'm sorry,' she said.

Steve wiped the blood from his mouth. 'How long's it been going on? You and lover boy next door?'

'Not long.'

'How long?'

'Since Louisa left,' she said. 'A few weeks.'

He straightened up, knocking a chair sideways, startling the baby.

'I should've known.' He kicked the chair across the kitchen, where it collided noisily with the stove. 'I should've known you were seeing another bloke.' He walked across the room and back again. 'Do you love him?'

William started to whine. She held the dummy in place with her finger. 'No,' she said. 'It's not like that.'

'What's it like, then?' He bent over her. 'Come on. What's it like?'

She shifted her chair away from him. She couldn't lie, now

she needed to. She was too exposed before him, after what he'd seen. But there was no way to tell him the truth about it either. She'd never seen anger like this before in her life.

'It's nothing serious,' she said.

'Nothing serious! What's that meant to mean?'

The baby began to cry and his dummy dropped to the floor. She held him closer, rubbing his back. 'Don't make me say it,' she said.

'It's just sex, is it? Is that what you mean? Just sex in our kitchen when I'm not home?'

Keeping her eyes on the boy, she nodded, once.

He went to the window and looked out at Joe's house, breathing hard. 'God help me if I see his bastard face. I don't know what I'll do.'

A cupboard door beneath the sink stood ajar and he kicked it shut, so hard it sprang open again. He stood back, kicked it again, harder, and then again, until it swung loose from its hinges. In her arms the baby wailed.

'I know you don't want me in bed.' He took a beer from the fridge and lifted the lid off with his teeth. 'You don't want me that way, not any more.'

'I felt under pressure to get pregnant,' she said. 'It changed things between us.'

Steve drained the bottle and slammed it down on the counter. 'Is that why you fucked the bloke next door?'

She looked into his face and saw pain behind the anger. She felt it as if she'd been hurt herself, the awful agony of it. It would be more than he could bear.

'Is it?' He was close to tears. 'Is that why you fucked him?'

'Don't, Steve.'

'Don't what?'

'I've never heard you use that kind of language.'

'No?' He put his hands flat on the kitchen table. 'I guess it's a day of firsts, isn't it?'

'I'm sorry.'

'No, you're not. I know you're not sorry because I saw you.' He pointed to a spot on the lino. 'You stood right there with your eyes shut and you grabbed that bastard by the neck. And when you saw me, you took your time letting go of him. D'you know that?'

She looked away, flooded with shame, and he held her by the chin, turned her face towards him.

'You're just sorry I interrupted you,' he said.

'That's not true.'

'I think it is.' He stepped away from her. 'I think you want rid of me and you don't have the decency to say it.'

She stood, settled the baby on her hip and tried to find the right words. He looked at her like a drowning man. She didn't know if she could hold onto him now, or if she should.

'I did feel that way for a while,' she said. 'I started to think I'd stopped loving you.'

He dug at his eyes. 'I knew that. I felt it.'

'I started to think maybe I couldn't love anyone.' She took a step closer to him. He didn't move away. 'I've always had this fear, that I'm like my mother.'

He shook his head at her. 'Meaning what?'

'Meaning I'm selfish and cold.' She felt tears coming. 'What if we had a baby and I didn't love it enough? What if I felt nothing at all?'

'I must have told you a hundred times you'd make a good mum—'

'That's because you've got me on a pedestal. You worship me and I don't deserve it.'

He considered her, scratching the dry blood on his lip. 'I can't argue with that.'

'You always loved me too much.' She rocked the baby, who was quiet now. 'I do love you. You might not believe it but I do, in my way.'

He stared down at the bags of shopping, spilled over the lino where he'd dropped them earlier. 'I ought to walk straight out of here, Mandy. Give me one good reason why I shouldn't get the hell out of here.'

'I don't have one,' she said. 'But I'd like you to stay.'

'Would you?'

She nodded, and he sobbed with undisguised relief. She reached out to him and he shook his head, turned away from her. He was dry-eyed when he looked at her again.

'I want you to respect me.' He picked the chair up from the floor and slammed it down. 'Can you manage that? Is that asking too much?'

She shook her head. The baby stirred and she lifted him up. He was drowsy, half asleep. She kissed his eyes, his cheeks.

'I'll help you raise him,' she said. 'If you still want that.'

Steve looked at her guardedly. 'Do you mean that?'

She nodded. 'We could adopt him, like you said. Stop hiding him away.'

'I thought you didn't want the baby. You said it was a crazy idea. He's not ours, you said.'

'I want to give you what you want.' She stepped closer to him. He took the boy from her and rocked him until he settled in against his chest. 'I know how much you want a family.'

'He has a mother,' Steve said. 'A family of his own who love him.'

'He'll have a better life this way, won't he? Isn't that what you promised his mother?'

'I promised that to a lot of people over the years.'

'This time it'll be true,' she said. 'We don't know where he'd end up if we let him go, do we? He might get taken to one of the Homes.'

Steve fell quiet and Mandy stood beside him, watching the baby sleep. She had a whisker of a chance, she figured, to hold onto her marriage. She'd said things in the past few minutes that she'd never have said, if not for the shock and regret, the honesty that came with pain. It might have been the scare she needed.

'I'll give it my best shot, Steve. If you think you can forgive me.'

He kept his eyes on the baby. 'You mean the world to me, Amanda. I don't suppose I can stop feeling that way.'

'Let me make it up to you, then. Let me try.'

He gave a small nod. She took William back from him. His little face was hot against hers.

'I'll murder that bastard if he comes near you again. I'll kick him all the way back to England. He'll wish he never came to this country. I'm bloody serious.'

She swayed with the baby in her arms. The yard was falling into darkness. The tea trees were misaligned through the broken pane in the back door.

'He'll stay away now. He doesn't want me really. He wants his wife and child back.'

'And what about you? Will you stay away from him?'

She nodded, and reached out to him again, took his hand in hers. This time he didn't move away.

33

Sydney, 1967

Joe sat down on the deck and caught a burst of birdsong from the trees at the end of the yard. A myna bird, he thought, catching sight of one, its black head and brown body. He wasn't sure how he knew the name. Louisa liked birds, she was always pointing them out. Maybe that was it. Or Isla might have told him; she was clever that way, remembered everything. He loosened his tie. Every thought in his head took him back to his wife and child. Not to mention that baby crying next door. A man could lose his mind.

He ground out his cigarette in the saucer he was using as an ashtray. Mandy had used him, he could see that now. She'd wanted out of her marriage. Grounds for divorce. She'd probably timed the whole thing so Steve would come home and find them like that. Just as he'd started to get sweet on her. Next thing he knew, he was getting thumped and she was standing there holding a baby, someone else's black baby, telling him to go home. He'd thought he was going to die. He undid his collar and rubbed at his neck. Shame his right arm was out of action. He could have hit the bastard harder.

They'd been jumpy about the baby. It was one of those kids that Steve had to remove for work. It had to be. Steve must have liked the look of it and decided to keep it for himself. It probably wasn't official. It was outrageous when you thought about it. He knew he'd get away with it because he was a copper and he knew the right people. And the kid's family had the whole system stacked against them.

Joe stood, shut the back door behind him and reached for the whisky. Poured it quickly, a big one, hand shaking a bit but this wasn't too early in the day. Almost five-thirty. He'd put a full day's work in – his first in over a week – and he'd earned a drink a dozen times over. The others would be in the bar by now, downing the schooners before they went home to the wife and kids. The second glass was smaller and he didn't rush it. Even found some ice. Steady hand. No need to get drunk.

The lounge room was a tip. Dirty plates on the coffee table and a stain on the carpet where he'd knocked a bottle over. The ashtrays were all full. He disgusted himself. The whisky was no solution but it was all he had to lean on, now that Mandy had let him down. The evenings were long and it was too quiet; even with the TV on he couldn't forget he was on his own. The house had an echo to it. Every footstep was amplified.

He sat down on the couch, leaned back and looked at the blank TV screen. Stan had taken some of his workload off him. He'd been good about it and his kindness had made it worse somehow, more humiliating. It was a challenging job, Stan had said. It was looking like the architects had changed their minds again and the proscenium arch in the major hall would have to be dismantled. It would be an Opera House whose major hall was a concert hall, not suitable for opera. The men were complaining, walking off site saying they'd had enough, and a few months back he might have joined them. He'd been an idiot to think he could rise up the ranks on something like this.

He slopped whisky over his shirt when the phone rang. Six o'clock. It wasn't Stan, this time. He put his glass down and looked at the phone, his mouth sour with fear and hope.

'Hello?'

'It's me, Joe. It's Louisa.'

The shock of her voice went through him like cold water. Jesus Christ, he might cry.

'Can we talk? I've been calling for days but there was no answer.'

He gripped the receiver. 'I want to talk to Isla.'

'She's asleep.'

'Wake her up.'

'She's been unwell. I don't want to wake her.'

'Unwell?'

'She'll be fine. She's been checked over by the doctor. It's flu, that's all. She's over the worst of it.'

His words were trapped in his throat. 'I want her back,' he managed to say. 'She should be here. This is her home.'

'Can we talk, Joe? Please.'

The line hissed between them and Joe stood on the rug, arms outstretched, phone cable pulled taut. 'You didn't even tell me where you'd gone. Can you imagine how scared I was?'

She was quiet. The silence clogged his ears.

'Did you hear me?'

'She saw us, Joe.'

He dropped his arms to his sides. 'What?'

'Isla saw us. That night.'

'What did she see?' He had a feeling he knew. His stomach turned over. 'Lou? What did she see? What night?'

'The night I went to Mandy's. We argued and it got physical.' Her voice was small, hesitant. 'I don't know if you remember.'

'No. I blacked out.'

'That's what I thought.'

'How bad was it?'

'Pretty bad.' She was crying. 'What kind of parents are we, Joe?'

'You should have told me.' He reached for his glass. 'Is she all right? Did she say anything?'

'She hasn't mentioned it. She's been distant with me. I think it scared her.'

'Of course it scared her.' He drained his glass and let the warmth fill his head.

'We're not right together, are we?'

He sat down on the rug and fought the tears, swallowed them back down. 'Don't say that, Lou.'

'You said it yourself.'

'I was angry with you.' He rocked forward, holding the empty

213

glass between his feet. 'I'm sorry I said that. I'm sorry about what happened that night. I hate the idea that Isla saw it.'

She was quiet a long time. He thought of Isla on the beach, treading water in the ocean beside him.

'Will you come back?'

There was a flare on the line and he wondered if she'd heard him.

'I can't come by boat,' she said, when the line cleared. 'The baby's due in April. I don't want to give birth on a ship, Joe.'

He sucked air through his teeth. 'Jesus, Louisa. There'll be no money left if you fly back.'

'Don't be angry with me.'

'Did you have to take all the savings?'

'I thought I'd need money to live on,' she said. 'While I was looking for work.'

He rolled the glass between his feet. 'You had it all planned out, then. Didn't you?'

She was crying again. 'I don't want to come back. Not if you're angry with me.'

'I'm not angry.' He hung his head between his knees and tried to say it like he meant it. 'I'm not angry, Lou. I know things have been bad between us.'

'Will you stop drinking?'

Jesus Christ, she wanted him to roll over and beg. He stretched the fingers of his broken hand, curled them as far as he could and stretched them again. 'I'll cut down,' he said. 'I'll give it a go.'

'We both miss you,' Louisa said. 'England doesn't feel like home. It's freezing cold and Isla hates it.'

'I'm pleased to hear that.'

'We need to stop fighting.'

'I know.'

'I'm scared that we can't.'

He put his head on his knee and tried not to think of the way she'd planned it all, the note she'd left him while he was at work. Coming home to find them gone.

'We can,' he said. 'There's a baby on the way, Lou. We're a family.'

She was still crying. He held the receiver to his ear, sorry and guilty and at the same time, empty. Sometimes, he thought, love and guilt felt the same.

34

Sydney, 1997

The wooden chair is wet under Isla's jeans as she sits down with her coffee. The sky is grey, the deck damp with recent rain. She slept badly. Every night since the trip to Ropes Crossing she's woken in the early hours, full of fear. She tells herself, as she lies awake, that she's scared *for* her dad, not *of* him. She fights the creep of doubt. When she can't rest she walks through the house, looking for him, this man who might have killed. When she finds him passed out on the couch she thinks, it's not possible. Surely not.

She can hear the breakfast news from the radio in the kitchen: Tasmania has decriminalised homosexuality. There is talk of a referendum on whether Australia will become a republic. She blows on her coffee. In the kitchen, the radio snaps off. The flick of a lighter. A glass bottle meets a hard surface.

'I thought I heard you out here,' her dad says, stepping out onto the deck.

He pulls up a chair and puts his mug down on the table. It's not yet seven-thirty but his eyes are foggy, unfocused. Drunk.

'My boss wants me back at work,' she says. She keeps her eyes on the Hills Hoist where her costume is hanging after yesterday's swim. 'He left a message on the machine, asking when I'll be back.'

Joe reaches for the ashtray and rests his cigarette on the edge. He sits back in his chair. 'It's been good to have you here. Shame your mother didn't stick around.' There's a slur in his voice. 'Just you and me, in the end.'

She can't look at him. The gulls are flying inland from the beach. 'I need to ask you something, Dad.'

'Fire away,' he says, too loudly. 'What's on your mind?'

'Are you sure Mandy left with Steve? They moved away together?'

He finishes his cigarette before he replies. 'Where's this coming from? Haven't we talked this over already?'

'I don't think so. Not really.'

'I thought we had. I thought I'd told you they moved away. Wasn't I clear about that?'

Isla makes herself face him. He stares back at her, drunkenly belligerent.

'You don't believe me,' he says.

'I think you might be sticking to your story.'

'Lying, you mean? Is that what you think?'

'Maybe.' A cool wind blows in from the south, spinning the Hills Hoist, lifting her costume into the air. 'Maybe you told me the same thing you told Mum when we got back from England. Mandy and Steve moved away.'

'They did.'

'Please don't lie to me, Dad.'

He drains the contents of his mug, opening his throat, tipping his head back. It's not coffee. Isla knows the burn in his chest as he swallows, the warmth in his head.

'I'm not lying,' he says.

'Steve Mallory says you are.'

He becomes very still. 'What?'

'He says he left without Mandy. He left her behind with you. He's told the police you're lying.'

'And you believe him?'

Her throat aches. 'I want to believe you.'

'But you don't.'

'I think you might be keeping something from me.'

He pats his pockets for his cigarettes, lights one with a shaking hand, smiles at her unconvincingly.

Surely not, she thinks. Surely not.

'I'll tell you something, Isla. Something I didn't tell you before.'

'Go on.'

'Steve Mallory took a baby. An Aboriginal kid. A baby boy.'

She looks away. 'You already told me about that. I know he removed kids.'

'But he kept this one.'

'What are you talking about?'

'Little black fella. Screamed all night,' he says, leaning danger-ously out of his chair to gesture towards the yard next door.

218

'Screamed all night and half the day too.' He rocks back towards her on his chair.

'I don't see what this has got to do with Mandy.'

'You don't want to hear it. Nobody ever does.'

'I want you to tell me about Mandy.'

He stabs at the table with his forefinger. 'This is about him. Steve Mallory, the bloke whose story you're swallowing. He kept a baby for himself. He wanted a child of his own so he kept one.'

She takes a mouthful of coffee and lets him talk, half listening.

'He gets to have a family,' Joe says. 'Never mind about the family he broke up.' He lifts his mug and finds it empty.

'Steve doesn't have a family. He's on his own.'

'Who told you that?'

She wants to tell him: I went to see Steve and he badmouthed you. He tried to turn me against you. There's a time she would have said that. She would have known whose side she was on.

'I've been asking around,' she says. 'Trying to get to the truth.'

'Have you?' He is quiet for a moment. She can hear the rasp in his chest. 'You think I'm making things up?'

'I think it suits you to think Steve was a monster.'

He leans forward across the table. 'And what do you think?'

The wind picks up, blowing rain against the house.

'I think he left Mandy behind in Sydney, with you.'

He rises, knocking the table, sending his mug rolling onto the deck. 'Why don't you go back to London, Isla? Why are you hanging around here? Why don't you go and pack your bag?'

'Am I wrong?' She stands next to an upturned plant pot, earth scattered at her feet.

'These bastards can all go to hell. I'm done with the lot of them.' He turns and points wildly at the neighbouring houses, the long backyards, the hedges and flowerbeds. 'Your mother can go to hell and your brother can go with her. I don't need any of them.'

'Am I wrong, Dad?'

'I didn't think you'd turn on me, Isla. You of all people!'

He reaches for the bunting that droops beside the kitchen window. It comes away as he pulls on it, trailing across the deck, shabby and soiled. He kicks it, and it wraps itself around his foot.

'Watch out.' She steps forward to break his fall and he crashes into her arms, almost knocking her sideways. She feels his weakness, his frailty as she holds him upright, hears the whistle in his chest.

He stands, holding her arms for balance. 'Don't ask me that again,' he says.

35

Sydney, 1967

Mandy regretted her visit as soon as she walked into Joe's kitchen. She shut his back door behind her and kept a grip on the handle.

'I won't stop long,' she said. 'Steve's nodded off. I wanted to check you were right.'

He was leaning uncomfortably over the sink, working at the tea stains on the inside of a mug with his good hand. Half a dozen dishes stood brightly upright in the drying rack and several whisky tumblers, washed and rinsed, were drip-drying upside down in orderly rows. This is a man, she thought, whose wife is on her way home.

'Looks like you're busy,' she said to his frowning profile.

'Thought it was about time I got the place cleaned up. It's not as hard as it looks, once you get started.'

She noticed the faded purple bruising at his neck. 'Look. My husband nearly killed you. I'm sorry that happened.'

'I'm fine, Mandy.' He looked at her distractedly. 'It seems to have knocked some sense into me.' Beneath the soapy water, the gold band on his ring finger caught the light.

'I'm pleased to hear that.' She looked around her at the clean floor, the freshly wiped surfaces. 'You turned over a new leaf, is that it?'

'I'm expecting Louisa back soon. And Isla. Don't want them getting home to a filthy house.'

'That's great news.' She kept her voice bright. 'When do they arrive?'

'Louisa's booking the flights today.'

'They're flying back?'

'The boat's too slow, what with Lou being pregnant.'

'Of course.' She reached behind her for the door handle. 'I've missed Isla. Be good to see her.'

He wiped the suds from his hand onto his shirt. 'All worked out nicely, didn't it?'

'Did it?'

'I think so. My wife's coming home with my daughter. Your divorce should come through soon. I'd say that's a big success all round.'

She stared back at him. 'What?'

'Don't think I haven't worked it out.'

'I don't know what you mean.'

'Last week. You let me think Steve was at work.'

'Did I?' She brought her hands to her face. 'Oh God, I didn't mean to do that. I lost track of how long he'd been out of the house.'

'Don't bullshit me, Mandy. You must have known he'd be back any time.'

'I forgot myself.' She flushed hot at the memory. 'The last thing I wanted was for him to come home.'

'Is he giving you a divorce?'

'What? No.' She tried to make sense of his face. 'No, we're going to try and make a go of it.'

His eyebrows lifted. 'He's sticking around?'

'We're giving it a go. I don't want to divorce him. I swear to God, Joe. You got the wrong end of the stick.'

His eyes moved over her face. 'Could have sworn you'd set me up. Grounds for divorce.'

'Don't be daft.' She tipped her head, tried to soften him. 'No need for anything like that. We were a comfort to each other, you and me, weren't we? A port in a storm. Nothing serious.'

He swung on his heel, back to the sink. 'Was there anything else? Don't want Steve coming over here looking for you.'

'There was something—'

'Best you don't come back over. Let things settle down.'

'Right.' She couldn't catch his eye. 'Joe, I—'

'I'll be ready for him, if he sets foot on my property.' He looked out the window to Mandy's yard, pointing. 'He'd better keep his distance.'

'He's asleep, don't worry. He was up in the night with William.'

He tipped the dirty water out of the bowl. 'Who's William?'

'The baby.' She cleared her throat. 'I wanted to talk to you about that.'

He became still. 'The baby I saw you with? Little black kid?'

'That's him.'

'What's that all about?'

She stared down at his lino and tried to get her thoughts in order. He was making her nervous. 'I was hoping you'd keep it to yourself,' she said. 'About the baby. Just for now.'

'Why's that?' He turned and leaned back against the draining board, staring straight ahead.

'It's easier that way,' she said. 'We're hoping to adopt him, but until then—'

'You want me to keep quiet about it?'

She nodded. 'Please.'

He raked his fingers through the stubble at his jaw. 'You want to implicate me in what you've done?'

She swallowed. 'No. I mean.'

He turned to face her. 'You realise it's hell to have a child taken from you?'

She opened her mouth to reply but her mind was blank. He stood up straight and she took a step back.

'At least I know where my daughter is,' he said. 'I know she's safe, with people who love her.'

'William's safe with us!'

'At least Isla wasn't taken by a stranger.' He raised his voice, speaking over her. 'At least she wasn't taken from me, God knows where, by some bloke who thought he'd be a better parent than me. At least I have that to be thankful for, don't I?'

She felt three inches tall.

'Don't ask me to keep quiet.' He slammed his hand down

on the counter, and she yelped. 'He's not yours. You need to give him back.'

'It's not that easy, Joe. He could be taken to one of the Homes if we don't keep him.'

'Can Steve take his pick of these kids?' He gestured out at the yard. 'Is that the way it works?'

'It wasn't like that. He was—'

The telephone rang in the hall. They both turned to look at it.

'Hang on.' Joe crossed the room, glancing over his shoulder at her. 'I need to get that,' he said.

Mandy stood in the kitchen, holding the door handle. She felt cold with shock. She was a fool for coming over here, expecting – what? She'd thought he might still want her, if she was honest. She'd thought she might have to let him down gently.

'Have you booked the flight?' she heard him say. His voice was loud and bright. 'When are you coming?'

She stayed where she was and listened. His silence was ominous, it seemed to her. A long silence was always bad news.

'What?' She heard him swearing under his breath, and the flame of his lighter. 'I thought you said you were going to book it.'

He picked the phone up and took it into the lounge room. Mandy trod across the lino and stood at the kitchen door.

'Louisa, listen. If this is about that night, about what happened, I swear to God it won't happen again. I had more whisky than I should have. I want you to know, I'm cutting down on the drink. I'm going to make some changes.'

Mandy stood perfectly still. She thought of Louisa, the day she'd sat at her kitchen table, swatting at flies and talking about a down payment. And that Friday night she'd come over and cried into a glass of brandy. Maybe it wasn't only homesickness she was running from. Maybe she'd been holding something back.

'It won't happen again, Louisa.'

Mandy backed up through the kitchen.

'Louisa, don't say that. Don't go. Don't hang up.'

She pulled his back door shut. She heard him shout, something angry and non-verbal. Then the metallic clamour of the telephone hitting the wall. Louisa wasn't coming back, by the sound of it. She stood on Joe's deck, looked across his yard, over the bright line of shrubs that separated the two houses, to where her husband stood with his arms folded, sending a dark shadow across the paving stones.

Mandy walked round to her own yard, conscious of Steve watching her. She could see how it looked to him. She felt guilty and ashamed, although she'd done nothing wrong.

'You look guilty as hell.' He stood on the back step, blocking her entrance to the kitchen.

'Let me in, will you?' She stepped up to the door but he didn't budge.

'I thought you might have had the decency to stay away from Joe Green.'

'I went to have a word with him, to ask him to keep quiet about William.'

He hit the door frame with the palm of his hand. 'You said you'd stay away from him! It's what we agreed!'

'I'm sorry. I was scared he might dob us in.' William was waking from his nap; she could hear him, chatting and squealing to himself. 'Let me get him,' she said, stepping up to the back door. 'Let me go to him, before he gets cranky.'

He stood aside for her and she felt the anger in him as she passed. His chest revved with it like an engine.

'I'm not a fool, Mandy,' he called out. 'I'm onto you!'

William smiled at the sight of her and lifted his head. She lay down on the bed next to him and messed his hair so his curls sprung up. Her breathing settled in time with his and she listened to his chatter, her hand on the small of his back.

'I ought to stick with blokes your age,' she said, her head next to his on the mattress. 'The rest are too much trouble, d'you know that?' She lifted him under his arms and let him climb over her.

'We agreed you'd stay away from that bastard next door.' Steve was in the hallway, barely visible at the edge of the door frame. 'Why can't you stick to what we agreed?'

She sat up, tried to see his face. 'I'm sorry I went over there.'

'Not as sorry as I am.'

She ran her fingers over the soles of William's feet. Steve moved to the side of the room and stood with his back to the window.

'It's been a week, Mandy,' he said. 'One week it took for you to go running to him. Maybe you'd have gone sooner if I'd turned my back.'

'He saw the baby, Steve. I wanted to explain –'

'I want you to avoid him like the plague. Do you hear me?'

She nodded, keeping her eyes on the baby. She'd messed up again, going over to see Joe. Steve had seemed a bit more like his old self these past couple of days and she'd stopped treading so carefully. It was early days, but. She'd have to give it time, be patient.

'If you see him in the street I want you to cross the road,' he said. 'If you see him out in the yard I want you to look away.'

'He lives next door, Steve. I see him every day.'

He shifted from foot to foot, breathing noisily through his nose. He was less familiar since he left the force. He smelled of the house and the products they used around the place: bleach and carbolic soap. She wondered when he'd last gone further than the backyard.

'I've been thinking. Maybe we should move away,' he said. 'Away from him next door. Somewhere nobody knows us.'

She went to protest and thought better of it. 'I love it here,' she said, as calm as she could manage.

'We could tell people William's adopted if we moved away. People would accept it.'

She caught something in his voice. 'Did you speak to Ray about William?'

'Not yet.'

'I think you should call him. The longer you leave it, it's more likely he'll get a call from the Home.'

'I can't get hold of him,' he said, deflated. 'I think maybe he's mad at me, for quitting the job. I left five or six messages and he hasn't called back.'

'He'll come good, won't he? After all you've done for him.'

'But what if he doesn't? What if he wants us to give William up?'

'You said he'd arrange an adoption!' She forgot to be calm. 'You said it could all be arranged, we just had to ask.'

'That was before, Mandy. When me and Ray were on good terms.'

She pulled the baby into her lap, closed her eyes and let him grab at her hair, her face.

'We'd be better off making a new start.' He said it firmly. 'Maybe move south, to Victoria.'

'We've lived here since we got married, Steve. I feel at home here.'

'I know that.'

She kept her eyes shut. 'I need to think about it.'

'You want to stay near to Joe Green?' His voice rose. 'You want to keep running over there every time I shut my eyes for half an hour?'

'That's not it, Steve.'

'What, then?'

'My dad won't know where I am if we move away.' She looked up at him. She could just make him out. He had a strange look on his face, like he despised her, like he was hard at heart.

'You could call him, Mandy. Pick up the phone.'

'I did. The line was disconnected. I wrote letters too but he never replied.' She felt his irritation. 'You know how he is.'

'I know he's never liked me. Can't say I care too much if we don't keep in contact.'

'He likes you fine.'

'I'm not good enough for his daughter, but.'

'That's not true.'

'He as good as said so once or twice.'

This was true, although it wasn't personal, it was just her dad's way. He'd taken against Steve before she'd even brought him home. It had hurt him, watching her drift into Steve's orbit, her loyalties tipping. It had been a dry summer like this one and she'd never been so happy or so sad. Steve had worn his police blues the day he'd proposed, nervous and uncomfortable but brave enough to stand on her verandah with all her brothers watching, to ask her dad for her hand. He'd taken a ring from his pocket and she'd loved him completely. She remembered the feeling. No one else had existed.

'He can't help the way he is,' she said.

'You can write him with the new address, when we're settled.'

She wouldn't see her dad again. She had a feeling about it, that he was lost to her. When she thought of him she thought of his hands, the way he'd cracked crayfish shells for her with his thumbs, lifting out the white pipes of meat.

'I don't like to think of him on his own,' she said.

'It's his choice, Mandy. Let the old bastard stew on it.'

She pedalled William's legs and he looked up at her, uncertain, a whine in his throat. She lifted him up. It's all right, she said to him, in her head. It's only Steve, he's not as bad as he sounds. The boy clung to her and stamped his feet in her lap.

'You'll have to trust me again some time,' she said.

'Don't push me, Amanda. You'd be wise not to push me.'

He moved past her into the hall. She thought he'd moved away when she heard his voice, softer than before. 'Told you you'd make a good mum.'

She let that go. The TV came on in the lounge room and she heard Abigail Walker out the front, shouting down the street for her kids to come inside for their tea. Mandy stood, shunted the baby up her hip and walked with him through to the kitchen. It was getting dark in there, the yard was shady, and she couldn't think how to fill the evening, what to do with herself. She made up a bottle and took William out to sit on the striped garden chair under the passionfruit vine. A light came on in Joe's kitchen and his words returned from earlier: *he's not yours. You need to give him back*. She knew it was true. And at the same time, it was unthinkable. It horrified her now, to think she might have let him go.

For the first time in days she wanted a cigarette. She sat back in the chair and watched the boy drink his milk down, his fleshy limbs, the tightly packed life in him. When had she fallen for this child? It must have crept up on her, but she felt it in that moment like a shove from behind, unexpected and alarming.

She stood, held William tight against her and took him back inside the house.

36

Sydney, 1967

Mandy walked up and down Bridge Street with her shopping bag on her shoulder. It was still early. She'd picked up eggs and milk and she had enough of everything else at home to last a day or two. If she wasn't careful she'd have no reason to go out tomorrow. The house was an uneasy place to be right now. She'd got in the habit of walking to the shops and back to avoid Steve's company while William slept. Every day she stretched it out by another ten minutes.

She stood in the line outside the bakery for a while, but the shop was too hot once she got inside and she realised she couldn't stomach a pie, after all. In the end she joined the smaller line in the milk bar on the corner and got herself a malted shake. She wasn't sure she wanted that either, but she sat down in a booth and watched a group of boys playing pinball, glad of the noise and movement. The laughter. It was good to hear laughter.

The table was sticky where someone had spilled a drink. She budged up to the far end of the seat where the table was cleaner and waved away the flies that circled overhead. She stirred her drink with the straw and took a sip. Someone shouted out an order from the bar and she jumped, nearly choking, and thumped herself on the chest until she got her breath back. Her heart raced.

It wasn't working out how she'd hoped. Steve wasn't moving on from it. If he hadn't seen her with Joe, if he'd found out some other way, he might have been able to box it away. Instead he was letting it eat at him. Brooding in the house like a caged bear. He could hardly look at her.

The baby was their only hope. He gave shape to the days, forced them out of bed, gave them something to talk about. She must be the last person on earth to catch on that babies were the glue for a marriage. Someone they could both love. And they did both love him. The kind of love you don't recover from, that flips between joy and fear. She'd been wrong, thinking she didn't have it in her to love a child. And she'd fallen harder because she hadn't seen it coming.

She managed half of the malted shake and decided to leave the rest. It was hot in here, despite the ceiling fans, and she couldn't relax. The flies were insistent, gathering at the far end of the table where the spilled drink had hardened. She swiped at one of them, hit it mid-flight, and her hand fizzed with the impact of its small, hard being, the brush of its wings.

A decision had formed in her head by the time she reached the bus stop. She would tell Steve they should move south,

233

like he'd suggested. She'd send the new address to her dad once they'd found somewhere. It was never going to sit easy that he'd cut her off, that he was on his own in that old house on the edge of Toowoomba with only the chooks for company. But she had to pick herself up and concentrate on her marriage. She took the bus up to the end of Bay Street instead of walking the last stretch as she did most days. She'd be back in time to see William as he woke from his nap. He wanted her these days, when he woke. He held his arms up and reached for her. She curved her arm against her body, anticipating his weight.

David Walker was practising his violin again, sending his plangent notes down Bay Street, along the parched hedges and lawns, over the shadecloths in Doug's front yard. The weatherboard houses on the ocean side of the street were looking dirty in the morning sun. It was the water restrictions, she figured. Nobody wanted to fill a bucket and scrub the boards down, not in this heat. Even Doug's house had a tide of grit under the window. His roses were doing well, but. She nodded hello at him, standing out the front with his shears, like always. Across the street, the new house was nearly finished, three doors along from the Walkers'. It was twice the size of her place. Two storeys and a space at the side for a private garage. Parking on the street wasn't good enough for some people.

She dropped her eyes as she passed Joe's house, in case he was home. She'd promised to avoid him like the plague, and she was doing her best. Eyes to the ground, all the way up to the gate, just to be on the safe side. Her key was in the lock before she noticed the windows. She'd opened them all wide before she went out. Today was the first day in weeks she'd felt a fresh southerly come in. But he'd shut them all.

'Steve?' She could hear movement in the kitchen, but no answer. 'Steve? Why'd you close the windows?'

The movement in the kitchen stopped. She poked her head into the second bedroom and found the curtains drawn in there, the bed bare; a small, wrinkled imprint in the sheets where William had lain.

'Steve?'

She threw her bag down on the carpet in their bedroom. If he wasn't speaking to her it was going to be a long day. She'd been hopeful not ten minutes ago, full of plans. All of it withered in the atmosphere of the house. The wardrobe doors were ajar and she crossed the room to close them. It was too quiet in here. Something nagged at her. She stood in front of the wardrobe and threw the doors open wide, scanned the contents. Several hangers were bare. Steve's shirts, the ones he wore most often, were missing. The jacket she'd given him for Christmas was gone too.

Mandy looked around, trying to think through the shock. There was space on the dresser where there had been clutter. She pulled the drawers out and looked inside. Only her things remained. Steve's shirts, socks, underwear, shorts, were gone. All of it.

'Steve?' Her voice was thin. 'Steve! What the hell is going on?'

The kitchen door opened and Steve's footsteps approached, slow and heavy. She could hear William's agitated breathing, the squeak of his dummy.

'I was going to leave a note.' Steve stood in the bedroom doorway with a box under one arm, William balanced on his hip. 'Forgive me, Mandy, but I didn't have the stomach to say goodbye.'

She couldn't speak. She shook her head and stayed where she was by the dresser with the drawers standing open. Steve looked at her as if from a great distance.

'I'll come with you,' she said. 'We can move to Victoria, like you said.'

He hitched William further up his body. 'I'm leaving you, Mandy.'

'You don't need to go.' His words registered as she spoke. It was impossible, what he'd said. She raised her voice. 'I decided, while I was out. We can move. I came home to tell you I made my mind up.'

'I'm leaving you.' He stared back at her. 'I've put up with enough. More than a man should have to put up with. I'm a mug for sticking around as long as I have.'

'But I'm keeping to what we agreed! I'm giving it my best shot, like I said I would.'

'It's not working. You must know it's not working.'

She pushed all the empty drawers shut, making the dresser shake. The framed photo of her dad fell forward, knocking bottles and jars to the floor. 'You were going to leave while I was out! After all we've been through together. All these years!'

'I'll write to you when we're settled.' He turned and left the room.

'Where are you going?' She followed him into the hallway. This was moving too fast. 'You can't do this. I won't let you.'

'My mind's made up.'

He was facing away from her, trying to turn the latch on the front door. The box under his arm was too big to free his hand.

'Please,' she said. 'Please don't do this. Just give it a bit more time.'

'You're too late,' he said, groping for the latch.

'Let me take him.' Mandy held her arms out to William. The boy looked back at her: watchful, alert, beautiful. She had half a mind to grab him and run. 'Here, let me hold him while you do that.'

Steve turned to face her. 'Are you crying?'

She nodded and wiped her face with the backs of her hands.

'Here.' He crouched down and let the box drop to the floor. 'Hold him.'

William wrapped his arms and legs around her. She held him close and cried into his hair, tried to remember the heat and shape of his body against hers. She did not know how to live if he took the baby from her. She had been half alive before. 'I'm sorry about what happened with Joe. I've been trying to make it up to you. I swear if you give me another chance I'll do better. I'll never let you down again.'

Steve looked down at the box at his feet, which was full of milk and nappies. He rubbed his thumb and forefinger over

237

his eyes. 'I know you're taking the Pill. I found the pack in the bathroom.'

The hope leached out of her. 'I swear nothing's happened with Joe since—'

'Don't.' He kept his eyes on the box. 'Don't. Please.'

'I'll stop taking it,' she said, desperation making her voice rasp. 'If you'll stay, I'll stop taking it. We can move away and we'll be a family. We can bring William up together.'

'You let me believe we were trying for a baby. All those months. You were on the Pill the whole time.'

She held William tighter. 'I wasn't ready,' she said.

He opened the door and picked up the box. 'I need to get on the road. Got a long drive ahead.'

'I'm sorry.' She followed him outside. The truck was full of boxes and bags. He must have been packing from the moment she left that morning. Her nose was running and she wiped it on her sleeve. 'I'm so sorry, Steve.'

He threw the box onto the back seat and slammed the door shut. 'I'll give you a divorce. Best thing for both of us. No point prolonging it.'

She walked around the truck to where Steve was standing. 'You want a divorce?'

'It's the best thing.' He thumped the roof of the truck with the palm of his hand. The veins were pronounced at his temples. 'I need to build my life back up, Mandy. I need to get out of this.'

Steve moved to take William from her and she took a step backwards. Her throat was tight, her words painful. 'Will you at least tell me where you're headed? I need to know where you both are. Please.'

He considered her a while. 'Marlo,' he said, eventually. He held his hands out for William. 'I thought we'd head for Marlo.'

'The cabin?'

'That's right. Not sure how long we'll stop there, mind. Depends how long it takes to sell up.'

'Sell up?'

'The house.'

'What?' Steve reached out again and she turned away. Her blouse was soaked through with her own sweat and the boy's body heat. 'You're selling the house?'

'That's right. I'll give you half of whatever I get for it. I've left some cash on the kitchen table to last you till then.'

'Steve, I don't want this. Please don't go.'

Steve put his hands under William's arms and peeled his body away from hers. She let out a moan as he did it, a noise she didn't recognise. The baby's warmth stayed in her fingers and she held them to her face. Her moan became deeper and louder until she was sobbing from the base of her throat and she couldn't speak and there were no words anyway, she had nothing left to say. She reached out to Steve, gripped his arm, but he shook her off. The coldness in him was impenetrable. She was making a scene in full view of the whole street and he seemed barely to notice.

He put the baby in a blanket box at the foot of the passenger seat and handed him a teether. She knelt down at the side of the truck, her knees burning on the bitumen, and kissed the crown of the boy's head. She let him grab her hair, her clothes. She wailed into the soft pit of his neck.

'Will you calm down, Amanda?'

She stood and made an effort to catch her breath. She wiped her face. 'Are you trying to punish me?'

He slammed the passenger door and walked around to the driver's side. 'The bills are all paid up in advance,' he said, as if she hadn't spoken. 'I'll be in touch when I've got the house on the market.'

She stood hopelessly by as he climbed into the truck. He was a stranger to her. This was the way he was when he took children away; she could see it now, the man he became. Focused and powerful, ruthless. Was this the man William's mum had met? Was this how she felt?

'Don't do this!' She screamed at him, gulping for air. 'Please don't go!'

Bay Street was bright and calm, indifferent. A few yards away, Douglas Blunt snipped rhythmically at his hedge.

Steve shut the door of the truck behind him. The pane squeaked as he lowered it and then she heard him calling her name. He held his arm outstretched through the window as she approached, his palm turned upwards. She took his hand and he gripped it.

'I tried to write this down for you but it wouldn't come out right.' He didn't look at her. 'I love you, Amanda. You're all I ever wanted in a woman.'

She crouched down beside the truck and pressed his hand against her face. 'Stay, then.'

'I can't forgive you.' He still wouldn't look at her.

'Take me with you. We'll start again together.'

'The sight of you kills me.' He took his hand away and turned the ignition. She caught a burst of William's throaty babble through the opened window; his legs kicking rapidly against the box.

'Take me with you!'

He didn't look back. Her body buckled as the truck reached the corner of Bay Street. She couldn't watch it turn out of sight. She sat in the street with her arms wrapped around her knees, her shoes sinking into the hot bitumen, the sun burning the back of her neck.

37

Sydney, 1997

'This house is a mess,' Joe says.

Isla keeps her back to him, busying herself at the sink until she hears him leave the room. She sweeps crumbs from the counter into the palm of her hand and she thinks of her grandmother, the way she would saw through a loaf of bread and lie the slices beside each other under the grill. She thinks of buttered toast and milk that has frozen in the bottle. In the bedroom her dad opens drawers and cupboards and slams them shut again, cursing. She scrapes plates into the bin and thinks of the cold English house where they were hiding from him, huddled together on the other side of the planet in a place where he couldn't reach them.

'How am I supposed to find anything?' he says from the bedroom.

She stares out at the yard and sees the long grass, the fallen leaves. From the bedroom down the hall her dad starts to cough,

242

swearing louder than before as the fit passes. She wraps her arms around herself and waits.

Joe reappears, half dressed, at the kitchen door. 'I'm missing something,' he says.

'What is it?'

'Something important.'

She feels him watching her as she pours water into the percolator. 'What did you lose?' She looks up at him. He is an old man, thin as a bean in his work pants and singlet.

'A watch,' he says. 'I kept it in a drawer.'

'I didn't know you kept a spare one.'

'Have you seen it?'

'No.' She stares back at him. Beside her, coffee drips into the jug.

'Now who's lying?' he says.

The telephone rings in the hallway. He lets it ring twice before he turns to answer it.

'This is Joe Green,' he says. 'Can I help you?'

A long silence follows. Isla wipes the table, straightens the chairs.

'Are you sure it's Mandy?' he says. 'I mean. You're sure it's her body?'

Isla drops the cloth into the sink. She stares at it, the crumbs clinging to it, the grit around the plughole. She wonders if she should rinse it out. She feels weak, she can't reach for it.

'Where was she found?' Joe says.

She turns and leans back against the sink. She can't clear her head. Can't stand.

'I will,' he says, and then, 'No. I'll come to the station.'

She hears him replace the handset. She crosses the room, lightheaded. The coffee is ready. She needs sugar and teaspoons.

'Was that the police?' She sounds scared. She clears her throat, stares into the cutlery drawer.

'It was that Inspector Perry bloke.' Joe searches the room for cigarettes, finds them on the windowsill and lights one with desperate impatience, dropping the spent match on the floor. He shoves his trembling hand into his pocket. 'They think they found Mandy's remains on file. Whatever that means.'

He paces the room as she pours coffee into two mugs. He sits down and stands up again.

'They want me to go down the station,' he says.

She puts the coffee on the table and sits down heavily. She remembers to breathe. 'Are they sure it's her?'

He nods. 'I think so.'

'You think so?'

'He sounded sure.'

'When are you going to the station?'

'Soon. Later.' He reaches into the cupboard beneath the sink and pulls out the vodka he keeps there, behind the bottles of detergent. 'He wants me to go today.'

She looks at her coffee as he drinks. She doesn't want to see him lift the bottle to his mouth, the urgency as he swallows. He's breaking a rule. For as long as she can remember her dad has drunk silently behind closed doors, hiding these bottles with red and gold labels, burying the empties in the bin. At family parties he would nurse a single bottle of beer all night;

at the dinner table he sipped cola. His privacy protected him from shame. And she had followed his example when the time came, finding hiding places of her own.

He wipes his mouth with the back of his wrist and she thinks, is this it, then? Is this where we stop pretending?

'She died thirty years ago,' he says.

Isla stares at him. 'Did she?'

He nods at the phone in the hallway, his eyes glassy. 'They found her in '67 but they couldn't identify her at the time.'

'Dad, I think—'

'The cop said her body was found on the beach, here in Sydney. Near Maroubra.'

'Maybe she drowned,' Isla says. 'She might have—'

'Strangled,' he says. 'She wasn't in the water when she died.'

She swallows coffee, burning the roof of her mouth. She spills it as she puts it down. 'I think you should get a lawyer.'

He covers his eyes. 'There are things I can't tell you, Isla.'

'Why?'

'I don't want to lose you.'

'What are you saying?'

'You're all I have.'

She runs her fingers over the chips in the formica table, the flecked yellow pattern that covers its surface. He drinks again from the bottle, and she feels his fear.

'Will you get a lawyer?'

He nods.

'Don't say anything, Dad.' She feels sick. She wants to be

numb. To keep pretending. 'Don't let them push you into saying anything. They want you to think they've got you.'

He pulls out a chair and sits down, facing away from her. He holds the bottle between his legs.

'Dad, are you listening to me? Don't say anything, will you?'

He lifts the bottle back to his mouth. His cigarette has burnt down in the ashtray and the filter drops forward, still glowing. He pushes the bottle towards her and she catches it as it slides across the table. She picks it up, feels its familiar heft.

'I won't say anything,' he says.

38

Sydney, 1967

Mandy noticed the red dust caked over the fenders of his car before she noticed Ray at the wheel. She weighed up whether she could turn back into the house without him knowing she'd seen him. Whether she cared if he knew or not. She was too slow: he caught her eye and waved, rolled the window down.

'Steve home?' He parked at the front of the house, leaned towards her through the window.

'No,' she said. She took off her gardening gloves and walked up to the gate. 'He's gone.'

'When d'you think he'll be back? I could do with a word.'

'Steve shot through.' It was a shock, saying it aloud. She checked the tremble in her voice. 'He took off a few days back. Just went.'

He opened his car door and stood on the footpath in front of the gate. Mandy had forgotten the size of him. He was the tallest man she'd met in her life. Bad posture, but. He'd wind up with aches and pains, she thought, later in life.

'I'm sorry to hear that, Mandy.'

'It's been quite a shock. You can imagine. I'm surprised he hasn't spoken to you about it all.'

He took his hat off and his eyes dropped to the footpath. 'He left a few messages for me. I kept meaning to call him back.'

'It's a bit late now.'

'I didn't think. I'd have called right back if I'd known.'

'He thought you were mad at him for leaving the job.'

He fanned himself with his hat. 'He did leave me in a bind if I'm honest.'

'He worked like a dog for you. Nine years, Ray.'

'He was a good man.' He nodded. 'A good worker.'

'The job got to him. He let it pull him under.'

'It's not easy, that's for sure.'

'It's not right.' She stepped closer to the gate. 'That job you had him doing. Going out there and taking kids away. That's not right, Ray. Steve was doing something he knew was wrong and it near finished him.'

Andrea Walker flew past on her bicycle, ringing her bell, and Ray lifted his hat to wave at her.

'I didn't know you felt that way,' he said.

'It took me a while to see it,' she said. 'I wish I'd seen it sooner.'

He hung his head. A fly settled in a thinning patch of his hair and he brushed it away. 'The job needs doing, Mandy. Nothing I can do about it.'

'He considered you a good man,' she said. 'Didn't want to let you down.'

'I know that. I wish to God I'd called him back.'

She could take a dislike to this man, she decided, standing there in the midday sun with that shifty, weasel look to him. Small, hard eyes. She could see him squirming with guilt and she was glad about it.

'You don't know where he might have headed?' he said.

She hesitated. 'Why d'you ask?'

'Just there was a bit of business needed clearing up. I could do with speaking to him about it. If you have an address?'

She felt sweat running down her spine. 'What was it regarding? I could ask him if he gets in touch.'

'He was meant to drop a child off at the Home down in Nowra. They tell me he didn't show up. It's causing me a head-ache, that's all. Need to keep the paperwork straight.'

Andrea Walker flew back past in the other direction, skimming Ray's wing mirror. She was getting too tall for that bike, Mandy thought. Her bare legs were bent almost double.

'He was always very reliable, Ray. Never shirked on a duty. You know that.'

'I do.' He lowered his voice. 'He's not in any trouble? Nothing I should know?'

Mandy shook her head. 'I reckon he'll be in touch if he needs you,' she said. 'Make sure you take his call if he does.'

'Righto.' He double-tapped the word out on the gate. 'Tell him to call me, if you hear from him.'

'He took the truck,' she said. 'Don't suppose you'll get that back.'

'No.' He got back in his car, bent right over to get his legs in. 'That truck had seen better days.'

She waved him off and he waved back through the window, swerving to miss Andrea. She was getting to be a menace on that bike. Mandy faced the house and caught a glimpse of Joe Green as his curtain dropped back against his window. She crouched down and turned the soil over with the trowel; kept her eyes down till she felt him move away.

39

Leeds, 1967

The phone was ringing. Isla picked up the receiver and held it to her ear. She heard a rustling noise, like the radio when Grandma was turning the buttons. She sat down on the bottom step and leaned against the bannister with the receiver on her shoulder, head tilted sideways, the way her mum did it. She pushed her fingers through the twists in the flex. Behind the noise there was a tiny voice, she thought. Sometimes it came clear and then it went away.

She moved up onto the second step, away from the kitchen sounds down the hall. Mummy and Grandma were cooking and talking, putting plates on the table. She gripped the receiver in both hands and moved her mouth close to the small, circular holes.

'Hello,' she said. It made the radio noise spin and whistle when she spoke. 'Hello hello.'

'Hello?' The small voice came closer. 'Who's there?'

Isla moved to the far corner of the step with her back to the wall, her knees up tight to her chest. The noise in her ear crackled and then stopped. The quiet was listening to her. She sat very still.

'Hello?'

She knew that voice. She sat up straight. 'Daddy?'

'Isla? Is that you?'

She smiled and nodded. In her ear she could hear his breaths. 'I answered the phone,' she said.

'I'm glad you did. I nearly put it down. I thought there was nobody there.'

'It was me.'

'I'm glad it's you. Very glad.'

Isla wound the flex around her arm and tried to think of something to say. 'I'm at Grandma's.'

'I know.' The phone started to hiss again and his words were quiet. 'I miss you, Isla.'

She waited for the hiss to stop. In the kitchen her mum was telling Grandma something about hair. *He cut his hair*, she was saying. *Cut it all off, like a soldier.* Isla thought of Daddy's soft skin and his hard bones.

'You still there?'

She nodded and pulled the flex tighter. It left white, curling marks on her arm. 'Are you still my dad?'

'Of course.' There was a pause. 'Of course I'm your dad, love.'

'Are you coming to get me?'

'Oh, Isla.' He was quiet for a long time, although the hiss had stopped. 'I don't think I can.'

Isla unwound the flex slowly from her arm. Her hand had puffed up pink and her arm was circled with curled indents.

'I don't like England,' she said.

'That makes two of us.'

'Why do people want to live in England?'

'That is a very good question. I have no idea.'

She ran her finger over the deepest indents, near her wrist, which were pleasingly ridged and slightly sore. From the kitchen she could smell sausages.

'You ok?'

Isla nodded.

'You're not crying, are you?'

'No,' Isla said, although she thought she might.

'Good girl.'

Grandma was calling her name from the kitchen. Her tea was ready, she was saying. Come and eat. Isla wasn't sure she was hungry. She'd been hungry when the phone rang, looking forward to the sausages. She couldn't think of anything she wanted, now.

'I'd come and get you if I could,' Daddy said. 'Do you know that?'

Isla nodded again, because she did know this.

The kitchen door opened and Grandma was shouting up the hall. Isla stood and leaned around the bannister with the receiver behind her back. 'Coming,' she said.

Grandma didn't move. She wanted her to come right away, please, because the food is on the table. Isla turned and carefully, quietly, put the receiver down in its cradle.

40

Sydney, 1967

'No need to get dressed up on my account.'

Joe Green stood on Mandy's verandah, looking like an unmade bed. His shirt was buttoned up wrong and his hair had grown. Curls were forming near his ears.

'Is he out?' He glanced down at the patch of oil in the street where Steve's truck had been.

She nodded.

'Can I come in?'

No, she thought. He was unshaven and his eyes were off. Something not quite right about him.

'I spoke to Isla on the phone.' He looked imploringly at her. 'I rang the house yesterday and she answered.'

She opened the door and stepped back to let him in. 'Come through,' she said, leading him into the lounge room. Too much history in the kitchen. 'I just made coffee if you want one?'

'Anything stronger?'

She raised an eyebrow. 'It's ten-thirty.'

'I'm not keeping regular hours, Mandy. I'm not sleeping too well.'

She went to the kitchen and found a beer at the back of the fridge, one of the stubbies Steve used to drink. She opened the bottle and stood there a minute with the fridge door open, leaning into the cool air. She had a nervous feeling, like she'd made a mistake and it was going to bite her. Joe cleared his throat in the lounge room and she tensed, nearly dropping the beer.

He was sitting on the arm of the couch when she went back in, his ankle resting on his knee. He took the beer wordlessly, closed his eyes and drank most of it down.

'You look like a truck hit you.'

He ran his hand through the thick hair at the back of his head. 'It's knocked me, Mandy. Talking to Isla knocked me back.'

'How is she? What did she say?'

'She asked me to come and get her.' He looked at her, incredulous. 'That's what she said. She wants me to bring her back home. She doesn't want to be in England.'

'What did you say to that?'

'I said I don't think I can.'

'Was she all right? Did she understand?'

'Don't think so. She hung up the phone on me.'

'Did she?' Mandy almost smiled for the first time in days. 'Maybe the line cut out,' she said, seeing Joe's face.

'She must think I've let her down.' He drained the rest of

his beer, holding the bottle to his mouth a while after the last drop was gone.

'She's too young to understand,' Mandy said.

He played restlessly with the beer bottle, picking at the label. 'Louisa changed her mind about coming back here. You might have guessed.'

'Did she say why?'

'Second thoughts. Doubts. Maybe she wants to play with my head.'

Mandy thought of the phone call she'd overheard. *It won't happen again.* 'She'll come round,' she said. 'You might need to give her a bit of time.'

'She's got me by the balls, Mandy. I'll have to sell up and go to England if I want to see my kids.'

There was a slur in his voice. A delay between brain and mouth. 'Joe, are you—?'

'You stopped wearing it,' he said.

'What's that?'

He reached for her arm, circled her wrist with his hand and moved his thumb over the pale strip of skin. His hand was cool. She felt the desire in him and it unsettled her. She'd started this and she didn't want it now she had it. There were names for women like her.

'Your watch,' he said.

'It wouldn't start again after I wore it in the water.'

'That's a shame.'

'Should've taken more care of it.'

He kissed the inside of her wrist. 'You were beautiful in the water that day,' he said. 'You know how to lift a man when he's down.'

She let her arm hang heavy and he dropped it. 'You sure you don't want coffee?'

'Not right now.' He pulled her closer against him. 'How can I go back to England, when you're here?'

He kissed her. He tasted metallic, of beer and cigarettes. She stood rigidly before him as he lifted her blouse.

'I think I could make you happy,' he said. 'We could make each other happy.'

'Let's take things slowly,' she said, but he didn't seem to hear her. He held one hand between her legs, moved his fingers over the seam of her jeans. She tried to want him, to go with it, but she didn't like the smell coming off him. Alcohol and stale sweat. She'd liked the buzzcut and the suit.

'Let's go to bed.' He kissed her neck.

'Joe, I—' She twisted away from him, involuntarily. 'Steve might come home.'

'What?' His hand was inside her bra.

'He's only gone down to Bridge Street. He'll be back soon.'

He pulled back. 'Why didn't you say?'

'I thought you wanted to talk. About Isla.'

She pulled her blouse down and he freed his hand, after a pause. 'You should have said earlier.'

'Sorry.'

He stood, and his balance almost went. He *was* drunk, then. Maybe half drunk, half hungover. Her eldest brother had gone this way with the grog: drinking in the mornings to stop the shakes. There'd been no helping him.

'Why isn't he at work?'

'He quit.' She took a step back from him. 'He got to the end of the road with the job. Stuck at it longer than he should have.'

'Sounds like a good decision.'

'You should go.' She took a step towards the door.

His eyes moved over her. The ceiling fan droned overhead.

'I don't want him to find you here, Joe.'

'I've been thinking. Since my hand's so much better, I might like to have another word with your husband. Might be a fairer fight this time round.'

She forced a small laugh. 'Don't be an idiot.'

He looked at her. 'You reckon I'm an idiot,' he said.

'I didn't mean that.'

'My wife thinks I'm an idiot. And now you think so too.'

'Joe, all I meant was—'

'You want to get rid of me. I can see that. I remember a time when you didn't want that. I remember when you wanted me to stay.'

He stepped around the coffee table towards her. Through the open window she heard Andrea's bicycle bell.

'Do you remember that, Mandy?'

''Course I do.'

'I fell for you. D'you know that?' He smiled; a strange, loose smile. 'I did. That makes me an idiot, doesn't it?'

'No. Not at all. I—'

'You don't feel the same. Of course you don't. What was it you said?'

She shook her head.

'A port in a storm.' The smile fell from his face. 'A port in a storm. Nothing serious. That's what you said.'

She stared back at him. She didn't dare move. He had a detached look to him, like his mind had snapped.

'Look, Joe. I think maybe you're cut up over Isla and you had a bit to drink. We all do it.' She kept talking, afraid of the silence behind her voice. 'Maybe you should go and sleep it off. Come back when you've sobered up and I'll make you a coffee. We can talk.'

'That's a good idea.' He looked around the room, slowly, considering. 'Let's do that. Let's drink coffee and talk. A port in a fucking storm.'

Still he stayed where he was. She tried to smile and his eyes hardened. Fear crept up her back.

'Where is he, then?' he said.

'He went for milk. I think you should head home.'

'Maybe I'll wait for him.'

'Look, Joe—'

'I think I'll wait here with you.' He met her at the door, standing close, not quite touching. He tipped her chin back with his finger. 'Nothing serious. Right?'

'Steve's going to blow his stack,' she said.

'I'm ready for him.'

'I don't think that's a good idea.'

'I'll be the judge of that.'

'Joe, please—'

'I can handle him.' He shouted it and she shrank back against the door. 'Did you hear me, Mandy? I can handle him. I'll be ready this time and he'll—'

He turned his head from her, hearing something, a noise out on the verandah. A knock at the door.

'Let me get that.' She pulled away and went to the door, lightheaded with relief. She hoped to God it was Doug, needing a lend of her rake.

'D'you want to come to a party at our place?' Andrea Walker stood on the verandah, smiling, half her teeth missing. 'It's for my birthday, next week.'

'A party?'

'I'm going to be ten,' Andrea said. 'The party's on Saturday.'

Mandy felt Joe behind her, moving into the hall. The door to the lounge room clicked shut. 'You'll be ten? How fantastic. I'd love to come to the party.'

Andrea scratched at her thigh, hitching her dress up. 'What about Steve?'

'Steve?' She widened her eyes at the girl. 'What about him?'

'Can he come to the party?'

'Sure. I'll let him know.'

'Mum said he shot through,' Andrea said. She poked her tongue through the gap where her left canine had been. 'He packed up all his gear and drove off.'

Mandy stood wordlessly, hot and panicked, her mind racing. Andrea's bike lay sideways on the footpath and the street was quiet, bright with roses, azaleas, bottlebrush.

'I don't know where your mum got that idea.'

'She saw him packing his truck. And he took that black baby and all,' Andrea said.

Mandy heard Joe shift his feet behind her. She stepped out onto the verandah into the dense heat. 'Maybe I'll come and have a word with your mum. Is she home?'

'She's at the doctor's. The baby's got colic.' Andrea looked up at Mandy. 'You got a lemonade?'

Mandy shook her head. She felt tears coming and she blinked them back. 'Not today, sweetheart.'

'I'll tell Mum you're coming on Saturday.' Andrea ran down the steps and picked up her bike. 'I'm getting a kitten,' she yelled, throwing her leg over the crossbar. 'You can see it at the party.'

Mandy watched Andrea go. She kept her back to Joe and looked up and down Bay Street, the flat normality of it. The tiles were hot under her house shoes. She waved at Doug, out on his front lawn with a watering can. He raised a hand and turned his back.

'Thought he went to get milk,' Joe said, from inside the house.

She didn't look at him. 'He left me. I didn't want to say.'

'Why not?'

'I don't know.'

'You don't know? When did he go?'

'About a week ago.'

He pushed the door open wider. 'Come back inside. You look hot.'

She shook her head.

'I think you should tell me what happened.'

'He packed his truck and left. What else is there to say?'

'You can't stand out there all day,' he said.

She turned to face him then. His eyes were red-rimmed. 'Why don't you just go home, Joe?'

'I want to know where Steve went.'

'Why?'

'I'm interested.' He moved back slightly, out of the light. 'I'm disappointed I won't get to see him today. You got my hopes up.'

'It's a place called Marlo, in Victoria. His family own a beach cabin down there.' She wiped sweat from her face and the tears came unexpectedly. She cried into her hands.

'What about the baby?'

'What about him?'

'Has he taken him down to – where was it?'

'Marlo.' She wiped her nose on her wrist.

'That's it,' he said. 'So nobody knows where the kid came from. Fewer questions. Is that the idea?'

'Think so.' The street was perfectly still, the sun close overhead. She couldn't stand here much longer. 'Will you go now?'

'That's not very friendly.'

'You've outstayed your welcome, Joe. Can't you see that?'

From the corner of her eye she saw Doug turn towards her. The red of his watering can, the blue of his sun hat. She waved at him, smiling and crying. She hated the thought of Doug seeing her like this. The mess she'd got herself in. But she was running out of ideas.

'I'll scream,' she said, still waving. 'If you don't get out of my house, I'll scream.'

He stayed where he was. She drew in a deep breath.

'All right. Jesus.' He stepped into the sun beside her and stooped down to speak into her ear. She heard him swallow, the muscles tensing in his throat. 'I don't like being lied to,' he said.

'Go away, Joe.'

His lips brushed her ear. 'I'll see you soon.'

He straightened up, unsteadily, and walked down the steps to the gate.

She fell into the house, shut the door behind her and put the safety catch on. Her hands were slow and clumsy. She stood with her back to the door, tried to get her breathing steady. She could still smell him: sour skin, stale smoke. Jesus, he was only next door. Yards away.

In the kitchen she took the back door key from its hook. She locked it, put the key on the kitchen table and sat down. Could he force the door? Would he do that? The pane was cracked anyway, it was hardly secure. She sat where she was, facing the door, and cried. The sky outside was cloudless, the trees lush and green, the vine heavy with fruit for the first time in years. She watched a lizard run along the windowsill. If she turned her head she'd see Joe's yard, the edge of his deck, his shrubs.

She went to the sink, turned the tap on full and put her

head and shoulders under the cold water. She filled a glass and drank it down. It occurred to her to call the police. She could speak to Ray direct and tell him – what? The bloke next door was blotto, he'd refused to leave and he'd scared her. She knew she wouldn't do it. Not because Ray wouldn't listen but because she was to blame.

The envelope of cash Steve left her was still on the table. It was heavy-looking, full of notes. She counted it twice, sorting it into tens and twenties. The house was quiet, just the rattle of the fan, a dripping tap in the bathroom. Three flies circled the room, trapped and stupid, throwing themselves at the windows.

41

Sydney, 1997

Isla knocks on Douglas Blunt's front door. She stands up straight, runs her fingers through her hair and smooths it down. She cups her hands around her mouth to test her breath. Today she is holding onto the wagon by her fingernails. A part of her sits in a bar with a whisky on ice, waiting.

'Isla?'

Doug is standing in his front yard, wearing his low-brimmed sun hat, despite the chill in the air. His shorts bulge at the hips where he's tucked his shirt in.

'Thought I heard you,' he says.

She walks back down the steps to meet him. 'I need to know what you told the police,' she says.

'If you're going to lay into me again—'

'I'm not. I won't.' She holds her hands up. 'I need to know what happened.'

'I think you should ask your dad.'

'That's not as easy as it sounds.'

He hitches his shorts at the back. 'You won't like it.'

She nods. 'Tell me anyway.'

'I remember that summer better than you might think,' he says. 'First year on me own since Emily passed. I was between jobs. I didn't know how to fill the time.'

'Sorry to hear that,' she says.

'It was bloody hot. No rain for months. I was out here a lot, keeping myself busy with the plants and the veggies. I saw all the comings and goings.' He nods at his veggie patch, the trowel and gardening gloves set down on the grass. 'Your mother took you back to England for a long while. Your dad was here on his own. A man gets lonely. I can understand that.' He pauses. 'I know it's not easy to hear this kind of thing.'

'I know my dad's no angel, Doug.'

He smiles uncomfortably. 'Joe was round at Mandy's place the minute Steve was out of sight. Steve was away with work for days at a time back then. Took him a while to figure out what was going on.'

'Did he leave her?'

He pulls at a protruding twig in the hedge. 'Last time I saw Steve Mallory he was packing up his truck to leave. I saw Mandy standing there trying to talk him out of it. She made a bit of a scene.' He nods up the street. 'And he drove off without her. Left her behind.'

'Are you sure? He didn't come back for her?'

'I didn't see Steve again,' he says. 'You sure you want to hear the rest?'

She nods and looks away, at the bare shrubs along the edge of his lawn where he's cut his roses and hydrangeas back. In a bar somewhere, she orders another drink. Ice knocks against the glass.

'Mandy was here on her own for a while after Steve left. I saw your dad coming and going out of her house. They didn't bother hiding it. Kissing on the verandah, that sort of thing.' His face colours and he looks down at the grass. 'It was getting to the end of the summer by then. Still hot as hell. Mandy liked to hang her laundry out in the sun. Sometimes she'd be out the front, giving the plants a bit of water. She always waved and said hello. Then one day I didn't see her. I looked out for her like always but she didn't come out into the yard. Same the next day. And then I saw your dad coming out of her back door.'

He falls quiet. The afternoon stops. Isla thinks she might throw up, here on Doug's lawn, among his clippings and gardening tools.

'I was in the backyard,' Doug says, 'looking across to the Mallories' place, and I saw him leave Mandy's house. He locked her back door behind him and went into his house. He didn't see me. I went and knocked on Mandy's door later on but no one answered.'

'Did you see Mandy again?' She hears how desperate she sounds.

'No, love. A day or two later, you and your mother came back.'

She covers her mouth, swallowing bile. 'Didn't anybody wonder where she went?'

'I know I did. It never sat easy with me, that she didn't say goodbye.' Doug smiles weakly at her. 'Nobody wanted to upset your mum, Isla. She had a new baby soon after she got back. Nobody wanted to tell her that her husband played away, God love her. We didn't mention the Mallories and we got on with our lives. You know how it is.'

'I think I do.'

He scratches his head through his hat. 'Sorry.'

She lets herself out of his gate, leaving him kneeling on the grass, gathering leaves and twigs into a bucket. She stops at the corner where Bay Street meets Dawson Place and vomits into the roots of a lemon tree. Across the street, someone pulls the roller blind down in their front room. The houses are smug looking, she thinks, with their neat exteriors, dark windows reflecting shrubs and hedges. This is the community she grew up in, where people know everything and say nothing. A man can kill a woman and his neighbours will look away. She vomits again, wipes her mouth and sobs loudly for her dad, whom she no longer believes in, whom she still loves. She turns towards town, where she will find her seat at the bar and she will stop thinking and remembering. It will all stop, finally. She quickens her step.

42

Sydney, 1967

There was an inch of instant coffee left in the jar. Joe filled the kettle and lit a cigarette, sat at the kitchen table waiting for it to boil. He didn't want coffee, but he'd poured all the alcohol in the house down the kitchen sink half an hour ago. He was shaking a little and his bones were aching. Chattering teeth. He'd have to take a shower before he went anywhere, find a clean shirt.

He went to the back door and found himself trying to catch sight of Mandy. She hadn't come outside in a while to hang out her washing or sit under the vine. He didn't like that he was standing here hoping to see her. It was getting to be a habit.

She'd got under his skin. He could think of nothing but how to make up for that day he went over and outstayed his welcome. A dark shame washed through him at the thought of it. He remembered her face, the way she'd looked at him. He hoped it wasn't as bad as he feared. Hard to know, with his memory shot to pieces and the constant shadow of self-loathing, the sweaty distortions between drinks. But he had a feeling he'd scared her. He'd been a fucking creep. He clenched his fist, the not-quite-healed one, and the pain was a brief distraction. He would make it right. He needed to wipe the slate clean, to overlay that day with a new, better one.

The kettle rumbled. He looked again across the yard into her kitchen but there was no sign of her. It was getting dark. When she didn't appear he opened up the drawer next to the stove, the second one down with all the odds and ends: the dishcloths and the can opener, the cotton reels and paperclips. He felt around for the keys, the ones with the string looped through them, with *Steve and Mandy* written on a cardboard tag. He knew they were there, he'd only checked this morning, but he kept returning to them, rattling them in the cave of his cupped hand.

He spooned granules into a mug and lifted the kettle. He poured, missing the mug, and splashed scalding water over the counter and his bare foot. The pain was clean and thrilling, and in shock he thumped the counter with his broken bloody hand. Fuck it. Fuck it. He hopped across the room and back, found a damp cloth and threw it over his foot. It hurt more than his head, which was something. He sat and shut his eyes a moment, let the room spin slowly, let the worst of it pass. The cigarette he'd lit earlier had burned down in the ashtray so he lit another one and picked up the coffee, managed a sip and put it down before he burned himself again. His scalded foot was starting to blister. A livid red welt across the skin.

The coffee was harsh on his empty stomach but he sipped it

anyway. He had two calls to make and he needed to make them sober, to say the right thing. He'd come to hate the phone these past few months.

He took the coffee through to the lounge room. The TV was on – Harold Holt talking about Vietnam again. He turned it off. It was dark but he didn't want to open the curtains and look at the state of the place. There was a scrap of paper somewhere, a note he'd written to himself after he left Mandy's place, so he'd remember what she'd told him. He felt around on the couch, found a cigarette burn and a sock. He lay down, pushed his face into the filthy cavity behind the cushions and allowed himself the darkened, private knowledge that he would go to the bottle shop after he'd made these calls. He would replace the bottles he'd tipped down the sink. He would not be able to stop drinking and the best he could do was to manage it.

Sitting up, he looked at the phone on the coffee table next to him. The note was there, where he'd left it. He picked it up, dusted away the cigarette ash. But first he dialled the UK number from memory.

'It's me,' he said, when his wife picked up.

'Joe? It's early here. Everyone's asleep.'

'I can't live without you.'

A pause. He thought of Mandy, the way she'd lain back for him on her kitchen floor with her jeans around her knees. The way she'd unbuttoned her blouse that day; the way she'd held him by the neck. Her smell.

'I love you,' he said, with his head full of Mandy. 'I love you so much.'

'Do you mean that?'

Her voice offended him. He held the receiver away from his ear. 'Come home, Louisa. I'll make you happy if you'll come back. I'll stop drinking. I'll never drink again.'

'Will you forgive me?' she said.

'Of course I'll forgive you.'

He put the receiver down on the carpet when she started to cry. He waited, drank some coffee. He'd divorce her once she was back in the country with his daughter. He'd get a solicitor and throw the bloody book at her.

'We'll come back,' Louisa said, eventually.

'Do you mean it this time?'

'Yes,' she said. 'I love you, Joe.'

There was a moment of interference and then he heard her say goodbye. He cut the line off with his finger, muting the bell.

The second call would be easier. He picked up the scrap of paper and dialled the number he'd written down, next to the words he needed to remember: *Marlo. Beach cabin.*

'I want to report a crime,' he said.

43

Victoria, 1967

Steve woke early with the cold. William stirred beside him and he pulled the blanket up to cover the boy's chest and shoulders. He spread his jacket over the top – the good one he got for Christmas with the quilted lining. William gave a throaty murmur, sighed and slept on. Each morning it was a little cooler. The wind came in off the ocean, shaking the window in its frame and rattling the door. They wouldn't be able to stop here much longer.

He lay beside William and watched the light brighten through the gaps in the timber. This time of day was hardest. His head wandered off to dark places. He found himself remembering specific children, their names and their voices; the things they'd said when they figured out they weren't going on holiday, after all. Sometimes they all came to him at once in symphony, but mostly it was one at a time, with a clarity that made him want to rip his skin off. Today it was the boy with the pale green

273

eyes – Dale, his name was – who'd kicked and yelled for the first few hours and tried to jump from the truck when he'd told him the truth as they'd turned off for Kempsey. Steve lay on the bed feeling Dale's bare foot against his spine, kicking the back of his seat as he drove. The sound of him shouting and howling. Trying the doors.

William wasn't going to make up for it all, he knew that, but it was a start. He sat up straight in the bed, his back rigid at the thought of it. He was going to do right by this child. He would give him everything.

The boy shifted again and turned his head, his mouth pressed sideways against the mattress in a loose pout. There was a flush in his cheek, Steve thought. He held his hand to his forehead and felt heat there, not too bad but he lifted the covers off him just the same. The jacket had been too much, that was it. He put his milk in a pan and set a low flame beneath it.

He pulled the curtain back from the small window. The sun was up. A wide blue sky with nothing in its way. The beach was empty; just a few gulls down on the shore. They didn't see many people: the odd surfer, or the occasional tourist clambering down over the dunes from the road. The locals knew to avoid this stretch of water, where the Snowy River flowed out to sea, meeting waves ten feet high from the south. You never knew when the current would shift, when a southerly would pick up. More dangerous than beautiful, to most people's minds.

Mandy had loved it here. He'd brought her down to be

sure she was the woman he should marry, to see how she felt about this place that for him was perfect. She hadn't wanted to leave.

'Come on, then.' He lifted William onto his knee. His nappy was wet but he was hungry, so he let him drink his milk. 'Wait there,' Steve said, once he'd finished. He sat the boy down on the floor with the empty bottle. 'Let me get your clean nappy. Get you nice and dry.'

William sat with his legs outstretched and hit the bottle against the timber floor, laughing at the noise. Steve stood and watched him. He'd be crawling next. All that strength in his small body, all that life.

'You're getting big, mate,' Steve said.

The boy held one arm in the air and shrieked in reply.

'Getting noisy, too.'

William laughed. He had a helpless laugh when he got going. Steve leaned forward and tweaked his little nose between his fingers, making him laugh harder.

'You're a big, noisy bloke, ain'tcha?'

The boy fell quiet and his face became preoccupied. There was a bad smell.

'Oh, mate. You didn't.'

He did. The stink was something shocking. Steve opened the door and let a cool breeze in off the ocean. The clean nappies were strung out to dry at the window, so he lifted one down and caught a clear view of the beach. There was somebody there, crossing the sand. A man was walking towards them purposefully, looking up at the cabin, moving with great, slow strides. It was like looking at himself. Ankle boots, blue uniform; police badge.

Steve dropped the nappy to the floor. Fear thumped hard inside him.

William looked up at him and laughed, cocked his head, expecting a response. Steve considered, in a panic, whether he could hide the child, if he could keep the cop outside, if he could meet him on the beach. William squealed, loud and high-pitched.

The cop saw him through the window and quickened his pace as Steve made for the door. The latch was stiff; he pulled it down but he knew it wouldn't hold and there was no time to find the key. He heard the cop's feet in the sand, getting closer. His grunt of effort as he shoved the door from the outside. The latch snapped under his weight. Steve pushed back against him from the inside, feeling his equal force, his strength. The door inched open and the cop jammed his boot in the gap.

'Sorry, mate,' he said. 'You're going to have to let me in.'

The copper stood on the sand and caught his breath. His face was confused. Appalled. A white fella, holed up on a beach with a black kid.

'What's this about?' Steve let the door swing open and did his best to fill the doorway. 'This is private property.'

'We had a call,' the cop said, panting. He lifted his shoulder and wiped the sweat from his brow onto his sleeve. 'From Sydney. You got a little lad with you?' The cop looked past him into the cabin.

Steve heard William behind him, babbling to himself. The ocean crashed loud on the beach. The copper watched the boy, nodded once and returned his gaze to meet Steve's. He dug his thumbs into the small of his back. He was a big bloke, not in the best shape. He looked more tired than a walk across the beach should make you.

'He's a ward of the Welfare Board in New South Wales,' the cop said. 'Someone kicked up a fuss. Called a few times. We're tightening up the records.'

Steve considered charging past him, pushing him to the ground, running with the boy till he found a place to hide. But his legs were heavy; he could barely stand. 'This is temporary,' he said. 'This cabin. Just temporary.'

The cop looked at him blankly. A line of sweat ran down his face and dripped from his jaw.

'I'm waiting for my house to sell. We'll move on from here soon as the money comes through. Just a few more weeks.'

The cop shook his head and wheezed. 'My boss wants this kid out of his hair.' He thumped his chest with his fist and cleared his throat. 'Like I said, he's a ward of the Board in—'

'He's well cared for.' Steve's guts turned over. The cop was barely listening. He'd have seen people pull their hair out, soil themselves, drop to the ground and beg. 'He's like a son to me,' Steve told him. A wave broke on the beach, drowning out his words. 'I love him like my own son.'

Behind him, William started up a whine. The copper took in the size of the child; his weight and build. His nostrils flared with the stink of his nappy.

'Christ.' He leaned back from the door. Covered his nose. He turned his back, but Steve heard him. 'Filthy bloody animal.'

Steve stepped down onto the sand. He felt the insult personally. The shock of it returned the strength to his limbs, quietened his fear; reminded him that he was on the right side now. A cool breeze came in off the ocean and he breathed it into his lungs. He had to be smarter here, for William's sake. He was getting this all wrong.

'Look,' he said. 'I'm in this game myself. My dad was a cop before me and his dad before that.'

'You're a cop?'

Steve nodded. 'Nearly ten years, based in Sydney.'

'Why didn't you say?'

'You caught me off guard.' He jerked his thumb at William. 'I know this looks strange. He's a kid I removed myself a couple of months back. I got attached to him. I'm hoping to adopt him once I've got myself together.'

The cop looked at Steve a long time. 'It does seem strange to me, to be honest, mate.'

'I bet.' Steve managed to laugh.

'They didn't mention you were a cop when they sent me down here.'

'Must have been crossed wires somewhere.' Steve tried to swallow but his mouth was dry. 'You could call my boss, up in Sydney. Sergeant Perry. He's based at Parramatta. He'll vouch for me if you speak to him direct.'

He nodded slowly. 'He's signed this off, has he?'

278

'That's right. Got his permission before I headed down here.' He looked away, feeling the lie in his face.

'I don't know, mate.' The cop looked at his boots, weighing this up. 'Don't think I can walk away from here empty-handed.'

'Speak to Ray,' Steve said. 'You don't want to drive all the way up to Sydney with a baby if you can avoid it. Took me days to get down here with him, what with all the stopping and starting.'

William's whine became a wail. The cop turned and looked out at the steep face of the beach, the gulls settled on the dunes. There was no one about for miles. 'Maybe I'll leave it for today. Give you the benefit of the doubt.'

Steve gave him a nod, forced a smile. He gripped the door frame for support.

The copper looked at William with distaste. 'Do me a favour and keep him out of sight, would you? Don't go attracting attention to yourselves.'

'No worries,' Steve said.

'Sergeant Perry, was it? Parramatta?'

'That's the one, mate.'

The copper turned and started back towards the road, lifting his legs high to keep the sand out of his boots.

A call from Sydney. Steve let the phrase fill his head as he got the boy cleaned up. Mandy must have told them where they were. He needed to stay calm, keep that thought at bay for now. He wiped the boy down and noticed a rash across his belly and down his legs. Looked sore. He picked William up and felt the heat coming off his skin. Might be the start of a fever. He'd let him sleep a while. They'd have to wait till night-fall to load up the truck and get themselves ready to move on.

A call from Sydney. He sat on the bed and cried long and hard like a stupid bastard. William fell asleep on his shoulder, breathing hotly against his neck.

44

Sydney, 1997

The lights are on in every room when Isla gets home at midnight and the house has been turned upside down. She steps over a lamp which lies on the floor in the hall, its shade separated from its base. The table where the telephone stood has been turned over, upended on the carpet, surrounded by family photos, their frames smashed. Alongside them a ceramic jug lies cleaved open, its white belly exposed. She stands among the wreckage and wonders if she did this. It seems possible. She is three days into her relapse and the days are no longer distinct. She doesn't know where she's been, what she's done.

Each room in the house is ruined: broken crockery in the kitchen, the chairs turned over. Ornaments and mementoes crushed underfoot. In the living room, the TV is face down on the carpet. A bottle of Smirnoff lies empty on the couch. No sign of her dad. She doesn't know when she last saw him. He will be angry, when he sees this. She is alone here and she

Susan Allott

sometimes fears him. Everything between them has changed and the trust has gone. She doesn't remember why.

She picks up the phone and puts the receiver back in place. The answerphone is upturned beside it, flashing red, on and off. She stands beside it as the message plays. A British accent wants her to call him right away, regarding the apartment on Sinclair Road. It's urgent, he says. His voice is pompous. She hits delete.

There is a call she needs to make, something she needs to say. It fills her head. She lifts the receiver and dials the London number. The phone rings in the small flat in Hackney and she holds the phone tight against her ear, ready to hear Dom's voice.

'Hi,' the recording says. 'This is Dom and Isla's number. Leave us a message and we'll get back to you.'

She waits for the beep. 'Sorry,' she says. It makes her cry. She thinks of the mornings there was blood on the pillow. She broke his tooth the first time. Cuts and bruises. A broken nose. He never fought back. A good man, who tried to help her, and one morning he was gone. She listens to the message twice more and she tells him each time that she's sorry, she loves him, she hates what she did. What she is.

Pain wakes her in the early hours. She lifts her head and sees the broken jug, the lampshade. Her head pounds. In the bathroom she swallows painkillers, catching her face in the mirror above the basin. Sallow skin and pale eyes, like her dad's. She looks away, leaving an image in her mind of wild, outgrown hair: dark roots and brittle, copper-blonde streaks.

282

Isla leans into the bath and turns the tap for the shower. Pain fills her skull and she retches into the plughole. She strips, stands under the hot water and cries tears of self-pity, coughing and choking, her head pressed against the tiles. The last thing she remembers clearly is standing in Doug's front yard. The reluctance in his face as he told her what he'd seen. She stays there, replaying the conversation until the water runs cold.

She fills three black bags with broken crockery and crushed ceramics, eases photographs from cracked picture frames. She puts the lamp back together. By midday the house is clean, if damaged. She goes to her dad's hiding places and finds only empty bottles.

At lunchtime he walks through the door. She waits in the kitchen where she is cooking, drinking coffee, taking the day one minute at a time. He calls her name but she doesn't reply. He stays where he is. She hears him turning over the coins in his pocket; his cough. The strike of her knife against the chopping board.

'Isla?' He walks towards her. 'Isla?'

She wonders if he would hurt her, if he thought he'd lost her loyalty. If she would fight back. She imagines it: scalding coffee against his skin. Pushing him to the ground, her foot on his chest; her hand at his throat. She tenses with the possibility of it.

He pushes open the door. He looks gaunt. Almost sober. 'You cleaned the place up,' he says. 'I didn't expect you to do that.'

She stops what she's doing, holds the knife still. 'Did you smash the house up? Was that you?'

283

He looks down at his feet. 'I'm sorry you had to deal with it.'

'I thought it was me.'

He is surprised, confused. He pulls out a chair and sits down. 'I had a bad few days,' he says, looking around him at the clean surfaces. 'It won't happen again.'

She turns her back on him and slices through an onion. She sees herself in everything he does and it terrifies her.

'I got a lawyer,' he says. His chair scrapes against the lino and he stretches his legs out. 'They can't prove anything.'

45

Victoria, 1967

They'd have to move on today. As soon as the sun was up, he'd get their gear in the truck and get on the road. He'd wanted to wait until William's fever passed, so he was well enough for the long drive. But it hadn't passed. Steve knelt by the bed and moved his jacket up to cover the boy's shoulders. He might be a bit brighter when he woke. And they couldn't risk another day in this place. That cop could be back any time. He'd have spoken to Ray by now and Ray might have blown it, he wouldn't have known what to say. He might have told him Steve had left the force. His stomach turned at the thought of it.

He pulled a box out from under the bed. He was impatient, now he'd made his mind up. They could sleep in the truck until the money came through. They'd done it on the way down here, pulled over and grabbed a few hours, it wasn't too bad. William was sleeping a lot, these past few days. He'd barely woken, barely taken any milk. Maybe he'd take him to a doctor, somewhere they weren't looking for him. Kids got fevers all the time, he knew this; it was normal. He told himself not to worry. Don't get yourself worked up, Mandy would say.

It took less than ten minutes to fill the box. He grabbed clothes and nappies and the coffee mug he'd brought from home. He took the dishcloth and towel down from the hooks he'd hammered into the low beam at the back of the cabin, wrapped the cloth around his mug so it didn't break. He put William's bottles and his formula milk on top, where he could reach them easily. The last pack of biscuits and the instant coffee next to it. He looked at William, still and silent on the bed. He hoped to Christ he was going to be all right.

Mandy would know what to do. She'd know how to keep his fever down, how to nurse him. She'd know whether they should take the risk and get him to a doctor. He could see her now, giving him one of her scathing looks and picking the boy up, sorting him out with her calm confidence. And he despised himself for missing her, for the part of himself that wanted to forgive her, even now, after this betrayal on top of all the rest.

It was getting light. He lifted the jacket off of William, threw it on top of the other things in the box and stood there looking at him. A thought formed in his head, a terrible thought that made the cabin shrink around him. The boy was too still. Oh sweet Lord, he was too still. He dropped to his knees, lifted the sheets away with fumbling, slow hands, and picked him up.

William's head fell back. His arms were slack at his sides. Steve patted his face, lifted an eyelid to find a blank, sightless eye. He held the boy in his arms and shouted terrified, wordless sounds at the mottled rash across his skin, the floppy, unresponsive limbs; the resting beauty of his face. He was warm, still warm, but his body was limp and he had no strength in him, no muscle, no life.

He must have screamed. He heard a scream that must have come from himself, from his body. He laid the baby down flat, tried to bring him round, breathing into his mouth, pumping at his little chest, stopping only when he could not breathe himself, when his hope had gone and he needed only to hold him. He rocked him side to side, propped his head against his shoulder, but William's arms did not lift and his body was heavy and he was gone.

At some point Steve heard a sound against the door: a knocking that paused and repeated. He didn't know what it meant. Nothing held meaning beyond the four walls of the cabin. There was no future now. There was nobody else. He walked up and down with William, holding him close, shushing him, making soothing sounds in his ear. He knew the boy was gone but he could not bear it.

Sun streamed in through the gaps in the timber. The knocking at the door was louder now. Carefully, gently, he laid the child's body down on the bed and moved towards the sound.

46

Sydney, 1967

Joe let himself into Mandy's house through the back door. He locked it behind him, put the keys in his pocket and stood a while on the mat, taking in the room that still had her presence, her things left the way she liked them. Her open-toed gardening shoes by the door, angled the way she stood, with one foot in front of the other. Her apron on the hook; her pots and pans on the drying rack. One cigarette butt in the ashtray, smoked right down to the filter. You could almost convince yourself, standing here, that she'd just gone out to the shops.

He carried on through the house, walking in and out of the rooms, touching her towels in the bathroom; sitting a while in a chair where he found a newspaper with the crossword half done. He looked at the clues she'd filled in, the way her capitals strayed out of the squares. He'd never seen her handwriting before. There was so much they hadn't done together.

His head roared with whisky. It took a lot of whisky these

days to stop the shakes, to blunt the pain and regret. He longed to be blind drunk. To be oblivious. He'd strayed onto vodka, just once or twice in the mornings before work. There was no pleasure in it, but that wasn't the point any more. He felt his dad in him when he drank from the bottle and hid it behind the plumbing in the cupboard under the sink. There was nobody in the house to find the bottle but it was in his blood to do it this way, to become a furtive, careful, practised liar; an addict. He had fought it all his life and it had been futile.

In the bedroom he found it harder to forget she was gone. The lack of her was everywhere. He took his shoes off and lay down on the bed, lifting her pillow to his face. On the first inhale he caught the faintest hint of her, the clean smell of the vanilla soap she used. His hands closed around the pillow and he gripped it hard, pulled it close to his face and let out a painful, strangled yelp, the closest he could get to crying for her. All he'd wanted was to put things right, to make up for his mistakes and win her back.

He climbed under the sheets. When he woke the light had changed, the room was full of shadows. He stood and straightened the bedding, plumped the pillows. He pulled a blouse out of the wardrobe but it was too clean; it held the smell of the iron but nothing else. He picked up a hairbrush from her dresser; took the lid off of a lipstick and rubbed its brownish colour against his wrist. From a drawer he took a pink scarf, the one she wore in her hair sometimes. He wrapped it around his hand. It was exquisitely painful, the thought of her with her hair pushed back from her face, looking up at him.

He put the scarf back in the drawer. No mementoes. Louisa would be back any day and he was going to have to stop this. He couldn't divorce her, not now. He'd have to try to be the husband she wanted him to be. Some days he thought he could do it. He thought he might take comfort in her loving him. And by trying to love her back, maybe he could atone for all of this. Other days, he thought spending the rest of his life with the wrong woman might kill him.

In the kitchen he stood again at the back door and cast his eye across the room. He'd reached for the key, turned it in the lock, when he noticed Mandy's watch on the counter top, circling the salt and pepper. He picked it up, recalling how she'd worn it in the water the day he'd followed her down to the beach. That had been the sweetest time, the best it would be between them, if only he'd known it.

He put the watch in his pocket and locked her back door behind him.

47

Sydney 1997

The sky is dark and low over Agnes Bay and the beach is deserted. Rain is blowing in from the ocean. Isla walks into the water, glad of the cold violence of it, the insistence of the swell. She swims into the waves as they rise up and they drag her under, turn her body over, throw her out and pull her under again. She is not afraid. She gasps for breath, wrestles with the water; dares it to hurt her. Twice it flushes her onto the shore and twice she wades back in. She stops thinking after a long time. She doesn't know how long it takes, but finally she knows nothing but the ache in her limbs, the struggle.

She is surprised by the strength of the rip when it takes her. The fear is cold and sharp. The shock. She is farther from the beach than she thought and closer to the rocky headland that separates the bay from the open sea. Her legs are helpless against the deep, relentless tug and it will kill her if she struggles. It will take what's left of her strength and she will drown. She learned this as a kid: don't swim against it. Don't panic. Try to float, if you can. And like every other kid in the class she'd known that if it happened to her she would panic; she would fight it and she would die. She looks up at the sky and thinks, this is not what I want, after all. Not like this.

Her head goes under. She waits for the pain as her body hits the rocks. She waits for her skull to crack. She surfaces, gulps air into her lungs, goes under again and thinks she is dead now, she must be. She is so cold. The colours of death are ugly: green and pink, yellow and brown. They move before her eyes, viscous, rolling shapes, heavy and lolling. Fat, leathery petals like tongues.

Isla does not feel it when the rip lets her go. Wave after wave covers her, rotates her, throws her body down and backwards. She gives up. Her mind is tired. In the deep water, out beyond the break, she sees a darkened room. Her mother is on the bed, her father standing, the two of them struggling. She sees her mother draw her legs back, position her feet against his chest. She feels the power of the kick. It is a pocket of trapped energy, a dormant force, thirty years in the waiting.

She kicks. At the base of the wave, she kicks with all her strength. She surfaces, rolls onto her back, kicks again. Her mind is tired but her body is young and strong and her legs want her to survive, to kick angrily, repeatedly until her foot grazes sand. Then her knee, her elbow. She lies in the shallows and the sky clears above her, the rain stops. Her lungs contract and she coughs, retches, opens her eyes.

The beach is wide open before her. She vomits up saltwater, drags herself onto dry sand and retches again. At the water's edge, metres away, she sees her canvas shoes, her towel, soaked through but untouched. A gull lands close to her feet and picks at a dead crab. She tries to stand but her legs give way. Her head is heavy against the sand and the sun hurts her eyes. She lies still, shivering, coughing. The gull considers her and struts off.

It takes three attempts to lift the towel. Her hands have no grip. She manages in the end to throw it over her shoulder. She picks her shoes up and drops them again. They are too heavy; her fingers can't close around them. In the end she leaves them behind on the sand. At the foot of the coastal path she sits and gathers her strength. She watches the ocean for a long time.

The day is bright and calm when she reaches the top of the path, where the tea trees meet the backyards on the ocean side of Bay Street. Carol Taylor is out the back of her house, tipping the water out of her garden furniture. She stops at the sight of Isla and brings her hands to her face.

'Isla, dear God! You didn't swim in that, did you?'

Isla registers what she says but doesn't reply. She can't bear the sight of Carol, in her beige shirt and slacks. She misses Mandy, who was lively and magnetic. The sort of woman you noticed.

'Are you right, love?' Carol says.

Isla nods at Carol and looks straight through her to the kitchen, where Mandy used to sit at the table eating prawns dipped in vinegar, her nose peeling with sunburn. Isla knows now that Mandy disappeared from her life and nobody ever mentioned her. Her family grew around this need to forget. They worked hard at it, keeping busy, growing selfish, angry, disappointed. And beneath it all, was Mandy.

She pushes the back door open and stands on the mat. There are voices coming from the lounge room. She goes to the bathroom and picks seaweed from her hair, brushes sand from her skin. She takes a clean towel from the linen cupboard.

'You gave it to the police?' Her dad's voice. 'Did you want me locked up?'

Isla steps back into the hall, pushes the door to the lounge room open and finds her parents facing each other, her father standing, her mum on the couch. The room is a mess of coffee cups and ashtrays, fogged with smoke. On the coffee table, next to a stack of dirty plates, sits Mandy's watch.

Isla stands in the doorway. She wraps the towel tightly around herself. 'What's going on?'

Louisa looks up at her. 'Are you all right, Isla?'

'I'm fine.'

She stands. 'Are you sure? You look awful. Your lips are blue.'

'I'm fine, Mum.' She motions her mum to sit and joins her on the couch. Her dad is thin and drawn in his work shirt, his sleeves undone at the cuffs. He is edgy, twitchy, in the sore place between drunk and hungover. 'What happened?' she asks him.

Joe stabs a finger at the watch. 'Your mother wanted me in prison,' he says. 'She gave this watch to the police—'

'I know.' Isla cuts him off. 'Mum wanted the police to have it, in case it was important.'

Joe scratches at his jaw. He nods, slowly. 'You were both in on this, were you?'

Isla goes to speak but the shivers have returned and her jaw is chattering noisily. She gives a small nod.

'The police returned the watch,' Louisa says in her no-nonsense voice, her hands pressed together between her knees. 'They did all that DNA business and they can't prove it was Mandy's.'

'That's a shame,' Joe says, looking from Isla to Louisa and back. 'That scuppered your plan, didn't it?'

Isla rubs at her arms. Sensation is coming back to her fingertips, making them ache.

'Why are you here, Louisa?' Joe pushes up his shirtsleeves.

'I thought you'd want the watch back,' Louisa says. 'I thought you'd be missing it.'

'You waited till I got home.'

'I wanted to see you.'

'Why? Did you want to needle me?' Spittle flies from his mouth. 'Did you want to provoke me? Is that it?'

Louisa gets up and steps around the coffee table. 'I have something to say to you.'

'What's that?'

She stands square before him, chin up, shoulders back. 'I loved you for a very long time.'

He flinches, as if she had slapped him.

'Decades of my life,' she says. 'I gave up everything to come out here with you. I left and came back because you promised you'd change. You said you couldn't live without me. Remember that? And that was a lie.'

He draws breath to speak and she steps closer.

'Don't even think about denying it. Don't you dare deny it now.'

He rocks back onto his heels, away from her.

'I want to hear you admit it!' Louisa shouts, pushing at his shoulder with the flat of her hand. 'I know you aren't going to tell me what you did to Mandy or where she is. But I want you to admit that you lied to get us back here. And you let me feel guilty for taking the money. For trying to save myself.'

Joe runs his fingertips over the lines in his face, the grooves between nose and mouth. He nods.

'Say it!' Louisa screams at him, pushing at his chest.

'It's true,' he says, in a low voice.

Louisa pushes him again, with both hands this time, and he staggers backwards, falling into the armchair behind him. He looks up at her, sparrow-like.

'It's true,' he repeats.

'You bastard.' Louisa kicks at his shins, arms outstretched.

'Mum.' Isla gets up from the couch. She wants to scream but her lungs won't fill. 'Don't!'

Louisa turns and drops her arms. She is dry-eyed, her chest heaving.

'Leave him alone,' Isla says. She has a loud ringing in her ears. She can barely hear herself. 'I'm not going to stand here and watch you attack him.'

Louisa smooths her dress down, catches her breath. 'He's a liar. Just remember that.' She points at the watch. 'He's been lying for thirty years.'

Isla sways. Her limbs ache. 'Leave him alone.'

'Come with me,' Louisa says.

'I think you should leave.'

'What will it take, Isla? When will you stop defending him?'

Isla sits again, before she falls. She doesn't hear the front door click shut, or her mother's car pull away from the front of the house.

48

Sydney, 1997

Isla gets to Circular Quay as the Manly ferry is docking. She pushes through crowds of commuters, women with toddlers; day trippers. It's cold and bright, and the water is lit up by the sun. The Opera House gleams on Bennelong Point. She turns her back on it, walks up Argyle Street and stops on the corner of George Street outside the police station. Sydney's skyscrapers stand tall before her.

She pushes through the doors. At the front desk, a female cop has her arms wrapped around a stack of files. A couple of documents start to slide free and she bends her knees to catch them. The phone starts to ring beside her. 'Can I help you?' she shouts.

'I need to see Inspector Perry,' Isla says.

'What's it about?'

'Amanda Mallory.'

'Who?' She has neat, red hair that curls under her chin. 'Could you repeat that?'

'Amanda—' The phone stops ringing and Isla finds she is shouting into a quiet waiting room. She lowers her voice. 'It's regarding Amanda Mallory. Can I speak to Inspector Perry, please?'

The cop heaves the files back up her chest. 'Hang on,' she says, and carries them through to a back office, leaving Isla alone in the waiting area. Through the door she's left open Isla sees a bank of grey filing cabinets and a corkboard covered in notices. She smells cigarettes and reheated soup. She wants to retch.

'Miss Green.' Inspector Perry stands before her with his radio hissing at his belt. His freshly clipped moustache. 'How can I help you?'

'I have a few questions,' she says. 'Can we talk somewhere more·private?'

He lifts a side panel and nods for her to follow him. They pass more filing cabinets, boxes of paperwork, desks with files stacked across them. At least three telephones are ringing, each at a different pitch. He leads her into a large, windowless office and shuts the door.

'Please sit down,' he says, without looking at her.

Isla sits down opposite Inspector Perry. His desk is wide and deep. Mahogany trimmed, with a leather inlay. At the far side of the desk is a large black telephone. At the other end, a mountain of paperwork divided by metal trays. His chair is higher than hers, she notes.

'I wanted to ask about the body,' she says. 'The body that was found on the beach here in Sydney thirty years ago.'

'Yes.' He takes his glasses off and rests them on the table in front of him. 'What about it?'

'Was it Mandy? The body – was it her?'

'No. The Maroubra body turned out not to be a match for Mrs Mallory, after all,' he says, with an indifference that Isla does not believe. He returns his glasses to his face. 'They were the same age, height and so forth. But it seems the Maroubra woman had given birth.' He waves his finger at a non-existent window, as if the beach at Maroubra might be visible beyond the wall. 'Mrs Mallory's medical records showed she had no children.'

'Why did you call my dad and tell him you'd found Mandy's body?'

'We believed at the time—'

'You called him before you checked Mandy's medical records.'

'We may have been a little hasty.'

She sits forward in the chair. 'You were trying to scare him. You knew you didn't have Mandy's body but you thought you could force a confession.'

'That's a strong accusation, Miss Green.' He tugs at his cuffs. 'I can assure you that's not the case.'

The strip lighting flickers overhead.

'Are you still searching for a body?'

'None of the records in New South Wales were a match.'

'What does that mean?'

He smiles, as if she were a slow learner. 'It means we're closing the case.'

She is briefly speechless. Inspector Perry sits back in his seat.

'Aren't you searching outside of New South Wales?'

'No need.'

'Don't her family want the search to continue? Her husband?'

'Mr Mallory believes his wife is alive.'

She laughs. She doesn't know if she is relieved or shocked or something else. The case is closed. She can get on a plane, go back to her life.

'Steve thinks Mandy's alive?'

'He made a statement to that effect.'

'When?'

'Few days back. He contacted the station with some new information. It seems Mrs Mallory withdrew funds from a Sydney branch of the Commonwealth Bank early in 1968, shortly after their house was sold. She took a large sum out as a cash withdrawal. We checked the bank records. The amount matches.'

'How do you know that was Mandy?'

'Steve had moved away. He didn't return to Sydney.'

Isla thinks Inspector Perry is less bored than he appears. There is something sharp behind his weary disinterest. She thinks of Steve, close to tears that day in Ropes Crossing, saying he thought Mandy was dead.

'Why didn't Steve mention this before? He seems to have changed his story.'

'Miss Green, I'm not sure you understand.' He leans across his desk. 'It's over. Your father is in the clear. I'm grateful to your family for their cooperation. I know it hasn't been easy.'

The strip lighting ticks and buzzes. Isla stares at his tower of paperwork. The mahogany and leather of his desk.

'It's been a relief to Mrs Mallory's family. Her brothers. They've accepted that she chooses not to be found.' He spreads his hands out across the desk. 'I'm sure your mother will find it a comfort. I heard she was distressed by the police enquiry.'

'How did you know about that?'

'Mr Mallory contacted the station, like I said. He mentioned your visit to his place of work. He was sorry to learn of your mother's distress.'

'I see.'

He smooths his moustache with his fingertips. 'With the money she withdrew, Mrs Mallory could have left the country.' He says it in a fresh tone, smiling, as if she had just walked into the room. 'She could have settled overseas, changed her name. I'm sure she's living life to the full, wherever she is.'

Isla nods. It's over. She feels waves rising up, covering her head.

His radio bursts into life at his belt. 'I'll show you out, Miss Green.'

Isla stands, pushing her chair away. The radio cuts out, leaving a sharpened quiet where the noise had been. 'I'll see myself out,' she says.

49

Sydney, 1997

Andrea waves at Isla from the beach. She looks radiant, even from this distance, striding through the shallows in gumboots and cut-off jeans, her hair tied up. Her son runs alongside her in the wet sand. Isla waves back, shouts hello, although in honesty she'd been hoping to have the beach to herself. It's too early for small talk, for the questions about Isla's parents, the answers to which will be relayed back to Andrea's parents. The details of Andrea's perfect life. She wants to walk and think and enjoy the winter morning while the sun is low in the sky.

'Didn't know you were sticking around,' Andrea says, shouting over the wind.

'I didn't plan to.' Isla stands beside her and looks out to sea. 'I'm leaving next week. Back to the grindstone. My boss has filled my diary already.'

'You good with that?'

'Don't know.' She digs her heels into the sand. 'Can't put my life on hold forever, can I?'

Andrea lets foam wash over her boots. 'I was glad to hear Mrs Mallory's alive and well.'

'I know. Such a relief.' Isla smiles. It calms her to breathe the salty air and to think maybe it is as simple as that. She's alive and well. The questions in her head quieten.

'I went straight down the station, once I heard the things people were saying,' Andrea says. 'I said to Ray, I know I was only a kid, but I was out on my bike all the time, up and down the street. I noticed things, you know?'

Isla turns to her. 'Who's Ray?'

'Sorry, the cop. Ray Perry. Inspector Perry, these days.' She leans down and wipes her son's nose with a balled-up tissue. 'My parents know him from way back. He was the local cop when they first moved here.'

'This is the same cop who's dealing with Mandy's case?'

Andrea nods. 'I know he was as shocked as the rest of us, to think something might have happened to her. That's why he took the case. He wouldn't normally do the legwork himself.'

Isla stares back at Andrea. A gull calls out overhead. 'Did he know the Mallories back then?'

'Ray was Steve's boss,' Andrea says. 'Steve's been a mess since he left the force, apparently. Had a nervous breakdown, spent a bit of time in a mental health unit in the seventies.' She pulls a long face. 'Never got over the marriage breakup, Ray reckons.' She crouches down to take a chipped piece of abalone from her son. 'That's nice,' she tells him, turning it over to look at the colours on the inside. 'That's a beautiful shell, my love.'

'What was it you noticed?' Isla says. She watches the boy run off down the beach, stiff-legged in his red gumboots. 'You said you noticed things, when you were out on your bike. What did you notice? I can't shift this feeling Mandy might be dead.'

Andrea straightens up. 'I saw Mandy leaving,' she says. 'She left and started her life over. I saw her go.'

'When was this?'

'A few days before my birthday, in March. I remember it was early in the morning and I was out the front of the house by myself. I saw Mandy on the footpath. She waved at me.'

'This was in '67?'

'That's right. Not long after Steve Mallory buggered off in his big green truck and left his wife standing in the street. That was the talk of Agnes Bay for a while.'

'But Mandy was leaving that day? You're sure?'

'Yep. She stood beside me on the footpath and we chatted while she waited for her taxi. She said she was going to Marlo.'

'Marlo? Where's that?'

'No idea.' Andrea shrugs, pushing strands of hair out of her face. 'She didn't look so good, I remember that. And she was kind of sad, you know? But she said it would all be right when she got to Marlo.'

'Marlo sounds familiar.' Isla looks out to sea. 'Why does Marlo sound familiar?'

'Probably because I named my cat Marlo. You remember, the ginger tom? We had him for years.'

'Of course. That's right.'

'I got him for my birthday that year, when I turned ten. That's why it always stayed with me, I guess.'

'You're sure the cops know about this?'

'I went down the station to speak to Ray after your dad's birthday party,' Andrea says. 'There was a bit of gossip that day, once everyone was on the grog. I said to Ray, I was the last one to see Mrs Mallory, not Joe Green.'

Isla hunches her shoulders against the wind. 'The cops treated my dad as a suspect for weeks after that.'

'Did they?'

'They didn't say you'd seen Mandy leave.'

'Maybe it's because I was a kid back then, they think I got it wrong.'

'Maybe.' A wave wets Isla's feet and she steps back onto the dry sand. 'Do you remember much about Steve Mallory?'

'I was scared of him.'

'Were you?'

'All the kids were. Don't you remember?' She looks away, distracted by her son and a wet springer spaniel.

'Yes, I do,' Isla says. 'Why d'you think we were scared?'

'We all thought he was going to bundle us into his truck.' The spaniel runs to the far end of the bay, where its owner is walking towards them, waving a stick. 'My mum used to say, he doesn't take kids from nice families.'

'Did she?' Isla thinks this might be funny if it were not so unspeakably sad.

Andrea swoops and picks her child up from the sand, seconds

before the spaniel returns, faster and wetter than before. 'You can't take your eyes off them, can you? Not for a minute.' The boy wails in Andrea's arms.

Isla smiles and kicks at the sand.

'We should get back. Good luck in London if I don't see you.' Andrea turns away, her son crying on her hip.

Isla walks the full length of the bay, stands a while on the flat boulders at the base of the headland. Then she walks back against the wind, head down, hands deep in her pockets. She lets water soak into her boots. She feels sand and salt in her skin, in her hair. The sun rises in the sky.

50

Sydney, 1997

'Inspector Perry can't see you right now,' the female cop says, calling out across the waiting room. 'Sorry about that.'

'I can wait,' Isla says.

'I think he'll be a while.'

'I've got all day. It's important.'

'Is it regarding Mrs Mallory?' The phone rings on the desk beside her. She lifts the receiver and replaces it. 'You were here about her case last week.'

'That's right.' Isla recognises her: bobbed red hair. A look of veiled exasperation.

'The case is closed,' the cop says. 'I was looking at it earlier. We've been transferring all our closed cases onto a computer database.'

Isla holds out her hand. The cop hesitates. Her eyes glance over Isla's windblown hair.

'Isla Green,' Isla says, extending her arm across the desk.

'Sergeant Karen Dent.' She shakes Isla's hand. 'I'm not sure I can help you.'

'It's all right. I think I can help you.'

Sergeant Dent smiles. 'How's that?'

'I don't think Mrs Mallory's alive.'

Her smile falters. 'Why not?'

'She followed her husband down south, a week or so after he left. To a town called Marlo, in Victoria. I spoke to my dad about it earlier. He remembers the Mallories had a beach cabin down there.'

'Does he?' The cop lifts her eyebrows. 'Is he claiming to have witnessed Mrs Mallory leaving?'

'No. But my neighbour did. She spoke to Mandy as she waited for a taxi.'

Sergeant Dent nods. 'A woman called Andrea? Would have been nine or ten at the time?'

'That's right.'

The cop breathes in, displaying great patience. 'I don't think she could recall the exact date she saw Mrs Mallory.'

'It was a few days before her tenth birthday. Doesn't that narrow it down?'

'Do you remember the days running up to your tenth birthday?'

Isla leans forward across the desk to relieve the ache in her limbs. Her toes sink into her wet boots. 'Mandy told Andrea she was going to Marlo. Andrea got a kitten for her tenth birthday a few days later, and named it Marlo. She must have had that cat for twenty years.'

'I don't think there's a mention of her cat in the case notes.'

Isla looks pointedly at Sergeant Dent until she stops smiling. 'So you're not accepting Andrea's evidence?'

'We have evidence Mrs Mallory is alive. Whether she went to Marlo or somewhere else is irrelevant.'

'You're prepared to accept Mandy withdrew that cash from the Commonwealth Bank in '68?'

'I have no reason to question that.'

'Did you check it out yourself?'

'No.' Sergeant Dent shifts her weight from one foot to the other.

'Mandy didn't withdraw that money.'

'What makes you think that?'

'She didn't have a job. She had no money of her own. It's unlikely she had joint access to her husband's bank account.' Isla straightens up. She thinks of her mother, standing in the rain. 'I think Steve Mallory's lying.'

'The case is closed.' There is hesitation in her voice. A chime of doubt.

'I'm sure your case notes are very thorough,' Isla says. 'I'm sure there's a record of that withdrawal. And a confirmation from the bank that it was a joint account.

Sergeant Dent presses her lips together. The telephone rings in the office behind her. Someone laughs.

'Shall I tell you something I found interesting in Mrs Mallory's case notes?' She tucks a strand of hair behind her ear. 'I typed up an interview with your father that took place a couple of weeks ago, after a body was found that appeared to match Mrs Mallory's profile.'

'It didn't match her profile,' Isla says.

'But you're aware of the interview that took place?'

'Sure.'

'Are you aware your father stated, before his lawyer intervened, that he had some memory loss around the time of Mrs Mallory's disappearance, due to his alcoholism? He isn't sure, on reflection, that Mrs Mallory went down to Victoria with her husband.'

Isla nods. She feels a rush of fear.

'He has some recollection of being with Mrs Mallory in her home after her husband left. He admits he didn't take it well when she lost interest in him. And he admits he had a spare key which he used to access her home uninvited.'

Isla steps back from the desk. She runs her hands through the gritty roots of her hair.

'I imagine your father didn't mention that to you.'

Isla shakes her head.

'His lawyer stopped him, of course. We didn't get a confession. And without a body it might be difficult to convict.' She tilts her head. 'Are you all right, Miss Green?'

Isla feels the movement of waves, lifting her up and pulling her under. She needs to lie down.

'Can I get you a glass of water?'

'No, thanks.' She waits for the room to realign itself. She puts her palms down flat on the desk. 'I think you should reopen the case.'

'Your father would remain a suspect if we did that.'

'I'm not here because I think my dad's innocent,' Isla says. 'I'm here because a woman is dead.'

Sergeant Dent frowns at her. Isla rocks in her damp boots. She feels a little better.

'We need to think of our resources,' the cop says. 'We'd need to reallocate personnel.'

'Maybe you could find someone who isn't an old mate of Steve Mallory to lead on the case.'

The cop's skin flares red at her neck. 'What did you say?'

'I think you heard me.'

The blush spreads across her face. 'I'm afraid I have to get back to work.'

'Are you going to reopen the case?'

'Unlikely.' She steps back from the desk. 'Maybe it's time you moved on from this, Miss Green. Better all round.'

Isla lets the door slam shut as she leaves. She walks out onto George Street and heads towards the city, with the Harbour Bridge behind her. Australia Square is set back from the street, its concourse busy with office workers and shoppers, tourists, residents of the luxury apartments above the retail space. From the apartments at the top you can see across the whole city; an unbroken view, her dad told her, back when he was the construction manager in charge of the site and this was the tallest building in Sydney. Isla remembers the opening ceremony: her dad picked her up from school and she stood beside him on the new concourse in the shadow of the tower. The mayor cut a ribbon and talked about the Eora people who once lived here, before there were buildings and streets and traffic. Only a small number survived, he said. It caused a murmur among the crowd, an uncomfortable pause. She doesn't know why it has stayed with her.

She passes tables with wide umbrellas above them, people eating sushi and calamari, drinking cold white wine, laughing. She keeps walking.

51

Victoria, 1967

He wished he hadn't let Mandy hold the boy. She wouldn't let up sobbing and howling, slapping her hand against the timber floor where she sat with William's body lain out across her lap. Steve felt nothing. It should have been a comfort to find her at the door, but her presence was more of an irritant. He wished to God she would shut up.

'I should have come sooner.' She lifted her knees and brought William's small body to her chest. 'There's three buses a week. I should have left Tuesday. I don't know why I waited.'

Steve lifted the curtain and looked out. The waves were dark and low, coming in from the south-west. They'd have a pull on them, he knew. The river was fighting with the current not far from the shore. No surfers risking their necks out there.

'Tuesday was when he got sick,' he said.

'Was it?'

'Same day the police turned up.'

She sniffed and wiped her face with her sleeve. 'What?'

'You heard me.' He let the curtain drop.

She sniffed again, and her voice was high. 'When did it happen? When did he—?'

'He was breathing fine when I went to bed last night.' He didn't look at her. 'I always check him when I go to bed.'

'I know you do.'

He forced the words out. 'He must have died in the night. In the early hours.'

She got herself to her feet and laid the boy down on the bed. 'I wanted to hold him again. I wanted to ask you to forgive me and let me stay.'

He shook his head at her. 'Cover him up.'

She hesitated, brought her hands to her face. Then she pulled the sheet over William, smoothed it down, stroking the small mound of his head. 'What have we done?' She turned to face him. 'Steve, what have we done? We were meant to give him a good life.'

'Don't!' He shouted it. 'Don't say that! He'd be alive if it weren't for you.'

She wiped her face. 'What did you say?'

'I said, he'd be alive if it weren't for you. If you hadn't gone to the police, I'd have been able to get him to a doctor.'

Sea spray hit the window behind him. He stepped closer to her.

'Steve. I didn't go to the police.'

'Don't lie to me.'

'I'm not lying!'

He hated the sight of her, wide-eyed and mocking, like he was a fool. 'A copper turned up here.' He gestured to the door. 'He wanted to take him there and then. He told me –' he saw her flinch as his voice rose, '– they got a call from Sydney. Someone called from Sydney and let the police down here know exactly where we were.'

'It wasn't me.'

'Nobody else knew we were here, Mandy. It's not like this is the first place you'd look, is it?'

Her eyes changed. 'Oh Jesus,' she said.

'What is it?'

She looked at her feet. 'Oh God.'

'What?'

She turned from him and sat down beside William's body.

'Did you tell the police, Amanda?'

'No. But I might have told—'

'Who?'

'Nobody.' She covered her face with her hands. 'Nobody. I got confused.'

He stood behind her. She was lying again. He reached out and grabbed a fistful of her hair, jerked her head back so he could see her face. 'Who did you tell?'

'You're hurting me.' She tried to twist out of his grip. 'Let go of me, Steve. What are you doing?'

'Answer my question.'

She stood up and faced him, gripping his wrist where he had a hold of her hair. 'I'll answer your question when you let go of me,' she said, through her teeth. 'And not before.'

He gave her hair another tug before he let go. Rage surged in him. He stepped closer to her and she backed away. Every fibre of him was ready to blow if she said that name.

'I think I mentioned it.' She looked at him defiantly, without apology. 'I think I might have told Joe.'

He'd seen that look on her face before, in his own kitchen. A look of remorseless betrayal. He should have dealt with it then. He hit her hard, his fist meeting her face. Harder than he'd hit anyone in his life. Her head flew back and she hit the wall with a thud.

'Get up,' he said. He stood over her as she slumped to the floor. 'I said, get up.'

She moaned, something low and angry. Still she did not sound sorry. She opened her eyes.

'Get up, Mandy.'

She got to her knees. Blood ran from her nose. 'You know what, Steve?' She stood and pushed her hair from her face. 'You were right. You're not the good guy.'

He hit her again with all his strength and she landed hard, cracking her head against the beam. She tried to stand. For a second she stared at him, furious and unrepentant. Then she lost her footing, staggered sideways and fell to the ground. He stood over her.

'You have no right speaking to me that way!' He roared into

her face and all his rage rose up, years of it, flooding his head, his body. 'What makes you think you can speak to me like that?'

She let out a moan.

'Are you listening to me, Amanda?' He kicked at her chest, because she always did this. She left him alone when he wanted to talk to her, when he needed her to listen. He never could get through to her. 'Will you listen to me, for God's sake?'

She did not respond. He kicked her harder, again and again. He wasn't going to let this drop, not this time. He wanted to fight with her, to finish what they'd started.

'Mandy?' She was silent and still. He straightened up and caught his breath. The cabin was very quiet. He did not want quiet. He looked down her and bellowed loud enough to kill the moment, to stop this from being the end.

'Mandy?'

He knelt beside her, pushed her hair away from her face. The anger dropped clean out of him, leaving fear in its place, cold and sickening. Her eyes were half open, her lips parted. He held his ear close to her mouth. She might be unconscious, he thought. She might be breathing still.

'Mand?' He spoke softly, gave her a gentle shake. Blood ran from her ear, down her neck.

Steve stood, turned away from her, walked the length of the cabin and back. He didn't want to look at her, lying there with her head slumped forward, her body twisted. He was cold, sweating. He faced the wall and shouted aloud that she shouldn't have looked at him like that. She should have shown some respect. She had pushed him too far; she had taunted him.

But the rage had gone. He could no longer recall what she'd said.

He lay down beside her. It was Joe Green who'd caused this. He should have known. It had been a shock, hearing his name, hearing her say it. It had made him do this terrible thing.

He held her hand as her blood spilled out across the floor. He closed his eyes.

The sky was darkening over the ocean. He stood in the sand with William's body in his arms. Sea spray flew into his face. He'd known, before Mandy turned up, that this was what he would do. The thought had come to him, clear and undeniable, puncturing his grief. He walked out to the rocks where the water was deep and the current turned beneath the surface, kissed the boy, lowered him into the water and let him go.

He did not howl at the dark shape of William's body before it was swept away. He turned his back on the ocean and held onto the horror, pushed it down, because he was not done yet. The rocks were slippery under his boots and he fell, picked himself up and kept moving, ignoring the pain. There was a job to be done and it was best to get on with it. *Get the job done, Steve. It's not meant to be easy*. Who had said that? He reached the sand and a wave hit him from the side, sucking at the shingle as he moved across it. It would be hard to carry her body back up this way, to haul her onto the rocks and let the current take her. To see her pulled under. She never liked the water.

319

The wind took his scream away and he leaned into it, kept walking, unsure if he was screaming still. The hardest part of it was, he knew he could do it. The job would be done. He ran the length of the beach and went inside the cabin for his wife.

52

New South Wales, 1997

Isla stops the taxi on the street outside Scott's double-fronted garage. It's seven-thirty in the morning and the neighbourhood is quiet. Palm trees and ornate gateposts. Not a sound. She's been awake since five, waiting for the right moment to arrive, to catch him before he leaves but not so early as to irritate. She has rehearsed what she will say and how she will say it. Her heart gallops with nerves and caffeine.

'Nice place,' the driver says.

Isla counts notes into his hand. She smiles and nods. Scott's house is not the grandest in Bellevue Hill but anyone familiar with the suburb could figure that from his second-floor verandah he has a panoramic view of Rose Bay. They might assume he has a pool at the back of the house and possibly a tennis court. And they would be right.

She climbs the steps to his front door and rings the bell. For a minute there is no response and then a window above her slides open. From the balcony she hears her name.

'Isla? What happened?' Scott leans over the steel railing, his shirt open at the chest, holding a glass of orange juice.

'I'm all right,' she says.

'Hold on. I'm coming down.'

She steps inside when he opens the door. The entrance area is twice the footprint of her London apartment, with white marble flooring and an open staircase that curves towards the upper floors. The entire rear wall is floor-to-ceiling windows, looking out over the pool.

'I'm all right,' she says again. 'Everything's ok. Really.'

He looks at her doubtfully. His face shines from his morning shave.

'Sorry it's so early,' she says.

'Come in. Join us for breakfast. Ruby's in Singapore but Mum's home.'

'I'd rather not.'

'What's going on?'

'I need to go back to Ropes Crossing.'

He looks up at the ceiling. 'What for?'

'I need to speak to Steve Mallory again.'

'I thought that was over with. I thought we could all move on.'

'It's not over with.'

He shuts his eyes, breathes very deeply. 'Mum called that cop yesterday. She spoke to him and he said the case was closed. They think she's alive.' He rubs his thumb and forefinger, reaching for her name. 'Mandy. She's alive.'

'I heard that too,' she says. 'It's bullshit.'

'For God's sake, Isla.' He crosses to the staircase, shirtsleeves flapping. 'Look, I can't take you out there, if that's what you're hoping.'

'I can't stop thinking about it.' She follows him to the foot of the stairs. 'I think they closed the case to protect Steve.'

He looks at her like she's unhinged. 'Why don't you leave it? Dad's off the hook. Things are better left as they are.'

'I don't think so.' She stands beside him. He smells of soap, deodorant, shampoo. 'I'm going back to London next week and Dad's drinking himself into a hole. Mum's left him. A woman I cared about as a kid is dead.'

'None of that is your fault.' His face softens. 'You look like shit. Let me get you some breakfast, would you?'

'I don't want breakfast.'

'Have you been drinking?'

'No.' She shakes her head and the ringing in her left ear stops. 'I'm sober. I swear to God.'

He puts one socked foot on the stair above. 'I'm sorry, but I can't help you. I need the car. I have a business to run. People who rely on me.'

Behind him, Isla sees her mother through the ceiling-height windows, walking towards the pool in cream silk pyjamas and a matching dressing gown. She's holding a mug of coffee, treading slowly, her feet bare.

'Why don't you hire a car?' He stops to button his shirt. 'I can drop you at the rental place in town.'

Isla watches her mother walk around the pool, pausing to

look up at the house. She had hoped Scott wouldn't make this suggestion.

'I can't hire a car,' she says.

'Why not?'

'I lost my licence a while back.' She says it in the level voice she has rehearsed all morning.

'You lost—?'

'Don't lecture me.'

'Were you over the limit?'

She looks down at the grey swirl through the white marble floor and nods.

'When was this?'

'Six months ago. No one was hurt. But I wrote off the car.'

He is quiet until she looks at him. 'You could have killed someone. Or yourself.'

'I know, Scott. I'm so ashamed about it.'

'I should hope you are.'

She feels his disgust. She doesn't have the guts to hold his eye. She is grubby and useless in his bright, clean house.

'I need to get to work,' he says, climbing the stairs. 'I can't help you, Isla.'

'You can't or you won't?'

'Both,' he says, without turning round.

'Ask Mum!' she shouts after him, standing at the foot of his staircase. 'Ask Mum if she believes it.'

No reply. From the first-floor landing she hears a door close.

'Thanks a bunch!' She shouts it across the expanse of marble, into the domed cavity of the roof.

Sydney's well-groomed business class is waking up. Isla walks through the streets as they leave their houses, back their sleek cars out of gravel drives and head for the city. They eye her curiously: a black-clad woman with outgrown hair, lace-up boots, nowhere to go. She glares at them, hot and angry, a misfit, a black sheep. She is lost, which is just as well. She'd be in a bottle shop if she knew where to find one.

Behind her a car sounds its horn. She ignores it. She passes under palm trees and thinks she'll head for the coast. The houses are grander now, set back from the street. Sculpted lawns, pillars, ocean-facing balconies.

The horn sounds again and a car pulls up at the edge of the road. A metallic blue Ford Laser with its bumper bar hanging low on the passenger side. 'Get in!' Louisa shouts through the window. She leans across and opens the door. 'Come on. I'll take you to see Steve, if that's what you want.'

Isla stands a moment on the footpath. She loves her mother's car for being old and ugly, so incongruous in this suburb that she almost laughs.

'Get in,' Louisa says again, lifting magazines and carrier bags from the passenger seat. Isla catches a glimpse of her pyjama shirt, its silk collar visible under her jacket.

'Are you sure?'

Louisa revs the engine. 'For God's sake, get in.'

Isla lowers herself into the car, ignoring the grit in the stitching of the seat. Something yields softly in the detritus beneath her feet and she kicks it aside. Louisa accelerates. She's wearing a long green trench coat over her pyjamas. Isla has never in her life seen her mum leave the house looking so dishevelled.

'I didn't sleep last night,' Louisa says.

'Why not?'

She checks the mirror, changes gear, glances at Isla over her glasses. 'Mandy didn't withdraw that money.'

'I know.'

She taps the steering wheel. 'Why would Steve change his story like that?'

'That's what I want to ask him.'

'Have you spoken to Inspector Perry about it?'

'I spoke to his colleague, Sergeant Dent. She's as bad as him, in her own way.'

'What do you mean by that?'

'Neither of them want to know.'

Louisa stops at the Ocean Street crossing and lets the traffic pass. 'I can't understand it,' she says. 'Inspector Perry was so thorough.'

'He was Steve's boss, Mum. They kept in contact after Steve left the force.'

'That doesn't mean anything.'

'I think they tried to get Dad convicted. And when that fell apart they closed the case.'

The lights change and she moves forward. 'I don't believe that for a minute.'

'I do.'

'You've always had a problem with authority.'

Isla draws breath to reply and thinks better of it. She counts very slowly to ten. The sky clouds over as they drive through Edgecliff, across town and over the Harbour Bridge. The water is dark and choppy, the Opera House dour without the sun. They pass Luna Park, where Scott cried as a kid, terrified by a ride that held them to the inside wall of a large, spinning barrel.

'The Rotor,' Louisa says, as if Isla had spoken. 'I had to take him home.'

'I loved it,' Isla says. She'd stayed behind with her dad after her mum and Scott left and he'd let her go back on the ride. She'd never felt so brave and reckless and proud.

'You know the marriage is over, don't you? Whatever happens.'

'Yes.'

'He's not going to stop drinking.'

Isla looks out at the freeway, seeing nothing, wishing she'd stayed on the other side of the world, where her family had made sense to her. She'd been able to love them from that distance.

They head west, away from the city, speaking only to check directions or to comment on the traffic. Louisa holds the slow lane all the way, the steering wheel shuddering, and Isla looks out at the telegraph poles, recalling Scott's expression as he stood on the stairs in his socks, asking if she'd been over the limit. He fuses in her mind with Dom, the way he turned away from her, appalled, sick of her apologies. The wearing thin of love. She needs a drink like never before.

'Do you like your job?' Louisa says out of nowhere.

'Mostly.' Isla turns, and her eyes fall to her mum's feet. She's wearing cheap plastic thongs and her toenails are painted red.

327

'I'm good at it, I think. It forces me to be patient. Hours go by and I hardly notice.'

'Do they treat you well?'

'I can't complain.'

'Good money?'

'Not bad. I had enough saved for the deposit on an apartment. To buy a place. But I let it go.'

'You don't have to buy an apartment,' Louisa says. 'I know that's what everybody does in London. Doesn't mean you have to follow.'

Isla shifts in her seat. 'Are you giving me advice?'

'You don't have to take it.'

It's a bit late, Isla thinks, brushing crumbs out from under her jeans. 'I'll bear it in mind,' she says.

The traffic going into Sydney, on the far side of the freeway, has ground to a halt. It stretches into the distance: trucks and convertibles, buses. The freeway heading west is clear, open road as far as they can see, straight and endless, featureless. Isla twists the radio dial on the dashboard but can't find a signal.

'It's broken,' Louisa says.

Isla sits back in her seat. She suspects her mother wants to make conversation. She needs a drink.

'You know, I had a place at university,' Louisa says. 'I was going to study history, at Leeds. I'm not sure I ever told you that.'

'No. I'm sure you didn't.'

Across the freeway, from the midst of the congested traffic, a car sounds its horn, long and hard.

'I was going to have a career.' She laughs. 'I wasn't going to turn into my mother. Endlessly cleaning and cooking, looking after everyone else.'

Isla turns to Louisa, who is looking at the road ahead. A truck passes them in the outside lane and the car sways in the slipstream.

'Dad must have been very persuasive,' she says. 'To change your mind, I mean.'

'He was.' Louisa fights a small smile. 'He certainly was.'

'And then he didn't measure up.'

Her smile fades. 'That's one way to put it.'

'No wonder you were—' She daren't say it in case her mum pulls over and leaves her at the side of the road.

'Angry,' Louisa says. She checks the wing mirror. 'Miserable. Resentful.'

Isla looks at her hands. 'I might have felt the same.'

'That's generous. Thank you.' She lets another truck pass. 'I'm sorry, Isla.'

'It's all right.' She shuts her eyes so she won't cry.

'I don't blame you for hating me. The things you saw.'

'I don't remember much.'

'You were too young. You saw too much and you turned against me.'

Isla shakes her head. 'Don't.' One day she will ask her mother about what she saw. She will wait until she's ready, a day in the future when she is not so raw with it and her body does not scream for alcohol.

'I wish I'd done it all differently,' Louisa says. 'I wish I'd protected you.'

The tears come then and Isla wipes them with her sleeve. 'You should've gone to university.'

'Don't say that.'

'You'd have been a good student. I can see that. You'd have been happier.'

Louisa feels around in the side of the door for a pack of tissues and throws them to Isla. 'I thought I'd be happy, running off to Australia with your dad. We were going to leave all the old ways behind in England. It felt adventurous, like anything was possible.'

Isla blows her nose. 'How long did that last?'

'I was pregnant with Scott when I realised my life was going to be shaped by my husband. His choices, his decisions. Anything *was* possible, but only for him.'

Isla thinks of her dad, out cold on the couch with his shoes on, his face alert in sleep. She sees him in the white rage of his hangover, lashing out, clearing ornaments from the dresser with the sweep of his arm. She can't picture him sober or smiling. When she sees his face he is flushed with drink, his eyes fogged. Blood on the couch, on the carpet. Scott screaming.

She stares out the window at the white bark of the gums, their precise shape against the sky. There is an ache in her chest where something has shifted, something that has always held her upright.

'Turn off here,' she says, just in time.

Louisa makes the turn and the road narrows, the fibro houses appearing at the side of the road. Isla directs her to the community centre where Steve works. A few cars are parked outside already. Isla spots the woman who works at the front desk climbing the steps to the entrance and passing through the glass double doors.

They sit in the car and stare up at the building. Louisa buttons her coat and tucks the collar of her pyjamas out of sight. A red ute parks across the street and a man gets out, opens the boot and lifts out a crate full of files. He is short and broad, bald-headed, in the same blue checked shirt and jeans.

'That's him,' Isla says. 'That's Steve.'

Louisa leans forward. 'So it is,' she says. They watch Steve walk up the steps into the building. 'Are you sure about this, Isla?'

'No. But I don't know what else to do.'

'He was always such a decent man.'

'I'm not sure about that.'

'He had a horrible job to do. He always hated it.'

'I don't think that lets him off the hook.' Isla unfastens her seat belt. 'Come on.' She gets out of the car. Behind her she hears her mum slam her door shut, her thongs slapping against the bitumen. She waits, and they walk together into the reception area. The rows of plastic chairs are empty.

The receptionist swings around, considers them both, unsmiling. She runs a hand over her bleach-blonde hair. 'We're not open yet,' she says.

'I wondered if we could speak to Steve Mallory,' Isla says.

The receptionist leans forward, elbows on the desk, her hands clasped in front of her. 'Did you make an appointment this time?'

'I'm afraid not.'

'He's busy. Staff meeting at nine for an hour. Sometimes overruns. Could be a long wait.'

'I think Steve will want to see us,' Isla says.

'Don't tell me, it's urgent.'

'It is.'

'You gotta get back to London.'

'I do.'

Behind her, Louisa clears her throat. 'Do you mind if I use the bathroom?'

The receptionist takes a moment to respond, taking in Louisa's outfit; reaching around her molars with her tongue. 'We're not open,' she says, finally.

'We'll get back on the road once I've been to the loo,' Louisa says. 'Only I really need to go. Sorry.'

She rolls her eyes. 'Through the double doors and on the right.'

Isla smiles at the receptionist as her mum leaves them alone. The lanyard pass around her neck reads *Valerie*. Isla takes a leaflet from the desk and uses it to swat a fly.

'Sit down if you want,' Valerie says.

Isla sits near the doors at the back of the room and watches the ceiling fan rotate. Valerie sings to herself, low and melodic. From somewhere inside the building, Isla hears a man's voice: a tone of surprise. She can't make out his words.

She stands. Valerie is preoccupied, folding a letter into an envelope. Isla slips through the double doors, into a dark corridor with rooms leading off it on either side, the doors closed. Another corridor branches off to the right, leading to more meeting rooms and offices. Halfway down, a door stands open.

'Why did you do that?' Louisa says, from behind the open door. 'Why did you say she'd withdrawn that cash?'

Isla looks through a glass panel to see Steve standing by a long, narrow table, his crate of files at his side. Her mum stands facing him.

'I thought it might be best,' he says. 'I thought it might be comforting to her family. And to you.'

'I don't need to be comforted.'

'Your son said you were upset by the police enquiry.'

'I'm upset you told a pack of lies about what happened to your wife.'

His face changes. He remembers a different Louisa, Isla thinks. One who didn't fight back.

'Why did you do that? Your wife is missing. Why did you want the case closed?'

'Look, can we talk later?' He looks anxiously around the room. 'This is a bad time.'

'You haven't answered me.'

'I spoke to Ray,' he says, rubbing the back of his head. 'I called Ray and he agreed it might be kinder all round if—'

'Who's Ray?' Louisa says, raising her voice, stepping closer to him when he doesn't reply. Isla knows this moment, where her mother's switch trips. She can't see her face, but she can see the aggression in her stance, and Steve's defences going up. He won't crack now, Isla thinks. Not like this.

'I thought you'd be glad to have it put to rest,' Steve says, taking a stack of papers from a file.

'What happened to Mandy?' Louisa says.

He tries to move past her. 'I've told the police all I know about that.'

'You told Ray, you mean? Is he a friend of yours, this Ray? Is he the cop who's leading the case?'

'I need to get to a meeting.' He pushes past Louisa and through the open door, where he collides with Isla, sending his papers across the grey carpet.

'What the hell are you doing here?'

Isla waits as he gathers his paperwork. Louisa comes to stand beside her, incensed. Isla holds a hand up to quieten her. She looks down at Steve, crouched at their feet, cornered and scared. She needs to be careful, she thinks. For once in her life, she needs to be calm.

'There's something I forgot to ask you when I was last here,' Isla says.

'I told you what you need to know.' Steve stands, clutching his papers to his chest. 'I'm not going over that again.'

'Do the people you work with know about your past? The kids you removed?'

He looks past her. From the waiting room at the end of the corridor they hear Valerie singing, a little out of tune.

'I'm doing a good job here, Isla,' he says. 'Trying to make up for all of that, as best I can.'

'Do they know?'

'One or two of 'em do, yes. It's not something I'm proud of.'

'Do they know about the baby you kept for yourself?'

'The baby—?' For a second there is agony in his face. He shakes his head. 'What do you mean?'

'You took a baby and kept him. A baby boy,' Isla says, hiding her own surprise. She hadn't quite believed it until now. Behind them, the singing stops.

'You got your wires crossed, Isla,' he says. 'I don't know anything about a baby.'

'He was one of the kids you were meant to remove. An Aboriginal baby. You took him home instead.'

'Where'd you get that idea?'

'My dad told me. He remembers the baby. Hearing him crying.'

'Your father's a drunk, Isla.'

'That's true.'

He pauses, bemused. 'And he's a liar.'

'He took everything from you,' Isla says.

'That's right.' His papers bend against his chest. 'That's right.'

A set of lights switch on at the far end of the corridor. Voices in the distance. Isla feels the balance of the moment roll back and forth.

'He broke up your marriage.' Isla glances at Louisa, who is shocked and silent at her side. 'He told a lot of lies and got away with it. He kept his wife and family.'

Steve nods. 'I'm glad you understand that.'

'I think that's why you wanted to blame him, for killing your wife.'

The lights switch on overhead. 'I think you should get out of here,' Steve says.

'Did Mandy follow you down to Marlo?'

'Did you hear me?' He moves to push past them. 'Get out of my way.'

Isla does not move. 'Is that where you killed her?'

'I said, get out of my way!'

He barrels past them, his head down, and Isla lands with her back against the wall. At the turn of the corridor, Valerie stands waiting. Her bleached hair is yellow under the lights.

'Steve?' Valerie takes a step towards him. 'What's all this?'

'Sorry, Val.' He laughs, catching his breath. 'Got waylaid. We can start now.'

Valerie looks at the two women, then back at him. 'I heard what they said.'

'I can explain all that.' He strums his papers with his thumb. 'It's not the way it sounds, Val. Why don't we—?'

Valerie looks at Steve with a sadness that cuts him off. He shrinks a little, bowing his head.

'We trusted you,' she says.

He stays where he is when she walks away.

53

Leeds, 1967

Grandma slapped the top of the TV with the palm of her hand. Stripes were moving sideways across the screen, left to right. She slapped it again, harder, and a picture appeared: the *Blue Peter* ship. Grandma stepped away from the set and the stripes came back, moving up towards the top of the screen in a great rush.

'God in Heaven!' Grandma gave the TV a final whack, harder than before. The stripes thickened and slowed, and the picture blinked into clarity, this time with sound. 'Look at that!' Grandma did a dance on the rug with her arms in the air. 'I've got the magic touch,' she said. 'Did you see that?'

Isla sat forward on the couch. It was her favourite presenter, John Noakes, the one with the nice face who made her think of Daddy. He said he was going to make a luxury dog basket out of a washing-up bowl. From the hallway her mum was calling, asking for help with her suitcase.

Grandma sat down next to Isla on the couch. 'It's a shame we don't have a dog,' she said.

John Noakes had put the washing-up bowl on a piece of foam and was drawing around the edge of the bowl with a marker pen. Mummy was shouting again from the bottom of the stairs. She was packing to go back to Australia. They were leaving later today to go home.

'I'd better give her a hand,' Grandma said. 'Don't touch the set, d'you hear? It'll explode one of these days and we don't want you going up in smoke.'

Isla nodded, her eyes on the TV. John was putting the foam into the bottom of the washing-up bowl to make padding for the dog basket.

'Have you tried sitting on it?' Grandma said, talking to Mummy in the hallway. She shut the door behind her and in the same moment the stripes reappeared across the TV screen, rushing downwards this time.

Isla stood. From the hall she heard Grandma saying *I wish you wouldn't go.* Isla moved closer to the TV, willing it to work. She was going to miss the best part, where he showed you how to finish off the dog basket using a length of elastic and a stretch of material.

He's no good, Grandma said. *Haven't I told you he's a bad 'un.*

Isla summoned her strength, lifted her arm high and brought her palm down hard and flat on the top of the set, as she had seen Grandma do. The stripes widened temporarily, but the picture did not come back. Her hand stung.

Mummy and Grandma were talking more quietly now. Isla

raised her arm again and lowered it with greater force than before, delivering an almighty smack to the wooden frame. Her whole arm was throbbing now. She clutched it and watched as the screen went blank, apart from a tiny white dot in the centre. A high-pitched noise grew from somewhere at the back of the set, getting louder and higher as the seconds passed.

'Grandma!' Isla moved away from the TV in quick, backward steps. 'It's going to explode!'

There was no reply. Isla opened the living room door to find her mum kneeling on the suitcase. It was a new one: a big grey oblong that she'd bought because she wanted to take things with her. Grandma was sitting on the floor with her legs out straight, trying to close the metal clasps.

'The TV's broken,' Isla said.

Grandma didn't look up. 'Did you touch it?'

'No,' Isla said, miserably. Her arm was still hurting and she was scared by the thin, high sound coming from the TV.

'Are you sure now?' Grandma gave up on the clasp she'd been pressing down on. Mummy stood up and the suitcase sprang open.

'I didn't,' Isla said.

Grandma pushed herself up against the bottom stair and stood, pulling her apron tighter at the back. 'You'll have to leave some of these things behind, Louisa. It's a suitcase, not a bus.'

Mummy stared at the case as if it had done something wrong.

'Let's have a look at the telly,' Grandma said. She followed Isla into the living room and switched the TV off. The high noise faded away. 'Let it cool down a while.'

Susan Allott

Isla wished she had thought of that.

'I think I heard you give it a whack,' said Grandma. 'Didn't you?'

Isla's skin became hot all over. 'No,' she said. She felt the lie as a big, quaking mass, pushing its energy into her limbs, making her more than a small person who was not yet five.

'I heard you,' Grandma repeated. 'I'm only fifty-two, lovey. I've all my faculties intact.'

Isla gripped her aching arm. 'Sorry,' she said, and she was small again, and not important.

'Why did you fib?'

'I'm not a good girl,' Isla said. She addressed the striped pocket of Grandma's apron.

Grandma knelt down in front of her so they were almost the same height. Isla put her hands into the pockets of her dungarees and let Grandma look at her.

'What in God's name makes you say that?' She squeezed Isla's face between the palms of her hands.

Isla did not reply. She made her hands into fists and pushed them deeper into her pockets.

'What is it now?' Grandma said. 'Tell me what's the matter.'

Isla didn't know how to explain what the matter was. She knew she had enjoyed hitting the TV, and she was only sorry about it because she was missing her show and her arm hurt. And she knew – this was worse than her aching arm – that Grandma was talking about Daddy when she'd said what she'd said. *He's a bad 'un.* She swayed forward within the clamp of Grandma's hands.

'Am I a bad 'un?'

340

'No, lovey. You are not,' Grandma said.

'But what if I am?'

Grandma dropped her hands into her lap. 'We have a way of dealing with this, where I come from.' She turned sideways and put her ear close to Isla's mouth. 'Tell me your worst secret. Go on. Say it very quietly. I won't tell a soul.'

Isla leaned in close against Grandma, who was warm and smelled of buttered toast. She considered what to say. She could tell Grandma that she did not like this big, cold house where everything creaked and shook. That she would be glad to leave. But she had a feeling Grandma knew this already and besides, it wasn't exactly true. She would not be glad to leave, because Grandma would be left behind.

Grandma tapped her ear. 'Out with it,' she said.

'I like Mandy more than Mummy,' Isla whispered. This *was* exactly true, and she knew it was very bad.

Grandma tapped her ear again. 'Don't you have anything worse than that?'

'Not really.'

'Well then.' Grandma turned to face her. 'Your secret will stay here, in my house, and I'll keep it safe for you. All right?'

Isla nodded.

'She must be terrific, this Mandy, is she?'

Isla nodded again. She would go and see Mandy when she got home and she would tell her everything about England. She tightened her fists inside her pockets. Wanting to go home was like waiting for your arm to stop hurting. If you thought about it too much it made it worse.

'You're nowhere near as bad as me,' Grandma said, standing back up. 'I'd say this calls for a dozen Hail Marys and a biscuit.'

In the hallway, Mummy had somehow got the suitcase shut on her own. She was sitting on it, with her hands resting on her huge, round belly.

'I wish I lived up the road in Sydney,' Grandma said. 'I could pop over to see you every day and we could get on each other's nerves, like normal people.'

'But you won't come,' Mummy said. 'Will you?'

'Haven't we been over this a hundred times?'

Mummy put her face in her hands.

'I hope to God I'm wrong,' Grandma said, and she led Isla by the hand into the kitchen.

54

Sydney, 1997

Isla stops at the top of the coastal path to look down at the beach. It's windy down there and the waves are crashing in from the south. The sand is covered in seaweed and foam, driftwood; a large hunk of polystyrene. It's not the best morning to say goodbye. She stands for a moment breathing the fresh air, but the wind is too strong. She walks through the yard, kicking through the long grass, and lets herself into the house.

Her dad is in the kitchen, dressed for work. She moves around him, making coffee, tidying. He's hurt that she's leaving and too proud to say so, or to admit that he'd hoped she might stay. He's making a big effort, keeping a lid on the drinking, burying his empties in the bin. Her mother's house rules have been wordlessly reintroduced, despite her absence. Soon he will have no one to hide from. She is leaving him to face himself and she is more glad than guilty. Her bag is packed and waiting by the door.

She puts the radio on and tunes it to something neutral; a feature about a charity auction. Her dad lights a cigarette and opens the back door. The wind blows his smoke back inside and he holds the door open with his foot.

Princess Diana will be auctioning seventy-nine of her most lavish dresses, the radio announces.

'Generous of her,' Joe says. 'Hope she won't be left with nothing to wear.'

Isla turns the volume down low and the news of the auction buzzes quietly from the corner by the toaster. She sits at the table with her coffee and thinks of the basement flat in Hackney where she will open the windows and clear out the things Dom left behind. She will look for a new place, somewhere bright and airy. She will replace her lace-up boots.

'You sure you want to go back to London?'

The question disarms her. She'd expected him to dance around it a while longer. She'd planned to tell him she was conflicted, sorry to leave but also ready.

'I'm sure,' she says, instead. 'It's where I want to be, for now.'

'You could find work here. We have television in Australia.'

'I like London, Dad.'

'Don't know why.'

'You've never been to London.'

'We went through on the train, on the way to Southampton docks. That was enough for me.' He reaches for the ashtray and the back door slams shut behind him. The wind bends the trees at the rear of the yard.

'I thought you might decide to stay,' he says, sitting down.

She blows on her coffee. 'Maybe I'll move back one day.'

'No, you won't.' He rests his ankle on his knee. The smoke from his cigarette fills the room. 'I wanted to say, before you go.'

She waits. He's visibly shaking. His chest wheezes as he exhales.

'I'm sorry you got dragged into that business over Mandy,' he says. 'I didn't want that to happen.'

'You should have told me all of it from the start.'

'I didn't want you to know.' He looks at a place behind her head. 'Those weeks after Steve left, when Mandy was next door without him. That whole mess.'

'What whole mess do you mean?'

'I didn't take it well, when she lost interest. I should have backed off.' He taps his cigarette into the ashtray, although no ash has built up. 'I think I scared her.'

Rain blows hard against the window. He coughs and beats at his chest.

'Do you think you drove her away? Down to Marlo, I mean. To get away from you?'

He's pale when he looks at her. His skin is waxy. 'It's the last thing I wanted,' he says.

'But you did.'

'I think so.'

She puts her coffee down. It would be easy to console him. It would mend things between them. She shuts her eyes and sees ghost gums at the side of the road, their white bark and clawed branches. Blood on the couch, on the carpet.

'It's Mum you should apologise to,' she says.

'Too late for that.'

'I don't think so.'

'She won't forgive me.'

'That's not the point.'

He can't meet her eye. 'I should never have asked you to come home. I should have kept you out of all this.'

'I'm glad I know,' she says.

'Are you?'

She leans across the table towards him. 'I don't want to be like you.'

'Isla.' He reaches for her hand and she pulls back.

'I want to live as far from you as I can. I want to be as different from you as I can be. I'll do it if it kills me.'

He sits back in his chair. The radio plays a jingle, an ad for shampoo. Isla lets the moment stretch out. She has a weightless feeling, of shock and relief. She daren't speak in case she takes it back.

'That's probably for the best,' he says.

She stands, goes to the tap and drinks a glass of water. It's raining in gusts outside.

'What time's your flight?'

'Not till five.' She can't see his face. 'Scott's taking me for lunch first.'

'I'll head off to work in a minute.' He is formal, abrupt. 'Make sure you lock up behind you.'

She stays where she is, next to the radio and the clean plates in the drying rack. There is a loud knock at the door, an unfriendly rap. Neither of them moves.

'Is that your brother?'

'It can't be. Too early.'

He walks from the room without fully standing up, his shoulders stooped. She hears him talking to a woman on the doorstep, asking her inside. Isla turns the radio off and listens. She thinks she knows the woman's voice.

'This is Sergeant Dent,' Joe says, returning to the room.

Sergeant Dent nods at Isla, a little sheepish. 'We met.'

'Tea? Coffee?' Isla pulls out a chair. 'Will you sit down?'

She sits. 'Coffee. Thanks.' She smooths her hair, which is damp from the rain. 'I have some news,' she says.

Isla fusses with the percolator as the cop sits down. She thinks of the dark London flat, all those weeks ago; her dad's voice on the phone, talking about a woman he used to know. Across the room, Joe asks Sergeant Dent to continue.

'Steve Mallory gave himself up,' the cop says. 'He came into the station and confessed to killing his wife.'

Isla turns to fill the kettle, gives herself a moment with her back to them both. She has the ache of an old wound. It makes no sense to be floored by it now, when she's known for so long that Mandy is dead. She hears her dad exhale, and when she turns around she sees her own shock in his face.

'When did he confess?' Isla says.

'Early last week. Not long after your visit to his workplace. He was—'

'How did Mandy die?' She doesn't mean to interrupt, to snap. 'Sorry. Could you tell us what he told you?'

'Mr Mallory physically attacked his wife. She died from her

347

injuries.' The cop sits back in her chair, looks at them both. 'We found blood at the beach cabin in Marlo. The floorboards had been covered over but the stains were still visible under-neath. We ran some DNA checks which confirmed it was Mrs Mallory's blood.'

'Jesus.' Joe seals his mouth with his hand.

'We're searching through the records in Victoria for her body,' she continues. 'But we're not holding out much hope.'

'Why not?' Isla says. 'Can't Steve tell you what he did with her?'

'He took her body down to the ocean. The currents are dangerous on that stretch of beach. A body disposed of in those waters might not come back to shore.'

Isla waits next to the kettle as it boils. She thinks of Mandy's blood in the boards of an old beach cabin, covered over and undiscovered. Her body lost at sea. The huge silence that allowed her to disappear.

'Nobody looked for her,' Isla says. 'Not for thirty years.'

Sergeant Dent gives a sympathetic smile. 'It does seem extraordinary.'

'It does.' Isla smiles back at her. 'How long has your boss known about it?'

'I don't know.' She doesn't blink. 'I tried to check the records, for the bank withdrawal Steve Mallory referred to in his state-ment. It turns out the bank doesn't keep records going back that far.'

Isla lets this sink in. 'What does that mean?'

'It means that evidence was fabricated.' She looks away, shifts in her chair. 'Inspector Perry's taken some leave. He's thinking about early retirement.'

Isla laughs. There is an uncomfortable pause. Joe goes to the door and stands facing the yard, his thumbs in his pockets. He swears quietly. The glass rattles in its frame.

'Can I ask you both a question regarding Mrs Mallory?' Sergeant Dent takes a notebook from her pocket. 'It's just a small thing. It might not be important.'

Joe turns around. 'Go ahead.'

'Mrs Mallory's medical records suggest she had no children. Is that correct, to your knowledge?'

He nods. 'She never had kids.'

'You're certain?'

'Absolutely.'

'That's what we thought.' She makes a note. 'Thank you.'

'Why do you ask?'

'Mr Mallory said something which didn't quite make sense. He was very distressed. It's probably not important.'

Isla pours water into the percolator. 'What did Steve say?'

'He said they had a child.'

'Did he?' Joe stands straighter. 'What else did he say about that?'

Sergeant Dent puts her notebook into her pocket. 'I'm afraid I can't tell you any more.'

'I think you can,' Joe says.

'It's a sensitive matter, Mr Green.'

'Why's it sensitive?'

'I can't—'

'Did something happen to the child?'

'I really can't say.'

'Was it a boy?'

She eyes Joe speculatively. 'How did you know that?'

'I reported it, thirty years ago,' Joe says. 'I called the police and told them Steve Mallory took a child with him down to Marlo. An Aboriginal boy.'

The cop recoils. She tucks her hair severely behind both ears.

'It's not a small thing,' Joe says. 'It's important. I remember that kid.'

Sergeant Dent retrieves her notebook from her pocket. She looks from Isla to Joe. Everything slows down. Joe finds coffee cups, rinses them out, pulls out a chair. He is calm, measured; certain. His better self. Isla will think about this for a long time. It will be the memory she goes to, long after she has settled down and he is gone. She will think of the charge in the room, the sound of coffee dripping through the percolator, the cop with her notebook on her knees. It will come to mind sometimes when she smells his brand of cigarettes. She will nurture it, this moment, at the expense of the others. And she will think, he was not all bad.

Author's Note

People often asked me, when I told them I was writing this book, why a British writer like myself was writing a novel set in Australia. I usually replied that I had spent some time living in Sydney in my twenties and wanted to write about this beautiful country that was never quite home for me, despite my best efforts. I sometimes explained that the book was originally about a British woman called Louisa who left Australia for England due to her overwhelming homesickness – I was trying to tell her story, which was close to my own, and found myself telling a different story in the process. What I didn't often say, maybe because I didn't want to admit my ignorance, was that in writing and researching this novel I was educating myself about Britain's relationship with Australia and our colonial past. Having married an Australian, I'd come to realise I didn't know enough about it. The English state schools I attended in the 1980s didn't teach us about the violence our ancestors inflicted on Australia's First Nations people when the colony was settled. What I knew about Australia, despite studying twentieth century history at A-Level, was limited to the fictions of Ramsay Street and Summer Bay.

Australians of my generation tell me they were taught a narrative of Australian history in which the white settlers were brave pioneers, taming the wilderness and building a land of opportunity. The anthropologist W.E.H. Stanner, in his 1968 lecture 'The Great Australian Silence', talked about a partial view of history in which the experiences of Aboriginal and Torres Strait Islander people had been disremembered:

'It is a structural matter, a view from a window which has been carefully placed to exclude a whole quadrant of the landscape. What may well have begun as a simple forgetting of other possible views turned into a habit and over time into something like a cult of forgetfulness practised on a national scale.'

The silence in Australia appears to have lifted since Stanner's day. The narrative of white settlement has widened to include the massacres that occurred in the aftermath of colonisation in 1788, and the often brutal treatment of the First Nations people who survived. But in Britain I'm not sure this is the case. It seems I'm not alone among my British friends in this knowledge gap around Australian history and our part in it. A look at the current history syllabus options for British schools suggests not much has changed. One secondary school department head I spoke to confirmed that Australian history is not covered at all at his state school in the English Midlands, other than a brief mention of the First Fleet.

The forced removals of Aboriginal children depicted in this book took place after Australia became an independent nation in 1901. Nothing to do with the British, then? Except that the policy is underpinned by the ideology of the motherland. As Geoffrey Robertson QC wrote in 2008:

'Historical wrongs can not be put right by belated apologies unless there has been a genuine attempt to understand – then remember and condemn – the thinking behind the policies that have had such appalling results . . . For this reason, the UK Government should find a way to endorse the apology to Australian Aborigines, for whose suffering Britain has been in part responsible.'[1]

For anyone wanting to know more about Australia's Stolen Generation, I would recommend the National Library of Australia's *Bringing Them Home Oral History Project*, where the voices of hundreds of Australians have been recorded. The majority of those voices are people who were themselves removed as children, or whose family members were removed. Another moving account can be found in the film *Rabbit Proof Fence*, based on the novel by Doris Pilkington Garimara. The following information, derived mainly from the 1997 *Bringing Them Home* report, may also be helpful.

The Aboriginal and Torres Strait Islander people of Australia who were forcibly removed from their families during the period from 1910 until 1970 are known as the Stolen Generation. Nobody knows exactly how many Aboriginal children were removed from their families in this time. Many records have not survived, and many of those removed in childhood are now deceased. It is thought that there are people removed in childhood whose Aboriginality is not known, even to themselves.

The Australian Human Rights Commission has estimated that between one in three and one in ten Aboriginal children were forcibly removed from their families and communities. The Commission states that most Aboriginal families have been affected, in one or more generations, by the forced removal of one or more children. Children removed in this way were placed in institutions where they were at heightened risk of physical and sexual abuse.

Prior to 1940, Aboriginal children were removed on overtly racial grounds, with lighter-skinned children being targeted for removal in the hope they might lose their Aboriginal identity and 'merge' with white society.[2] From 1940 onwards, the removal of Aboriginal children was governed by Child Welfare legislation. To justify removal, children had to be 'neglected', 'uncontrollable' or 'destitute'. These terms were applied more readily to Aboriginal children than non-Aboriginal children, and poverty was often conflated with neglect[3].

In May 1967, Australians voted in a referendum which proposed two amendments to the Australian Constitution relating to Aboriginal people. The amendments were overwhelmingly endorsed and became law in August 1967. Consequently it became possible to count Aboriginal people in a census for the first time. A federal Office of Aboriginal Affairs was established and grants were given out to the states for Aboriginal welfare programmes.

In 1969, the New South Wales Aborigines' Welfare Board was abolished. The Aboriginal Homes at Kinchela and Cootamundra were closed soon afterwards, but the Aboriginal Home at Bomaderry in New South Wales was operational until 1980.

The *Bringing Them Home* report was the outcome of a national inquiry into the separation of Aboriginal and Torres Strait Islander children from their families. The report was tabled in Federal Parliament in May 1997. Over 600 Aboriginal people who had been removed as children, or who were the children of people who had been removed, were interviewed for the report. The report recommended that official apologies be made, acknowledging responsibility for the laws, policies and practices of forced removals.

In 2008, Australian Prime Minister Kevin Rudd issued a national apology to Australia's Stolen Generation. As yet, no apology has been made to Australia's Aboriginal and Torres Strait Islander people by the British government.

Notes

1 Geoffrey Robertson, 'We should say sorry too', *Guardian*, 13th February 2008
2 'Bringing Them Home, National Inquiry into Torres Straits

Susan Allott

Islander Children and their Families', Australian Human Rights and Equal Opportunities Commission, p. 25
3 'Bringing Them Home, National Inquiry into Torres Straits Islander Children and their Families', Australian Human Rights and Equal Opportunities Commission, p. 28

A note about language
The language used throughout this novel reflects the language of the period in which the novel is set and the views of some characters for whom racist attitudes were ingrained. Some of this language is not considered appropriate today, but is given in its historical context.

Acknowledgements

I sometimes look back and wonder how I managed to write this book. For most of the years it took me to write it, I was juggling a day job with bringing up young children. I was also learning how to write, which any author knows is a dispiriting experience, the words on the page never matching the brilliant thing we hold in our head. The answer is, I drew on the support around me, and there was a lot of it. I couldn't have kept going without the people who helped and encouraged me, and I'm enormously grateful to them all.

In particular, I want to thank the friends, family and colleagues who read the early drafts and gave kind and helpful feedback, even when those drafts were slightly dreadful. Thanks to Sheila Pallier, Charlotte Spencer, Catherine Rose, Nicki Bowman, Ed Elias, Emily Elias, Tilly Wright, Kit Hui and the Faber Academy gang, and of course my most steadfast writing buddy Francesca Jakobi. My thanks go out also to the talented teachers I was lucky to work with: Marian Husband, Edward Docx, Debi Alper, Emma Darwin, Esther Freud and Stephen Carver.

Huge thanks to my multi-talented agent Nicola Barr, who helped me to hone my story into the book I was trying to write all along, and took it out into the world with such energy. Many thanks also to Amelia Hodgson and the rest of the team at The Bent Agency for their ongoing support.

Thank you to my brilliant editors, Suzie Dooré in the UK and Kate Nintzel in the US, for their belief in *The Silence* and their considerable skill in bringing out its potential. Thanks to Ore Agbaje Williams, Rachel Quinn, Simeon Greenaway, Vedika Khanna, Ploy Siripant, Liate Stehlik, Jennifer Hart, Gena Lanzi, Molly Waxman, Jeanie Lee and the rest of the team at HarperCollins for their part in designing, producing and raising the profile of the book. Many thanks also to Caroline Ast of Belfond and to Ilaria Marzi of Harper Italia, for the wonderful French and Italian editions.

I'm grateful to Nadia Hanafi and Philippe Kerampran for their kind support with my author website, to Jon Bent for his input to the Author's Note, to Barb Taylor and Alecia Bof for their help during the final edits, to Charlie at Urban Writers' Retreat for her faultless hospitality, and to Alistair at Rye Books for sourcing me so many inspirational novels over the years. Thanks to the other three corners of the Book Square for knowing when to ask how the book was going and when to change the subject. Thanks to Writerful Books for the sensitivity read, and also to Stephen Buckley for his generous insight on the more sensitive sections of the book.

Thanks to Dad and Gillie for reading the early drafts and being so positive and encouraging. Thanks to Mum for reading and for helping in so many other ways, and for always believing I could do it. Thanks to my sister Sarah for being fabulous and for her ground-level marketing efforts. And thanks of course to my amazing children who can't remember a time when I wasn't writing this book, and have been my proud champions at each step of the way.

Finally, thanks beyond measure to my husband David, who has always understood and encouraged my need to write. *The Silence* has benefited from his 'very Australian' perspective, not to mention his eagle eye for continuity errors. I doubt it would have been written at all without his love and support, or his willingness to give me the space and time I needed.

I should finish by saying that among the many resources I used to research this book, the National Library of Australia's excellent web site was the most useful and exhaustive. I returned again and again to their oral history section, which is keeping alive the experiences of people whose voices might not otherwise have been heard. I've tried to do justice to those experiences within the limits of this work of fiction. Any errors or inconsistencies are entirely my own.

Questions for Reading Groups

1. What do you think the 'Silence' of the title refers to?

2. The author writes from multiple points of view in the novel, switching point of view in each chapter. Do you think this is an effective way of telling the story? Do you think any perspectives are missing?

3. Louisa tells Isla, 'We were going to leave all the old ways behind in England. It felt adventurous, like anything was possible.' How is the experience of migration depicted in *The Silence* and how does it play into the problems in Louisa and Joe's marriage?

4. The word 'sorry' recurs in the novel, and apologies sometimes come belatedly, or from the wrong person. Sometimes they are withheld entirely. Why do you think the word 'sorry' is important in *The Silence*?

5. Do you have any sympathy for Steve as a character? If so, how do you reconcile this with what he does?

6. Why do you think Isla's grandma asks her to whisper her worst secret in her ear?

7. Andrea Walker says, 'My mum used to say, [Steve] doesn't take kids from nice families'. Isla thinks, 'this might be funny if it were not so unspeakably sad.' What do you think Isla means by this?

8. At the end of the novel, Isla decides to remember her father as 'not all bad.' How is memory significant in *The Silence*?